THE HOUSE THAT HUSTLE BUILT

PART TWO

Buy

for Melodrama

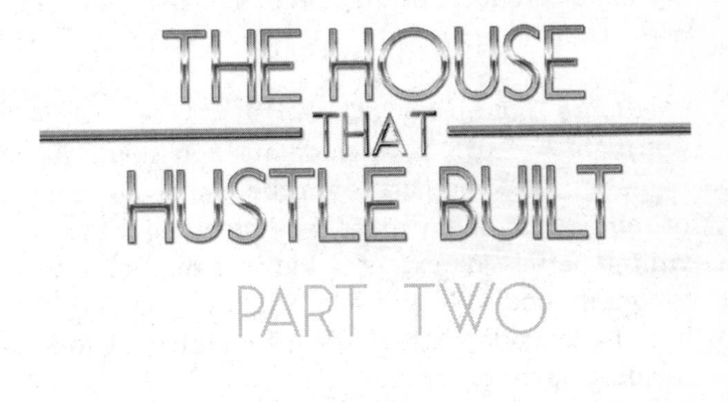
THE HOUSE
THAT
HUSTLE BUILT
PART TWO

NISA
SANTIAGO

This is a work of fiction. All of the characters, organizations, and events portrayed in this novel are either products of the author's imagination or are used fictitiously.

www.melodramapublishing.com

Library of Congress Control Number: 2015912275
ISBN-13: 978-1620780718

First Edition: November 2015
Mass Market Edition: May 2017

Printed in Canada

ALSO BY NISA SANTIAGO

Cartier Cartel: Part 1

Return of the Cartier Cartel: Part 2

Cartier Cartel: Part 3

Bad Apple: The Baddest Chick Part 1

Coca Kola: The Baddest Chick Part 2

Checkmate: The Baddest Chick Part 3

Face Off: The Baddest Chick Part 4

On the Run: The Baddest Chick Part 5

Unfinished Business: The Baddest Chick Part 6

South Beach Cartel

Guard the Throne

Dirty Money Honey

The House that Hustle Built

The House that Hustle Built 2

The House that Hustle Built 3

Murdergram

Murdergram 2

Killer Dolls

Killer Dolls 2

Killer Dolls 3

Mafioso

Mafioso Part 2

Mafioso Part 3

Mafioso Part 4

ONE

The room was dark and still. Cash sat hunched over at the foot of the bed, his face in his hands and elbows pressed against his knees. He was dressed only in his boxers, and looking troubled. It had been a long month. He was tired. Getting rid of those bodies had drained his last bit of energy, and the fact that he didn't have a clue who'd sent those niggas had him in a funk. His life was in someone else's hands, and they could decide his date of death. Cash shook his head at the thought, hoping to make it less true.

He sighed and sulked, whined and bitched each day. Cash was a grown-ass man acting like a spoiled child. He didn't care, though. Cash strongly felt that Pearla was the root of all his problems.

His cellphone vibrated from an unknown number. Cash quickly picked up. "Yo, who dis?"

"Cash, this is my only phone call," she said quickly. "I got knocked. These fuckin' pigs trying to send me upstate. You have to bail me out, son."

"Momma Jones! Are you fuckin' kidding me? Bitch, I hope you fuckin' rot in jail."

Cash hardly ever spoke to his mother so rudely. Never called her outside her name, but things done changed. When he'd needed his mother, she shitted on him. The only reason he was still cool with his father was because Ray-Ray had saved his life.

Momma Jones roared, "Who the fuck you think your bitch-ass talking to? Huh, li'l nigga! Now, I'm your momma! Your flesh and blood. So bring your narrow ass to central booking and get me out."

Cash didn't respond. He just held the line. He knew it would be a cold day in hell before he held her down again. She could sell her pussy, suck dick, or allow niggas to run up in her asshole for all he cared.

Momma Jones began to panic. She softened her tone. "Cash, son, you know jail is no place for your momma, right?"

"Um-hmm."

She exhaled. "So you gonna get me out?"

"Um-hmm."

"I love you, Cash. And I swear I'ma pay you back."

Cash hung up. He was about to go and tell Pearla about Momma Jones but then decided against it. Things weren't the same between them. She wasn't the same.

Pearla was in the bathroom. He could hear the shower running. They hadn't had sex in almost three weeks, which was a dramatic change from their twice-a-day habit. He'd once enjoyed her and she'd enjoyed him, but violence, financial despair, and other concerns had soured and diminished both their moods for any lovemaking.

A week earlier, Cash and Pearla got the shock of their lives. They were at home overseeing the last leg of the renovation when a certified letter came to the house stating that the home equity line of credit on their property was in default. Unless they came up with the nearly twenty-four thousand dollar past due amount, the bank would foreclose. The problem with the letter was that neither one had taken out any loan on the house. They'd paid for it in cash and thought they had an asset worth over a half million dollars.

The couple called the bank, did some investigating, and concluded that Poochie had drained the house of all its equity. She netted five hundred and five thousand dollars of money that didn't belong to her.

Of course Poochie denied that she had forged her daughter's signature and stolen the money, but the mailing address from the loan was listed as Poochie's last known address. When the loan went into default the bank finally sent out certified letters to all addresses, including Jamaica Estates.

Pearla got a lawyer involved to fight for her property, but it was going to be an uphill, expensive battle. Poochie had somehow found the property's deed in her daughter's lockbox, and to the naked eye the signatures on the documents looked authentic. In fact, Pearla and Cash were being treated as if they were trying to commit fraud.

The shower came to an end, and Pearla toweled off. For a moment, she wiped the fog away from the bathroom mirror and stared at her image, reflecting on past events. *What did I do wrong?* she asked herself. She exhaled heavily. She felt like she'd aged ten years. Who could she run to? Who could she talk to? No one. All she had was Cash, but at the moment, their relationship was rocky.

Pearla wrapped the towel around her fresh, clean body and knotted it near her breasts. She stepped out of the bathroom and saw Cash seated on the bed, looking troubled and distant.

They were staying at a motel because their house was too risky. Their room was small and cheap, but cheap was adding up.

"What's on your mind?" Pearla asked Cash.

"I hate that we put almost everything we had into that house, Pearla. It was a mistake paying so much for the repairs."

"What other choice did we have, Cash? We need to sell it and get the most we can for it. A busted-up place, bullet holes in the walls, the smell of death inside it—you think that would help sell it?"

Cash frowned. "We can only afford to stay here maybe a week more, but after that, either we move back into that house or live on the streets."

Pearla didn't want to hear either option, but she knew he was right. It was costing them nearly $300 a week at the motel, the cheapest in Brooklyn. However, that three hundred was helping Pearla to somewhat find peace of mind.

"I hope this real estate agent can help us get top dollar for that place," Cash said.

"They will. I know it's worth every bit of six hundred."

"We wouldn't be in this predicament if it wasn't for ya fuckin' mother," he reminded her.

"Why state the obvious, Cash?" Pearla knew he was frustrated and so was she. "You know, instead of sitting around here sulking you could have been a man and gone out and tried to raise the money to pay off the bank."

"And how was I supposed to do that?"

"Do what you do best. Steal cars."

"Is that your response? Your mom steals all our money and your response is that it's my responsibility to fix this shit? What about you? What about your hustle?"

Pearla shrugged. She didn't want to argue or dwell on the past. The fact was that she and Cash were drained and depressed. The court cases, family issues, and attempts on both their lives had taken everything out of them. Who could plot, scheme, and hustle under those circumstances?

Cash removed himself from the bed and went to his pants draped over the back of the chair in the room. He pulled out his pack of Newport. Briefly, he gazed out the window and caught Pearla's light reflection as she dropped the towel to the floor and started to get dressed. He wasn't even turned on by her nakedness or her shaved pussy.

Pearla sat on the bed naked and started to lotion her legs first. She took her time, working from her ankles up.

Cash turned around looking blank and said, "I'll be back."

"Where are you going?"

"I need to go for a walk and smoke."

"Now?"

"What's wit' all these fucking questions?" he screamed.

"Wait. What?" Pearla had no idea what was going on with him.

Cash snarled. "I'm so sick and fuckin' tired of your constant bitching!" He hurried out the room past Pearla.

Pearla sat there looking somewhat aghast by his sudden outburst. She didn't say a word. Yeah, they were in a very rough patch in life, but she felt soon it was all going to change for the better. Cash, however, was more pessimistic, always seeing the glass as half-empty.

She stared at the door for a moment and heaved a sigh. After taking that shower, her pussy throbbed. She'd thought that maybe tonight, she and Cash could finally have sex, make it feel like old times again between them. So much for that idea.

Cash walked out of the motel lobby and lit his cigarette. He took a few pulls and looked around. This area of Brooklyn was desolate and shady—a block away was the ho stroll, where prostitutes stopped cars and turned tricks. Two blocks away was the overhead freeway, where the traffic was sparse after midnight.

Cash walked up and down the block, smoking and pondering. He had his pistol concealed in his waistband, and the safety was off. He wasn't taking any chances. He walked toward the corner of the block and witnessed one of the sexily dressed prostitutes climb into an idling car. Quickly, the car drove off with an eager customer.

"Maybe I should have become a pimp," he said to himself. "Less fuckin' risk!"

He turned the corner and continued walking, trying not to stress about the meeting with the realtor the following day. Cash had five hundred dollars to his name. He thought linking up with Pearla and her hustling skills was going to be worth it, but it wasn't. Everything was going against them. If the meeting with the realtor was successful, and they could actually put the house on the market for six hundred, it would put their heads above water, give them a lifeline. If not, God help them both.

Cash walked by a few working ladies, who glanced at him in admiration. They quickly averted their stare, not knowing whether he was a pimp or not. He laughed to himself. Pimps had to keep their bitches in pocket. The fleeting thought of paying for pussy surfaced. Cash never had to pay for pussy in his life. He was too fly and handsome for that. He strongly felt pussy should always come free—that and water.

He walked around the block and stopped back in front of the motel, finishing off his cigarette and flicking it away. He lingered in front of the entrance and smiled to himself. He had a backup plan just in case things didn't go smoothly tomorrow. If push came to shove, he was ready to hit the panic button and eject, then pray for a smooth landing.

TWO

Cash and Pearla walked into the realtor's office and took a seat at her desk. The place had minimal décor, with pictures of family and friends on the desk along with her laptop, a window with a second-floor view, and her realtor's license displayed on the wall behind the desk.

The couple shook hands with the woman and took their seats. Pearla was ready to hear some projections.

The realtor, Megan Davis, had ten years of experience in the housing market and was supposedly good at her job. She sat in front of Cash and Pearla and said with a straight face, "The house will go on the market for three hundred and fifty thousand."

Cash and Pearla were shocked. That was a little more than half of what they were expecting to get for it.

Cash said, "What! Are you crazy? Three hundred *K*? That's fuckin' robbery! You know how much we paid for that crib?"

"You need to understand, real estate isn't what it used to be. Times have changed and it's still a buyer's market," Megan tried to explain.

Pearla wasn't about to accept that low-ball offer. She couldn't afford to, with what they owed on the HELOC. There had to be another way. She said, "We've put a lot of repairs into that house, and the location? It's definitely prime real estate."

They'd paid over $500,000 for that house, and at this rate they would lose all around.

"The market has shifted, Pearla. It's up and down; the only thing steady in this business is the trouble that it comes with."

Cash and Pearla weren't in the mood for jokes. Cash was furious. He glared at Megan and despised that she was taking their situation as a joke.

"Fuck this shit!" he exclaimed. "I think you tryin' to scam us! Ain't no way we gonna settle for that shit. Do your fuckin' job and get what we asked for."

Megan scowled his way. She sat erect in her high leather chair and fired back, "How about you stick to what you know—whatever that is—and let me do my job?"

Cash didn't like her attitude. He was tempted to jump over her desk and smack her hard enough to send her weave flying into next week.

"Do your job and be fair," he growled. *Bitch!* He added. "I know the real estate market has turned around; this ain't two thousand eight anymore."

"You're right, this isn't two thousand eight, but the market is still feeling the ripple effects from that year, and unless you're in my shoes, sitting in this chair, then you will not fully understand the inner workings of this market."

The agent continued to belittle Cash with her subtle, sarcastic remarks. She knew what men like him were about. They didn't know anything about real estate, simply buying homes with their illegal cash, thinking they could flip a house like they flipped coke. Of course the house was worth every penny of six hundred grand, but Megan had her own company on the side with her husband. As a realtor, Megan was able to prey upon desperate homeowners who needed to sell and quick. She would drown them in information about the soft market, push doom and gloom, and snatch their homes right up from under them. They would place that same home right back on the market within a week at full market value, making a killing.

Cash didn't trust Megan. He was good at reading people, especially females. Her mouth was saying one thing, but her eyes were saying something else. But what could he do? He didn't know the housing market; he was just a two-bit hustler who came up with Pearla.

Cash couldn't stand the sight of Megan anymore. He stood up abruptly, exclaiming, "Fuck this shit! I'm out!" and removed himself from her office.

Pearla sat looking dumbfounded. What now? What was she going to do? Megan Davis continued talking to her, seeing she was the only reasonable one in her office.

Pearla was hurting, though, trying to hold back her tears and hide her pain. She was losing everything. She had to stay strong. This was only a season, and she was going to get through this.

Cash lingered outside the three-story building, smoking a cigarette and fretting. He felt that it was time to hit that eject button, soar into the air, and parachute down someplace different and better, before he went down with the burning plane.

Moments later, Pearla walked out of the building with the realization of her situation written across her face—it was going to get ugly.

Cash didn't hesitate. He spun her way and shouted, "You fuckin' happy now? Huh? Look at the shit we in. We ain't got shit now, Pearla. We fuckin' broke!"

Pearla retorted, "I'm not in the mood to argue with you, Cash."

"Fuck that! You let that bitch inside there play me. Talk to me like I'm fuckin' stupid!"

"You played yourself!" she yelled.

"I'm done wit' this, Pearla! We shoulda just kept the eighteen grand and left that fuckin' house the way it was. We coulda used that money to start over, got us a new hustle. But, no, you always think that you know best, that you smarter than me. Like I'm stupid and don't know shit."

"So you think all of this is my fault? Oh, did you forget about Petey Jay, giving that stupid muthafucka three hundred and seventy thousand dollars of our money? You can't get much dumber than that. So, no, I don't think you're smart when it comes to business. I carried you, you stupid muthafucka! I helped build you up. If it wasn't for me, then you would still be a low-level car thief, making peanuts and lookin' stupid."

"Bitch, I didn't need you. I was good. *You* needed me." Cash had his hands clenched into fists, anger manifested on his face. He wanted to hit something, or someone. He knew if he didn't walk away, he and Pearla were going to start fist-fighting in the middle of the street.

"Bitch, fuck you!" he screamed. "I'll show you how much I fuckin' need you!" Cash stormed away from her.

Pearla couldn't hold on anymore. Her tears started to trickle down her face. She watched Cash hurry away from her, turning the corner, not knowing where he was going. She was ready to collapse on her knees and fall out. This wasn't happening. Her life wasn't supposed to turn out like this. She'd had it all planned out, but now it was all falling apart.

THREE

After being alone for two weeks in the low-end motel, Pearla realized that Cash wasn't coming back. Unfortunately, the cheapest place to stay was also the most dangerous. Pearla headed home and locked herself in the bedroom, the television on mute. Their light bill was way past due. They owed the electric company $500. It was money she didn't have. It was only a matter of time before she found herself in the dark. Pearla was becoming desperate. She knew she needed to do something.

For hours, she would lay in her bed in the fetal position under the covers, crying her eyes out. She barely got any sleep.

The large house was filled with unwanted and eerie sounds. There was no telling who was in the shadows waiting for her. The only thing she had in her possession to protect her was a .380 handgun. Death could be around any corner and where was her nigga?

She needed someone. She wanted Cash by her side, but he was showing his true colors. The man was selfish, had always been selfish. Pearla had thought they were in this together. Obviously, she was wrong. The minute shit got really rough, Cash abandoned her in a time of need.

Her anger, which had begun as a simmer, was now was bubbling inside.

It was a sunny day, but nothing was bright in Pearla's life. She showered and quickly got dressed. Before afternoon, she was stepping out her front door and climbing into her Bentley. She had to do something. The choice she was making did worry her, but she was desperate. Exhaling loudly, she started her car and then pulled away from the curb.

A half-hour later, Pearla lingered in front of her mother's new place on Rockaway Parkway in Canarsie, Brooklyn. The place, a two-story brick home with a wraparound porch and long driveway, was an upgrade from her last home. Pearla sighed heavily, gazing at the home and wondering if the money Poochie stole had paid for it.

Her mother had a new man in her life. Pearla heard he worked for the Department of Sanitation and made decent money. How any man could fall in love with Poochie was a mystery to Pearla, but word of mouth said that Poochie had always been a good fuck.

Now that Poochie had a new nigga in her life and she'd hit the jackpot with the HELOC, she wasn't coming around Pearla with her hand out. Poochie had someone else taking care of her now, and Pearla had become irrelevant, like a complete stranger.

Pearla climbed out the car and proceeded toward the front porch. A Lexus and Chevy Impala were parked in the driveway. She tried to look her best while seeing her mother. Though she was dead broke, there wasn't any need to look like it. She wore tight jeans, stilettos, and a classy halter-top. Her long black hair fell down to her shoulders, and her earrings and other trinkets were costume. Pretty much everything expensive she owned had been pawned off to keep up with bills, buy food, and take care of other household expenses.

The last thing she owned outright and of value was her Bentley. The bank could take her house, she could sell her diamonds, and her stomach could rumble from hunger and none of those issues could get Pearla to sell her beloved car. That car represented wealth, was a reminder of her journey, and allowed her to cling to the image she worked so hard to create.

Pearla was still a very pretty girl. Life was kicking her ass, but she was still standing. She had to swallow her pride and ask Poochie for help. There was no one else to ask, and her mother owed her for the predicament she'd put her in. She braved a smile and knocked a few times. She had no idea how things were going to play out. She'd never had a close, loving relationship with her mother. But when Poochie had needed something, Pearla was there to help her out.

The front door opened, and a middle-aged man came into her view. He was shirtless with a hairy chest, a thick, dark beard, a balding head, and a nice physique for his age.

He smiled at Pearla and said, "Hello."

"Hey. Is Poochie here?"

"And who are you?"

"I'm her daughter."

The man looked stunned. "Daughter? She never mentioned that she had a daughter."

Of course, she didn't, Pearla thought.

"Well, I'm Henry," he said, his hand extended.

Pearla shook his hand. She liked his smile. He had an easygoing demeanor. He stepped aside and allowed Pearla into his home and closed the door behind her.

Pearla took in their decor. The first thing her eyes rested on was the 60-inch flat-screen in the living room. Then the leather couches. Then the African artwork and statues displayed in the room. It looked like her mother was living large.

"She's in the bathroom," Henry said. "Have a seat and make yourself at home. I'll tell her you're here."

Henry went upstairs, and Pearla took a seat on the couch. She wondered what it would be like to live in a place like that. She had the urge to be held and taken care of. Being alone was scary. Pearla never had to be alone. She either had a boyfriend or was staying with her mother.

"What the fuck are you doin' here?" she suddenly heard her mother yell from behind. "How the fuck did you know where I was staying?"

Pearla turned around and saw Poochie dressed in a blue housecoat, her hair cut short, and wearing hazel contacts—new man, new look.

Already, Pearla knew it wasn't going to be easy. "I just came to talk," Pearla replied meekly.

"Talk? Talk about what?"

"I've missed you, I guess. How are things going?"

"Don't you have a fuckin' life? Why the fuck are you tryin' to be in mines?"

Pearla was taken aback. Now that Poochie had a little come-up, the bitch was acting brand-spanking-new again.

"So, it's like that, huh? You doing good from the sweat off my back, and I'm out the picture. How quickly we forget!"

"Forget? Forget what, bitch? What is it I'm supposed to remember?"

Pearla shook her head and sarcastically replied, "Remember how I looked out for you, maybe? How you fuckin' committed fraud and stole my house right out from under me. Why don't you remember that, huh?"

"Get the fuck out my house, Pearla! I done told you it wasn't me! And if you came here lookin' for a hand out, I don't fuckin' got it!"

Pearla knew it wasn't about to happen. Why did she bother to come anyway? She stood up, defeated and said, "You know what, I hope you fuckin' die! You ain't gonna never change."

"You think I owe you something?" Poochie hollered. "I don't owe you shit! You a fuckin' grown woman, Pearla. Act like it!"

Pearla pivoted and walked away. She wanted to punch Poochie in the face and knock her head off. How grown was Poochie when she always came around with her hand out begging? Whenever Poochie needed a place to stay and the rent paid, Pearla took care of it, even though her mother had always been difficult to deal with.

Pearla hurried to her ride, while Poochie was hollering and cursing, looking like a madwoman.

Poochie hollered, "I got mines, bitch, and you couldn't keep yours! You always thought you was smarter than everyone. Bitch, you wasn't!" Then she slammed the door.

Pearla needed to take a deep breath and lit a cigarette. The nicotine was comforting, but hearing from Cash would have been better. He had been MIA for two weeks, and she was starting to worry.

FOUR

Cash had Gloria in the deckchair position. He thrust his dick inside her, grunting and sweating like a slave picking cotton as he enjoyed her glorious insides. She was on her back, pivoting her hips so that her legs were in the air, and then she bent her knees while Cash fucked her from a kneeling position. Cash felt a sense of power having Gloria in that position, folding her, leaning in on her legs, improving his angle as he targeted her G-spot.

Cash took complete control of her arms and legs, so all she could do was lay there and take his dick. The Magnum condom he wore stretched like a rubber band inside of her. His strokes were long and deep, and she was getting wetter with every stroke. Her pussy was so wet, her juices trickled down from between her legs and onto the mattress.

"Ooooh! Fuck me, Cash! Oh shit! Fuck me!" Gloria cried out. "You about to make me come!"

Cash stared into Gloria's eyes as he thrust harder and harder. She clawed at his back, her pussy clamping down around his dick.

Cash continued to grunt. She was the perfect remedy to his problems.

"I'm gonna come!" he announced feverishly.

"Come, baby. Yes, yes, come in this pussy."

Gloria reached down and caressed his balls as he was pounding her. The stimulation he felt was overwhelming. Cash was in a bottomless daze, transfixed by his sexual gratification.

He thrust harder, clutching the bed sheets, and Gloria wrapped her legs around him tightly, the penetration intense. Her breathing was ragged, her chest heaved rapidly with heavy panting.

"I'm gonna come, Cash! Oh shit!"

Her body pressed into the bed, with each thrust from Cash she felt the weight of his body. She was ready to explode and so was he. A few more pumps inside the pussy and Gloria hollered from the orgasm that detonated inside of her, vibrating underneath Cash like she was receiving an electric shock. She held him tightly against her naked frame. The sounds that escaped from her mouth weren't English anymore, but alien. Her orgasm was out of this world.

Cash wasn't done yet. He continued fucking her. He was a machine. He definitely wanted Gloria to remember this dick, fall in love with it, yearn for it, so he went all out.

Fifteen minutes later, she had another explosive orgasm.

Gloria couldn't take it anymore. Her young stud was driving her up the wall. He felt so good.

"Come for me, baby. Come in this good fuckin' pussy!" she hollered.

A few strokes later Cash came deep in her. Luckily the condom caught his semen. Cash was sure he would have gotten her pregnant if it didn't. His nut felt never-ending. His load could fill a cup.

He panted, climbed out of the pussy, and collapsed breathlessly by her side.

For a minute, they both were speechless, relishing the experience.

"I need a fuckin' cigarette," Cash finally said, gazing at the ceiling.

She nestled against him and kissed him lovingly. "I'll get you one, baby. You want something to eat too?"

"Yeah, make me a sandwich."

Gloria kissed him on the lips, smiling at him.

It was too easy. He was having a great time staying with her. He enjoyed everything she had to offer, from her pussy to her home.

Gloria removed herself from his grasp, her dark skin glistening with sweat. Her body was thick in the right places, legs long, tits small, her butt plump, and her hair was a mane of flowing dreadlocks, wild and ethnic.

At forty-five, Gloria was Cash's cougar. She was easy on the eyes, especially for her age. He was half her age, but he figured age was nothing but a number.

Cash had lucked out meeting Gloria, whose place had become his new home. She didn't mind taking him in. Overnight, he was living like a king inside her three-bedroom home in Woodhaven, Queens. Feet kicked up and a three-course meal at the ready. He had everything he needed, from cable TV to a refrigerator full of food, a place to sleep, and some good pussy night after night. He wasn't thinking about Pearla and her bad luck ass.

He'd met Gloria a week earlier, the day he'd stormed away from Pearla after their meeting with the real estate agent. Her luxury BMW had caught a flat tire on Atlantic Avenue in Brooklyn. Cash was driving by and saw a damsel in distress. He immediately pulled over to help change her flat tire. Immediately, they sparked, having chemistry.

Cash had the gift of gab. She was mature and beautiful, and he knew she was interested in him by the way she looked at him. He knew her type—the older woman loving younger men. Everything about her gave her away, from her stare-down to her conversation.

He'd told her he was having a bad day too. He made her laugh. She liked to laugh. That same day they went to McDonald's for lunch.

"And what's your story?" she asked him.

Cash avoided telling too much of his business, since she was a stranger to him. It was easy to tell her lies, though.

"I'm a sucker for love," he lied. "I moved up here from Philly to be with this shorty and I just caught her sneaky ass still fucking around with her ex."

"What?" Gloria gasped.

"Yeah, and you think you're having a bad day."

"It just got better."

Gloria quickly became infatuated with him. Her eyes spoke volumes. Her touch was gentle and welcoming, and when her lips parted to speak, Cash thought about sliding his dick in between them.

Gloria was an assistant principal at Boys and Girls High School, and had been there seven years. But Cash knew her weakness—men like him; he'd been there and done that.

After lunching at McDonald's, they went back to her place and continued talking, while watching a movie. Cash quickly took in how she was living, and he wanted in. He didn't have two nickels to rub together, but he played it off and gradually smooth-talked his way into her world.

That night, they had great sex. He made her come multiple times, and she loved it.

Gloria donned a long robe and exited the bedroom. Cash lay in her bed, feeling pleased. He knew she would want to go at it again later on that night. Luckily, he had the stamina to satisfy her. The pussy was great, like a well-seasoned meal.

He reached over and picked up his cell phone. He saw the numerous missed calls from Pearla. He was purposely ignoring her. At the moment, he didn't want to deal with her. She was drama!

Pearla had left over a dozen messages on his cell phone and a few lengthy texts. Cash briefly looked at them and deleted each and every last one of her texts and deleted her voice messages. Out of sight, out of mind. "Fuck you!" he uttered.

He had a good thing going at Gloria's place. She had a good job, drove a nice car, and she had a really nice home. She was single with no kids and was ready to pamper Cash with whatever he needed. And she sucked dick like a porn star. Why would he want to go back to the drama with Pearla?

Cash also felt safe at Gloria's. No one knew where he was.

Gloria entered the bedroom with a turkey-and-cheese sandwich and a Pepsi. She tossed Cash a pack of Newports, and he lit up like a Christmas tree.

She sat near him, stroking his chest, kissing on his neck as he ate the sandwich she made. "You be good to me, and I'll be good to you," she whispered into his ear.

"Oh, baby, with treatment like this, I'll always be good to you."

She smiled.

After the quick meal, they went back at it. She sucked his dick, and he ate her out. And Gloria rode him to sleep. Cash didn't want to wake up from his paradise. Not ever.

Cash had the place to himself that morning and afternoon, since Gloria was at work. He made himself at home. She'd given him a set of keys and took him shopping for some clothes, and he permanently moved into her home without a second thought. If Pearla found out she would not only be furious but shocked.

What Pearla failed to understand about Cash was that he was who he was. When she met him he was a dude who liked to fuck, smoke a few blunts, and keep just enough money in his pockets to survive. Then she came into his life and pushed him to be a man he wasn't built to be—driving expensive whips, wearing expensive jewels, and fucking high-end broads. Not every dude was cut out to be on top. Cash wouldn't say that he didn't have any ambition, but he was hardly the ambitious type. While lying up in Gloria's house, he realized who and what he really was.

Cash watched cable TV and then raided her fridge, making himself a hefty breakfast. He needed to eat to get the strength to keep up with Gloria. Every night they fucked. Two weeks there, and there was no letting up. Cash didn't mind.

Cash sat in front of the flat-screen TV, watching music videos on BET. It was early afternoon, and he was bored. Since leaving Pearla, he'd become a homebody, becoming Gloria's plaything and manservant.

When she was at work, she expected him to keep her place clean and for him to cook. In exchange, she gave him a roof over his head, gas money, helped pay his cell phone bill, put food in his mouth, and gave him great sex. And she loved getting her pussy eaten out. What was there to complain about?

Cash got up off the couch and went toward the living room window. He gazed outside, taking in the quiet Queens block. From corner to corner there were short front yards with manicured lawns, each home with a driveway and a nice car. Everyone appeared to be at work. Cash felt like the odd ball out. Gloria's place wasn't better than the place he'd shared with Pearla, but it was cool.

As he stood by the window, he lit a cigarette and thought about his troubles. He still didn't know who was behind the attempted murder on him and Pearla, but his gut instincts told him that he had to get at Petey Jay and Perez the minute they got released from jail.

He wanted to connect with his former friends, Manny and Darrell, but he didn't know how well he would be received. He'd been selfish. He'd gotten rich while shutting them out. Manny and Darrell felt betrayed. They had always been a team. They used to have fun together, until Pearla came and poisoned the well.

Each day, his resentment toward Pearla festered. Had it not been for her and her grand schemes, he would have been living a great life, with money in his pockets, and most importantly, he would still have his childhood friends around. He'd traded them in for Pearla.

Luckily, Cash still had his ride, a piece of him from the good old days. His car and Pearla's were both completely paid for in full, all cash.

His mind was made up. It was time to get money again, and the quickest money for him with the least risk was stealing low-end cars, like he used to do.

FIVE

Pearla left her house and jumped into her car. Her gas tank was nearly on empty, but she needed to do the two-mile drive to the local supermarket. She had no cash on her, but that wasn't going to stop her from picking up the few things she needed.

Lately, she had been stealing from the local bodegas, which was simple. Usually there was a man behind the counter busy with another customer, so Pearla would walk inside the bodega, scope out what she needed, and snatch maybe a bag of potato chips, a bag of mini candy bars, some cookies, a few canned soups, and maybe bottled water. She'd stuff all her goods in a large purse and pay for a pack of gum. But that type of food wasn't filling. It was like cheap drugs, thrilling for the moment, but not lasting.

Pathmark had what she needed. She walked inside trying to look decent and not like some broke, down-and-out bitch that was up to no good. She grabbed a shopping cart and coolly walked into the supermarket. Like everyone else, she went up and down the aisles picking out what she needed. She picked out her meats and chicken, a few snacks, and some toiletries, keeping things minimal.

She made her way toward the self-checkout area and began scanning each item and loading it into the plastic shopping bags just as a paying customer would. That small amount of food was nearly two-hundred dollars.

Pearla took out a maxed out credit card and pretended to swipe it to buy time. She was waiting for the attendant in the area to get distracted and leave. Fortunately, it didn't take the attendant long to leave because no one wants to work. While the cashier skirted off to gossip with a coworker, Pearla began loading all her items into her shopping cart.

The checkout machine began to alert the attendant once those bags left the conveyor belt before the items were paid for, but Pearla was long gone.

Once outside and safely inside her car, Pearla was finally able to breathe. Boosting food was petty, but this is what her life had morphed into. Stealing pork chops and canned goods from the local Pathmark.

Things soon went from bad to worse, more like critical. The next day the bank placed a foreclosure notice on her front door. Pearla knew this day was coming, but somehow, she was still in shock.

CHAPTER SIX

Pearla sat in her cold, still bedroom and gazed out the window aimlessly, in a trance-like state. She was wrapped snugly in her blanket, the pistol in her hand.

"I'm tired," she said to herself.

Pearla was tired of living alone and scared. She was broke. She'd lost her hustle. She couldn't think straight. She had no friends or family, no man. She was embarrassed and couldn't be seen like this. She was in bad shape.

She lifted the .380 and put it to her head. The safety was off, and there was a bullet in the chamber. Her tears trickled down her face, leaving behind a river of pain.

"I hate them!" she said, bitterness and contempt in her tone.

She continued to stare out the window and knew it was her time to die. She closed her eyes and took a deep breath.

On the count of three. "One … tw—"

Ding-dong! Ding-dong! Ding-dong!

Suddenly, her doorbell sounded. Someone was ringing her bell incessantly.

Pearla's heart swelled up with hope. She thought Cash had come back to her after all this time. Would she be forgiving or angry at him?

She dropped the gun and ran downstairs and swung open the front door, only to find her neighbor standing on her steps.

Ms. Hicks, holding the foreclosure notice in her hand, frowned at Pearla and asked, "What is this? How can you allow your house to go into foreclosure, Pearla? What is going on with you?"

Pearla sighed heavily. She wasn't in the mood to deal with Ms. Hicks. The sixty-year-old white woman had always been pleasant, but they weren't best friends or sharing neighbors. They simply said hello to each other in passing; Pearla had her life, and the white woman had hers.

When they'd first moved in, she and Cash thought the bitch was a racist, but she wasn't. She was simply a snobbish bitch, skeptical about the young couple moving in next door to her.

"Pearla, you know this will only bring down all property value in the neighborhood."

Pearla didn't care about the neighborhood, she didn't care what the bitch had to say, and she wasn't in the mood to hear anything. She stood there looking a hot mess, wrapped in her blanket, her hair in disarray, her eyes red from crying continuously.

Ms. Hicks barged into Pearla's home. She'd had it with all of Cash and Pearla's antics.

A while back, there was the commotion and the loud

noise, and the strangers parked outside their home. Then there was their arguing in public, where Ms. Hicks was tempted to call 911 on the couple a few times.

"This used to be a nice neighborhood," Ms. Hicks uttered. "You can't come here and ruin what some of us spent years to build."

"I'm sorry." Pearla wasn't sure why she was apologizing to the older woman. What happened in her home was her business, not her neighbor's. If Pearla was herself, she would have cursed this bitch out.

Ms. Hicks looked around the living room. The house was dark, the blinds closed, and it was chilly inside the room.

"What is going on here, Pearla? Why is it dark and cold like this?" Ms. Hicks asked.

"I tried selling the place before it went into foreclosure, but I guess it's too late now."

"You were going to sell your home? Why?"

"I no longer belong here. There's too much going on."

Ms. Hicks was confused. "Where's your husband?"

"He's gone."

"Gone? Like he'll be right back?"

"No, he's gone, like he left my ass and he ain't ever coming back."

"I'm sorry to hear about that."

"You don't need to be sorry. Fuck him!"

"And are your lights off?"

"Ms. Hicks, why are you here? I'm moving. I'm getting kicked out my own home; the bank has it now. Isn't that what you wanted? The niggers are leaving. Shouldn't you be satisfied? Huh?"

"First off, I'm never happy when a couple loses their home. And I thought you said you were trying to sell it. What happened?"

"The realtor happened, that's what. I thought my house was worth more, but she explained to me that it wasn't."

"And how much did she say your house was worth?"

"Three hundred and fifty thousand."

"What?" Ms. Hicks gasped as if what Pearla had said was blasphemy. "This home is definitely worth more than that. Double."

"Well, I heard different."

"Who is this realtor?" Ms. Hicks wanted to know.

"This place on Hillside Avenue. I looked them up. They seem legit."

Ms. Hicks had her eyebrows raised in suspicion. Something Pearla was saying didn't seem right. She had been around a very long time. She knew the housing market and her community. She'd made it her business to know the price of all the homes on the block and around the area.

"You have to watch out for some of these real estate firms, Pearla. Some of them aren't what they appear to be. Some of them are unethical and will convince the seller to sell their house at a loss, and the buyer can actually be the real estate firm."

Pearla was listening.

Ms. Hicks added, "They'll buy your home for three hundred and fifty thousand dollars, and soon after that, the realtor will sell your house for triple that, seven hundred thousand or more. You have gotten scammed, Pearla. I hate to say it. They saw you coming."

Pearla couldn't believe what she was hearing. She thought she knew what she was doing. Before this incident Pearla thought she was Enron—the smartest one in the room. She had trusted her instincts, but Cash was right on all levels. The realtor was scamming them. Pearla should have listened and gone to another realtor to get a second opinion.

"You need to report them," Ms. Hicks said.

Pearla was still blown away from being ripped off. She felt so stupid.

Ms. Hicks continued to talk. She started to feel sorry for the young girl. She was naïve. She had been duped out of what was hers.

Once again, she asked about Cash.

"I don't fuckin' need him! He made his fuckin' choice!"

"I'm a divorced woman myself, twice now. I'd been with my ex-husband twenty-five years, and then just like that, he leaves me for some young whore," Ms. Hicks said out of the blue. She looked at Pearla. "There's one thing I know for sure about men—you can never depend on them."

Pearla wasn't in the mood to hear her backstory. She wanted to tear that bitch, Megan Davis, apart. She felt like a fool. Ms. Hicks tried to be comforting, but Pearla wasn't in the mood to be comforted. She wanted revenge.

"You need to fight this, Pearla. Don't let them take your home."

"How?"

"I can give you the number to a great lawyer. I've used him in the past."

Pearla didn't know what to think. Ms. Hicks was suggesting fighting in the courtroom, but she was thinking about fighting it the way she knew best, via the streets. Courts required lawyers, and lawyers wanted money, and money was what she didn't have right now.

After Ms. Hicks left, Pearla wasted no time picking up the phone and calling the bank. Ms. Hicks' visit had sparked something inside of her. When she got through to the bank manager, she explained her situation, telling him what had happened.

The manager simply said, "That is not our problem, ma'am. That's an issue between you, a lawyer, and your realtor."

"But I can come up with the money. Just give me a few more days."

"I'm sorry. The foreclosure has already been implemented. There's nothing else I can do. Unless you can come up with the money in seventy-two hours, then you will be evicted from the premises," he stated frigidly.

Pearla wanted to curse and scream. He was no help at all. She hung up and tossed her cell phone across the room while screaming into the air.

More tears fell from her eyes. The pain was heavy. There was no escaping the reality that she was going to be evicted from her home, penniless. All that money she had sank into it was now gone.

Pearla blamed herself. Had she started to hustle right after Cash left, then raising the money would not have been a problem. She'd wasted months in depression. She'd wasted time lingering on Cash. But now, with so little time, there was nothing left to do but accept the inevitable.

CHAPTER SEVEN

Cash easily popped the locks to a Buick Regal, slid into the driver's seat crouched low, and hurriedly hot-wired the car. It started with no problems. He put the vehicle into drive and drove off.

Stealing cars was a high that was never gonna get old for him. Sex was first, but stealing cars was right underneath.

Cash changed the radio to Hot 97, and Drake's "Make Me Proud" started to blare through the speakers.

"Damn, I love this shit!" he hollered excitedly, nodding his head, jamming to the song.

Gloria had kept him out of his element for too long—from behind the steering wheel of a stolen vehicle. His car was in the shop for brakes and service, so he needed a car to move around in. True, he needed the cash, but the thrill was much more appealing and stimulating.

Cash lit a joint, inhaled strongly, and made his way to Brooklyn. His sugar mama was at work, babysitting high-school kids. He couldn't take being cooped up in her house a day longer. It was easy to steal the neighbor's car and joy-ride for the day. It was the perfect day to link up with some old friends of his.

He cruised down New Lots Avenue, checking out the fine ladies walking the streets. He made a few catcalls at some as he smoked the joint. Being in his old neighborhood, Pearla briefly crossed his mind. He hadn't seen her since there was ice on the ground.

He found himself in his old neighborhood. East New York was bustling with people and traffic. The girls were out strutting through the hood in their summer outfits. With fall approaching, the ladies wanted to flaunt their summer clothing until the cold weather crept in.

Cash had his eyes transfixed on long legs, black skin, long weaves, and tight shorts. "Damn, I wish summer could be forever," he joked to himself.

He continued driving, turning the corners slowly and loving the attention he got in the stolen Buick. He made his way to Livonia and Rockaway Avenues.

He parked the Buick underneath the train trestle and got out the car. A turkey and cheese sandwich at the local deli was calling his name. He walked inside, ordered his sandwich, and bought a pack of Newport.

A beautiful woman quickly caught his attention. She was browsing around the store, minding her business.

Cash licked his lips. She was a cutie, nice body and long hair, something to play with. Her tight T-shirt accentuated her tits, and her short skirt showed off her thick thighs, which made his dick jump. He watched her keenly. She made her way toward the store countertop to pay for her bottled water and a pack of pumpkin seeds.

Cash stood to the side. She didn't pay him any attention. Before she could pull out her cash to pay for her stuff, Cash placed a ten-dollar bill on the countertop and said, "I got you, ma."

"You got me, ma?" She turned and looked at him like he was stupid. "I ain't your mother, and I can pay for my own things, thank you!"

Cash smiled. "Oh, my bad. I didn't mean to offend you."

"Too late for that."

"Okay, let me start over. You caught my attention over there, and I just wanted to get to know a beautiful woman. My name is Cash." He extended his hand out to her.

"Cash!" She laughed. "Really? That's your name?"

"Yeah. And what's yours?"

"My name shouldn't concern you!" she quipped.

Cash could only laugh. She was definitely a tough cookie to break. He quickly looked her up and down and tried to read her. He figured she had to be in her early thirties, probably with no kids, because her stomach was too flat with a six-pack. He assumed she had a good job, no husband because he didn't see a wedding band on her left hand.

The woman pulled out her own cash and paid for her items, shunning Cash's hospitality.

He continued to smile, having a sense of humor about the situation. He said to himself, *Damn, I must be getting rusty, losing my touch and shit.*

"Excuse me!" she hissed. The woman pivoted and walked out.

Cash stared at her big booty from the back. He wasn't about to give up so easily. A simple diss wasn't going to deter him. He tossed the clerk a twenty-dollar bill for his things and hurried out of the store, trying to catch up to the woman, who was walking toward the housing projects across the street.

Cash followed her. His ego a bit bruised, he felt he had to come harder with his game. He wasn't about to crash and burn like that. "Excuse me, beautiful," he hollered. "I just need one minute of your time."

She turned around with a nasty look. "You're a relentless muthafucka, aren't you? Look, little nigga, you're not my type. I'm not interested in you. I already have a man."

Cash felt he was every bitch's type. He continued to flash his golden boy smile at the difficult catch. It wasn't in his nature to strike out with women. He stood close enough to her, but not creepy close, giving her enough room to feel at ease.

"You don't even know me, beautiful, and you already judging me," he said.

"What part of 'I already have a man' don't you understand? You stupid, slow, or retarded? Which is it?"

"Damn, I'm just tryin' to show you some love."

"Nigga, I don't want your fuckin' love! I don't want anything to do with you. I don't want to know you at all! Just leave me the fuck alone! Bounce, nigga!" She turned and walked away, leaving Cash with egg on his face.

He'd never felt so embarrassed. He couldn't go out like that. He couldn't have this bitch playing him. He had to uphold his reputation.

As she walked away, he yelled out, "Fuck you, you dumb dyke bitch! You know who you dissin', bitch? Fuck you and your man! I got plenty of bitches. I don't need you!"

The woman stopped walking momentarily, slapped her ass, and palmed it, indicating for him to kiss her ass, and continued walking away.

Cash frowned. He was tempted to throw something at her.

"Damn! It must be freezing in hell for a bitch to diss Cash like that."

Cash turned around and saw Benny, an old childhood friend, laughing at the incident.

"Man, fuck that stupid bitch!"

"What you doin' up in the projects, Cash? You know niggas don't like you around here."

"I ain't worried about niggas around here," Cash replied, dryly.

"You should be. You done ran up on half these bitches in the projects, fuckin' everything that moves, from married to taken, and you know these project niggas ain't forget."

"I got better things poppin' off for me, Benny."

"Yeah, we ain't seen you around in a few months."

"That's because I got this nice cougar bitch in Queens I'm staying wit'. Bitch is an assistant principal at a high school. She takes care of me sexually and financially."

"What happened to Pearla?"

Cash waved her off, stating, "She old news."

Benny laughed. "You a trip, nigga."

Cash pulled out his fresh pack of cigarettes, and Benny didn't hesitate to ask him for one. Cash passed him a cigarette, and the two lit up.

Cash took a few drags and then asked Benny, "Yo, you know that bitch that was talkin' shit?"

"Yeah, she got a man, though. Some drug-dealing nigga name Rome. She don't be out like that, stay to herself. Believe me, nigga, you ain't the only one that tried to holla."

"That's a'ight. I'm gonna see that bitch again."

"You don't get enough pussy, nigga?"

"Nigga, there ain't no such thing as enough pussy," Cash said. "Nigga, you know, new pussy is always the best pussy."

Benny laughed. "Same ol' Cash."

Cash looked around the area, taking it all in. The streets of Brooklyn were always live. For the past four months, he had been held up in a relationship, living in the suburbs and forgetting about the fun he used to have. He quickly got over the rejection and was ready to work on meeting some new ladies in the area.

"Damn, Benny, I don't remember it being this many pretty bitches in the projects and in the hood."

"Yeah, they be out here, my nigga."

"I see. I see." Cash smiled.

"Yo, you drivin'?" Benny asked.

"Nigga, what you think?" Cash replied smugly.

Benny laughed. "Yeah, I shouldn't even ask. Your car-thievin' ass."

Cash nodded toward the burgundy Buick across the street.

"That's you?"

"Yeah, my ride's in the shop. Why you ask?"

"I just wanna know if you can give me a lift somewhere." Benny finished off his cigarette and flicked it away into the street.

"To where?"

"Just goin' toward Linden Boulevard. Don't feel like walkin' that far."

"A'ight, I got you."

Cash took one final drag from his Newport and tossed it. Then they walked toward the car and climbed inside. As Cash started the ignition, his cell phone rang. He looked at the caller ID and saw it was Gloria calling him.

"Here's my bitch calling right now," he said to Benny. He answered, smiling, feeling pompous. "Hey."

"Hey, baby. You home?" Gloria asked.

"Nah."

"Where are you?"

"I'm in Brooklyn, seeing an old friend," he said.

"Oh. Are you gonna be home when I get there? I'm gonna need help with dinner."

"Yeah, I should be there."

"You should, or you will? I don't need an ambiguous answer from you, Cash," Gloria replied gruffly.

"Okay, I will."

"Okay. And this old friend, is it a he or she?"

"He. My nigga Benny."

"Oh. Well, don't stay out too late. I'm gonna need you home like you promised."

"Okay."

"I love you, baby," Gloria said.

Cash sighed and faintly replied, "I got love for you too. Bye!" He hung up. He wasn't about to repeat the same words. He wasn't in love. Far from it.

Benny was smiling heavily at him. "That's the missus, huh? When is the wedding?" he kidded.

"Ha-ha! You got jokes, nigga. I ain't no one-woman man, never was, never will be. But that's the bitch I told you about. I'm stayin' wit' her until I get my shit right."

"She got you pussy-whipped, nigga?"

"Yo, don't no bitch got me pussy-whipped. That ain't even funny, nigga! I'm just playing nice because she being good to me. Damn, nigga, you know, it's a full-time job hustling these part-time women," Cash said proudly.

Benny laughed. "Same ol' Cash—One day your dick gonna fall off."

"It hasn't yet, and besides, I'm always using protection—no babies, no STDs, nigga. Clean bill of health!"

"Yeah, a'ight."

When they got closer to Linden Boulevard, Benny said to Cash, "Yo, when was the last time you saw Manny and Darrell?"

"It's been a while. Why?"

"Nah, just asking."

"What? They falling apart without me?"

"They just doin' them," Benny said.

Benny climbed out of Cash's car on Linden and Mother Gaston Boulevards. They gave each other dap, and Cash drove away, going toward the projects again. He had Manny and Darrell on his mind and decided to go see what they'd been up to since he'd been gone.

He drove up Mother Gaston Boulevard, cruising slowly, playing the music loud and continued to check out the females in passing. He turned on New Lots Avenue and headed toward his old stomping grounds around Dumont and Pennsylvania Avenues.

The minute he turned the corner, he noticed a group of males hanging out on the block and shooting the breeze, Darrell and Manny among them.

Cash drove their way and hopped out the Buick with a large smile then shouted, "My niggas, my niggas, what's up!" He had his hands in the air, excited to see them.

Manny and Darrell didn't return the same bright greeting as Cash. They frowned as he approached.

"This nigga here," Manny said dryly.

"What the fuck you want, Cash?" Darrell exclaimed.

"Oh, a nigga can't get any love from my boys?"

Manny hollered, "You a fake-ass nigga, Cash. We ain't fuckin' wit' you, nigga."

"What? Fake?" Cash replied, looking dumbfounded. "Who you talkin' to?"

Manny repeated, "You, nigga!"

Cash thought he was okay with his old crew, that nothing had changed, but immediately they started to shun him.

He noticed Manny was pushing a black-on-black Escalade with large chrome rims. Both men were dressed wearing fresh sneakers, sporting pricy jewelry, looking well off.

After he broke away to do his own thing, Cash thought his crew would crumble without him. For a long time, he was the alpha male, and they were his cronies. Now things done changed.

Manny and Darrel had continued to steal cars. Now they split the profits 50/50, three grand a car split between the two of them.

Cash said, "Yo, I came back to the block so we can do what we do best—get paid. I ain't fuckin' wit' Pearla anymore."

Darrell laughed. He looked at Cash jokingly like, *You serious, nigga?*

Manny said, "Do it look like we need you, nigga? We doin' fine without you. Get the fuck off the block, Cash. Niggas ain't gettin' money wit' you anymore. It ain't like you looked out for us when you had that thing goin' on in Miami."

Cash looked speechless for a moment. He couldn't remember far back enough to the time when he began stuntin' on them—that sweet time when his pockets were swollen and he was flying in and out of Miami with tens of thousands of dollars for stealing cream-of-the-crop cars, and never put them on.

Manny continued, "Yeah, nigga, stand there lookin' fuckin' stupid! You a foul muthafucka, Cash. And you a fuckin' snitch! We don't fuck wit' fake niggas or snitches!"

"Snitch?" Cash looked at them like they were crazy.

"You shitted on Petey Jay," Darrell chimed. "He locked up because of you, and you fucked over Perez—snitchin'-ass nigga!"

"I ain't no fuckin' snitch!" Cash replied vehemently.

"You ain't what, nigga? Fuck you, nigga! You ain't shit, nigga!" Manny stepped closer to Cash and put his hand in Cash's face. "What the fuck you gonna do? This my block now, nigga!"

"Yo, Manny, get your hand outta my face, nigga! I ain't the fuckin' one!" Cash growled at him, his fists clenched and face scowling.

The other males on the block stood around watching the tension between Cash and his former friends. The neighborhood and the streets all believed that he'd set up Petey Jay and did Perez dirty, after all that man did for him. Cash's name and reputation had turned into mud.

Darrell shouted, "Nigga, you pussy!"

"Fuck you too, Darrell! Y'all niggas ain't shit!"

"You a bitch, nigga! You ain't shit!"

"When Petey Jay comes home, you gonna see, nigga!" Manny hollered.

"I'm gonna see what, nigga? Cuz y'all niggas ain't gonna do shit!"

Manny and Darrell had a lot of hate in their eyes. It was inevitable that the argument would soon turn into punches being thrown.

Cash was ready to strike Manny first. His blood was boiling. He was seething. He shouted at Manny, "Do somethin', you faggot-ass nigga!"

Manny quickly reached into his waistband, removing a Glock 17, and pointed it directly in Cash's face.

Cash, caught off guard, didn't flinch. He scowled heavily, clenching his fist and teeth. "So, you gonna shoot me now, nigga? Huh?" Looking directly down the barrel of the gun, Cash saw his life flashing before him. He couldn't read Manny. Was he crazy enough to do it, pull the trigger and kill an old friend?

Darrell stepped in between the heated exchange, saying, "Yo, Manny, just chill."

"Nah, fuck this nigga!"

Cash continued not to flinch or move, scowling back at Manny. He didn't know if today was his day to die, or whether Manny was simply bluffing, trying to show off in front of everyone.

"Yo, he ain't worth it, Manny," Darrell said. "Besides, too many people watchin', and we already gettin' money, my nigga. Don't let this punk nigga fuck it up for us."

Manny lowered the gun. Inwardly, Cash sighed with relief.

"Get the fuck off my block, nigga!" Manny said.

Cash didn't say a word. He backpedaled and then pivoted toward the Buick. He climbed inside and drove away. He was fuming. Now there was another name he needed to add to his hit list. Cash was sure that if there hadn't been so many witnesses on the block, that Manny would have pulled the trigger and taken his life.

EIGHT

Boom! Boom! Boom!

"U.S. Marshals! Open the door!" a man shouted. "We're here to enforce an eviction warrant."

The loud knocking startled Pearla out of her sleep.

"U.S. Marshals! Open the door!"

Pearla's heart was stuck in her throat. She ran toward the bedroom window and glanced outside. She saw the marshals posted outside her front door: four white males dressed in their embroidered law enforcement jackets, looking intense.

Either she opened the door, or it sounded like they were going to knock it down.

"U.S. Marshals here for an eviction!" they continued to yell.

Pearla made her way downstairs with her heart in her throat. The eviction process had actually taken longer than Pearla thought, but now it was time to pay the piper. She had exhausted all her options. She opened the door, and the marshals poured inside her place with the eviction warrant.

"You and whoever else is inside here have a half hour to gather your belongings and vacate the premises," the tall white male said to her.

Pearla looked expressionless. She didn't respond, but did what she was told.

The marshals went through her place like they owned it. They placed a dispossess notice on her front door, and Pearla was forced to gather up whatever could fit inside her car and leave. Everything else was put out on the curb. She held back her tears and kept a strong face. The marshals were stern and cold. No apathy whatsoever.

Her neighbors stood outside gawking, stunned by what they saw.

As Pearla was being escorted out of her home carrying an armful of her clothes, she quickly locked eyes with Ms. Hicks. Then Pearla shouted out, "Is everyone enjoying the show? Huh? Is this amusing, seeing a woman evicted from her house, like some fuckin' criminal!"

Ms. Hicks shook her head and turned away.

Pearla didn't care for her opinion or sympathy anyway. She walked toward her car and stuffed everything she could carry from her home into the trunk and backseat, which was overflowing. She had never been so humiliated. The front of her home looked like a yard sale.

Once the car door shut, the engine started, and she drove away from the house, her tears started to fall like heavy raindrops. Pearla drove two blocks and completely broke down. She had to pull over. She couldn't drive or think at the moment. Where to go? What to do?

Pearla drove around aimlessly for hours, burning her gas but not caring. With dusk approaching, she found herself parked in front of Roark's place. She was back in the projects. It was the last place she wanted to be, but she was desperate.

It took time to put herself together, but she did, spending an hour in a public bathroom doing her hair, makeup, and correcting her outfit. Though homeless, broke, and desperate, she still had an image to uphold. She couldn't let anyone see her sweat.

She started toward the building, strutting in her red bottoms that had seen better days, but, still, they were Christian Louboutins and cost her a pretty penny last year. Pearla walked with her head up, prideful. However, underneath the image was a torn, broken woman. She was being put to the test, and she felt like she was failing.

As she was about to walk into the lobby, she heard blaring rap music from a passing car. Pearla turned just in time to catch a glimpse of Cash driving by with some young bitch in the passenger seat. He was all smiles, the male whore that he was.

A crushing feeling quickly crippled Pearla. She couldn't move. It felt like someone had taken a baseball bat to her stomach repeatedly. She wanted to throw up. It looked like he'd forgotten about her completely. Just like that, he was gone and she was left standing there taking all of the punishment.

Fuck him! she said to herself. He didn't want her then she didn't want him. She tried telling herself that anyway.

Pearla had to take a deep breath and remind herself why she was there—to get her life back in order, restart a hustle. Do better, be better! She was there to make amends with Roark. She needed her friend to go boosting again. She needed to put another crew together. And she knew it wasn't going to be easy.

She went inside and took the pissy elevator to Roark's floor. She braved a smile and knocked twice. The door opened, and Roark was standing right in front of her, looking unfriendly.

"What you doin' here, Pearla?" Roark asked with a frown and attitude.

"I came here to talk."

"About what? You have some nerves coming to see me after everything you did."

"What did I do, Roark? Huh?"

"You know. We gonna play this stupid game?"

"I thought we were friends."

"And so did I, but you leave to go live with Cash, forget about me, and Jamie's dead."

"I had nothing to do with that," Pearla lied. "And you know this!"

"I don't know shit," she spat. "What you mean, 'I know' like I'm your alibi or something?"

"I don't need an alibi, because it wasn't me, Roark. You sound stupid."

"People are talking, Pearla."

"And what are they saying?" Pearla looked at Roark intensely.

Roark didn't blink, but locked eyes with her former friend, doing her best to hold her own against someone she once looked up to and respected. "You is a grimy bitch, Pearla!"

"Is this the streets talking, or is this coming from you directly, Roark?"

"It's both. And I don't need you anymore, Pearla."

"You don't need me anymore," Pearla replied incredulously. "Without me, you would be nothing. I remember when you were afraid to steal a pack of gum from the corner store. I was the one that molded you and taught you how to boost the best shit."

"And you taught me well. But I came up without you."

"So now you think you a boss bitch?" Pearl said with contempt.

"Oh, you don't believe me? You need to come take a look for yourself," Roark replied with a smug look.

Pearla thought Roark was acting raucous. She'd never had that much mouth. She was a changed bitch, from her attitude to her wardrobe. Roark was dressed trendily in a short designer skirt and a low-cut top revealing her ample cleavage. She rocked diamond hoop earrings and a matching bracelet. Her hair was blown out and long. She even got a few tattoos, one across her left breast displaying the Gucci logo, and one with colorful roses and thorns intertwined, wrapping around her right leg and reaching down toward her knee.

Roark stepped aside and allowed Pearla into the apartment. The minute Pearla entered the living room, her eyes lit up. Roark's living room had everything in it—clothes, shoes, jewelry, coats, mink coats, and even electronics. It looked like Best Buy and Saks exploded and dumped all the good shit inside the small area. It was a den of hot goods.

Two young girls were seated on the couch, counting money. They glanced at Pearla but didn't say a word. They were dressed in designer clothing too, wearing bling and looking a bit hood.

Roark was standing on her own two feet instead of having to lean on anyone else. Her meekness and introverted attitude had been transformed. It seemed like she was the one wearing the crown now.

Pearla was shocked. The apprentice had now become the master.

"You see, I don't need you anymore, Pearla," Roark said. She stood behind Pearla with a condescending look, her arms folded across her chest.

Pearla just stood there, taken aback. This was a whole other level Roark was on. She wanted to ask Roark what she was doing differently that had her doing so well. Pearla was sure that her friends would've folded once she'd left the group.

Roark had a team of young boosters and was dealing with Chica to sell the product. She was also setting up the illegal marriages with Chica, having taken Pearla's place.

Pearla couldn't help but to brim with envy.

Roark walked by her and pulled out a wad of cash from a jar and started to count it. It totaled five thousand. "Showing is so much better than telling, ain't it?" Roark said. "What me and Chica got goin' on now, you will never touch it."

Pearla managed to smile. "What you got here is cute, but how long do you think it's gonna last?"

"Pearla, you need to stop hatin'. It definitely don't look good on you, boo boo."

"No hate, bitch," Pearla fired back, "just facts."

"Well, you wanna hear my facts? We're not friends, and we won't be ever again, because I don't trust you. You betrayed Chica and me, and Jamie's dead, so what makes you think you can just come back and act like everything's gonna be all good?"

"You need to worry about Chica. Now *she's* a grimy bitch. And like I said, I didn't have anything to do with Jamie's murder."

"All I know is she was fuckin' Cash, and then she was dead."

"You don't know shit, bitch!" Pearla exclaimed.

"I do know how to get paid, though. Right?" Roark quipped.

Pearla glared at Roark, but there wasn't anything she could do. For the moment, Roark was on top.

"Just leave, Pearla. I don't want you here; we're fine without you," Roark said.

"Laugh now, cry later," Pearla said.

"You threatening me?"

"Take it as you want it, Roark."

Pearla stepped out into the hallway, and Roark slammed the door in her face. Roark now felt she needed to watch her back too, or she might end up like Jamie.

It pained Pearla greatly to see Roark living large. After everything she did for that girl, Roark had the audacity to shun her and talk disrespectful. It was all good. Pearla planned on stepping back up and reclaiming what she once had.

The moment Pearla walked out of the lobby, she pulled out her cell phone and dialed Chica. She had to swallow her pride. It was time for them to have a talk. The phone rang several times on the other end until Chica answered.

"Oh, I know you ain't calling me, bitch!" Chica exclaimed. "Who the fuck you think you are? I just spoke to Roark."

"I just called to talk," Pearla said in a humble voice.

"Talk? Bitch, we don't have shit to say to each other. Fact, I don't have a muthafuckin' thing to say to you! You is a grimy fuckin' bitch, and I don't want anything to do with you. You understand, bitch? Fuck you! You is a two-faced bitch, Pearla! Lose my fuckin' number! After everything I did for you, and you backstab me, take my hustle, and wanna cut me out! Die, bitch! Die!" Chica hung up.

It was official. There was no one left. What goes up must come down. And Pearla came down hard.

NINE

Ooooh, eat that pussy!" Gloria cried out. "Don't stop. Right there. Yes, right there!"

Cash had his cougar bitch spread-eagle on the bed, flat on her back with her feet planted on either side of his shoulders, his mouth buried in her pussy, licking and sucking slowly.

She squirmed a bit, enjoying the pleasure. He boxed her clit with his tongue. He used both hands to caress her breasts at the same time. The combination was stimulating and breathtaking. Her clit and pussy were pulsating and wet like a river. She couldn't control herself.

"Oh God! You gonna make come, Cash!" she hollered.

The look on her face was sexually twisted. She clutched the bed sheets and moaned louder and louder. The sound of her thrill started to echo off the bedroom walls as she skyrocketed into total bliss.

"Damn, nigga! Ooooh shit! Ooooh! Yes!"

Cash was focused and committed. He needed to keep Gloria happy, but at the same time he was stressing about Manny and Darrell. He wanted to get back at them. He wanted to hurt Manny for pulling out a gun and putting it in his face like they were strangers.

In the meantime, Gloria needed to be pleased. Lately, she had been upset with him for not pulling his weight around the house, not cleaning or cooking, and leaving for hours in the day and coming back late at night. Cash could tell she was becoming frustrated with his behavior. Now wasn't the time to screw up his living arrangement.

Cash had no reason to complain, but he couldn't be domesticated.

"I'm gonna come, Cash!" She announced in breathless anticipation. She continued to squirm and placed her legs over Cash's shoulders, feeling her orgasm building. "Oh God, I'm gonna fuckin' come!" Shortly after, she exploded, squirting out like a water fountain.

Cash could only watch as she gushed out intensely, cooing and quivering. He smiled. *Job well done!*

The sex wasn't done yet. He strapped on a Magnum condom and went in. He needed his nut too.

An hour later, they both lit up a cigarette and lingered inside the bedroom. He had Gloria completely satisfied. With four orgasms in one night, he was going for a record. Most times, the sex made her stop complaining and distracted her from his imperfections.

Cash took a drag from the Newport and exhaled.

Gloria looked at him and out of the blue asked, "What do you do during the day, Cash?"

"What you mean?"

"Are you looking for work?"

"Pleasing you is work," he joked.

Gloria frowned. "Oh, so I'm work now? You don't like having sex with me?"

"Nah, I was just playing, sexy. I love having sex with you. You got that good pussy," he replied, trying to save face. Cash went over to her and kissed her lips gently. "You're beautiful, baby."

"Oh, I'm beautiful, huh?"

"Yes. And I want to be with you forever."

"Are you having sex with other women?"

"What? Nah."

Gloria had her suspicions that he was cheating on her, but she couldn't prove it. She wasn't looking too hard to flush out his infidelity. While she was at work, Cash wasn't shy about bringing different girls into her home—Rena, Gina, and Keisha. He would have sex with different women all through her house. Even the same bed they fucked in had been soiled with other women.

Gloria sighed. "I want us to work out, Cash."

"And we will."

"I want to trust you."

"Baby, have I given you a reason not to trust me? I'm here for you, and I'm doin' right. I'm out there looking for a job—which reminds me, I'm gonna need a couple of dollars for gas money. I got this job interview lined up tomorrow afternoon at this shop."

"Oh, you do? Where is it at?"

"Yeah, a friend of mines is trying to hook me up at this mechanic shop in Brooklyn. You know I like cars."

"I know."

"It sounds like the perfect gig—pays twelve an hour, and I get to do what I love," Cash fabricated.

"It sounds good, Cash. How much do you need for gas and lunch?"

"Fifty is cool."

Gloria removed herself from the bed butt naked and went to retrieve her purse from the dresser. She opened it, reached inside to pull out her wallet, and removed a fifty-dollar bill. She handed it to Cash.

He smiled. "You're perfect for me," he said. He kissed her passionately again. He was growing hard. He pulled away from her, looked down at his big erection and joked, "Look at that. He's hungry for you again."

Gloria smiled. "I see."

"You wanna go for a fifth time and try to break our record?"

She smiled. "I'm down!"

Her stamina in the bedroom matched his. Like Cash, she could never get enough of great sex. She needed his dick like a weedhead needed his high, and Cash knew it. Gloria had it bad for him. He made her weak. She was wise and intelligent, but Cash sometimes made her look like a fool.

Cash pushed her onto the bed on her back, and she immediately spread her legs for him, announcing, "Come and get it, big boy!"

He climbed on top of her and started another heated round of intense, sweaty sex with her. Cash made it his business to keep doing what she liked to keep her blinded from his true self.

Cash lay in bed sleeping while Gloria got up at six in the morning to get dressed for work. It was too early in the morning for him. Last night had him drained. He wanted to sleep and regenerate himself for later on.

Gloria got dressed in her dark blue pantsuit and heels, grabbed her belongings, and quickly woke up Cash.

"Don't forget to clean the bathrooms today like you promised, baby, and good luck on your job interview." She kissed him on the check and exited the bedroom.

Cash stirred around in the bed a little and went back to sleep. *How do they do it, the working people, get up so damn early every morning for a crappy job?* he thought to himself.

He was too young and too fine to work a regular nine-to-five job. Life was about having fun, going after the things you love full throttle, no holding back, living your dreams, becoming known.

Half an hour before noon, Cash finally lifted himself from the bed and went into the bathroom to take a long-held piss. The sun was out, and the day was warm. He thought about the fifty dollars he'd conned Gloria for. *Stupid bitch actually believed I had a job interview today.*

Cash had two things on his agenda. Keisha was one, and Brooklyn was the second. After washing his ass, he looked at the time and saw it was noon already. He called Keisha from his cell phone.

"Hey, beautiful. What you doin'?"

"Nothing," she replied. "Just chillin'."

"Come over and see me."

"You still at your sister's place?" she asked.

"Yeah! I need you right now, baby. I'm missing you."

"Okay, I'll be there in fifteen minutes."

"A'ight, cool. I can't wait to see you."

"Me too."

Cash hung up, smiling proudly. Keisha was his super freak. She was nineteen years old, had her own car, and worked retail at the mall in the evenings, so her afternoons were free for her to come by and play with him.

Cash hurried and got dressed and waited for Keisha.

It was one p.m. when the doorbell rang. Cash walked toward the door and peered outside. He saw Keisha. He smiled and opened the front door.

Keisha walked in looking scrumptious in a pair of tight blue jeans, a tight white shirt that accentuated her tits, and a pair of fresh white Nikes. Her hair was short and curly. She was too cute.

"Hey, baby," Cash greeted her with an intimate hug. "You miss me?"

"You know I did." He invited her inside.

The minute she was inside the living room, he couldn't resist feeling on her booty and trying to undress her.

"Damn! You miss me that much?" she said, giggling.

"Me and my dick."

Keisha giggled some more.

Cash didn't want to waste any time. He unbuckled his pants, dropped them around his ankles, and smiled her way.

He sat on the couch, and Keisha plopped in front of him on her knees and without a word, she began stroking, licking, and sucking his hard dick.

Cash moaned, loving his life right now. He palmed Keisha's head while she was performing, pulling on the back of her neck to take his big dick as deep into her mouth as possible. Keisha sucked and sucked.

Afterwards, he practically ripped off her clothes, threw her against the couch, and fucked her hard, all the while ignoring Gloria's phone calls and staring at her picture on the fire mantel.

Cash pulled Keisha's hair and spanked her ass, and Keisha screamed, his big dick thrusting inside of her.

When Cash came, he pulled out and shot his load all over her back.

After they fucked they raided the fridge. Keisha kept him company until four p.m., having to be at work before five.

Cash hurriedly cleaned up after she left, made a dinner of spaghetti and meatballs for Gloria, and pretended he had a long day looking for work.

He was going to milk the cow until it went dry.

TEN

The rain hammered down on the streets and on Pearla's parked car like a hail of bullets on the dark chilly night. The storm wasn't letting up any time soon.

A flash of lightning lit up the dark sky, and thunder boomed powerfully above. Visibility in the street was almost zero, but Pearla had her attention absorbed at the front porch on the Brooklyn Street in Canarsie.

She found herself in a very dark and ugly place. She wanted to make her mother suffer. Pearla couldn't stop thinking about Poochie. "That fuckin' selfish bitch! I hate this bitch!"

The .380 in her hand was loaded and cocked back. She eyed the house and noticed there was only one car in the driveway. She was waiting and contemplating doing the unthinkable. She needed to get the pain off her chest. She wanted to teach Poochie a hard lesson. Cash too. They'd both abandoned her when she needed them the most.

The rain continued hammering. Traffic on the street was little to almost non-existent. Her stomach growled, and her sanity felt like it was fading. It almost felt like she couldn't cry anymore, but then someone would be able to squeeze another tear from her eyes, hurt her more, make her feel like shit when she was already hitting rock bottom.

A blue Lexus pulled into the driveway. The headlights turned off, and the engine was killed. The driver's door opened, and Poochie climbed out with an umbrella in one hand and a bag of groceries in the other, trying to hurry out of the rain.

Pearla, without delay, removed herself from her car and marched toward Poochie with the gun gripped firmly in her hand. The rain hit her skin like it would go right through. She looked impermeable to the weather. She was mad and completely numb to the harsh conditions. She wanted revenge. She was transfixed by Poochie's action, watching her mother hurry onto the porch.

Pearla hurried her way. Before Poochie could reach the front door, Pearla called out to her, "Poochie! You fuckin' selfish bitch!" her voice filled with disparagement.

Poochie spun around and was wide-eyed.

Pearla outstretched her hand and trained the gun at her. She was unmoving, focused on wanting to seriously hurt her mother.

Poochie hollered, "Pearla, what the fuck is wrong wit' you? You crazy?"

"I hate you, Poochie!"

"Pearla, look, you need to calm down and lower the fuckin' gun!"

"I came to you for help, and you shut me out. But when you needed me, I was there!" she yelled.

"I'm not a nice person, Pearla. You know this. I know I can be a bitch. But I love you. You're my only child."

"Oh, now you fuckin' love me?"

"I do, Pearla. I did for you by tryin' to make you fuckin' strong to live in this cruel world. If I babied you, then you wouldn't have become the woman you are today. I didn't want a weak daughter. I always envied you, Pearla. You were always able to stand on your own two feet. You never needed a man to support you. But you always had one around. You were an entrepreneur. You're a leader, Pearla."

"Fuck you! You just sayin' all this shit because I got the fuckin' gun!" Pearla, her face scowling, stepped closer to Poochie.

"Listen to me, Pearla, you kill me and you think your life will get easier?"

"I don't give a fuck right now. My life ain't shit right now!"

Poochie took a deep breath. "That's not true. You, you're a born hustler, Pearla. You can always rebuild."

"Rebuild with what? Where's my fuckin' money!"

Poochie looked panicky. She didn't want to die. She was helpless. "Don't do this, Pearla. You're not weak like this."

She didn't want to listen to Poochie's feeble attempt at trying to save her own life.

The heavy rainfall continued to drench Pearla. She looked like a wet dog. She locked eyes with her mother.

Do it! Just do it! she kept telling herself.

Why did she hesitate? Poochie shouldn't have seen it coming. It would have been easier to shoot her in the back and flee. But Pearla wanted to see the look on her mother's face.

Pearla held the gun steady. She was focused. From where she stood, she couldn't miss Poochie at all.

"I raised you to be a strong woman, but now you want to be a killer?"

"Admit it!"

"Admit what?"

Pearla gritted her teeth. "Where. Is. My. Fuckin'. Money!"

"It's all gone, Pearla. All of it. And I'm sorry, but that's the truth."

Suddenly, something startled Pearla. It was the sound of thunder exploding in the sky.

Then the gun went off. *Boc!* The bullet shattered the front window.

Poochie screamed, "I'll pay you back! I promise! I can give you a couple hundred dollars a month. Please, Pearla, don't do this!"

Pearla couldn't do it. She just couldn't take her mother's life, even though it felt like Poochie had already taken hers. She took off running back to her car and got in.

Unbeknownst to Pearla, her mother had every dime of the half million dollars she pilfered stashed in the attic of Henry's house. She would have died before she would have given it up.

ELEVEN

Through her windshield, Pearla noticed the traffic cop standing near her car writing her a ticket. It was early morning, and the city was just coming alive.

"What the fuck!" Quickly, she put on her sneakers and rushed out of the car to confront him. "What the fuck are you doing?" she yelled.

"Ma'am, you're parked illegally in a handicap zone."

"What? I was in the fuckin' car. I was sleeping!"

He continued writing, ignoring her.

"You couldn't see me inside the car?" She shouted with her tart breath in his face. "You saw me lying down in the backseat. All you had to do was tell me to move!"

He continued writing.

"Seriously, you gonna write me a fuckin' ticket?"

"It's my job," he stated absently.

"Fuck your job!"

He removed the ticket from his book and attempted to place it against the windshield, but Pearla stepped in between him and her car, fuming.

"I can't afford a ticket right now. Can't you see I'm

sleeping in my car? You can't give me a break? C'mon!"

"I'm just doing my job, ma'am. If you have a problem with the ticket, you can contest it," he proclaimed, sounding like a robot.

Pearla huffed and puffed. She snatched the ticket from his hand and tore it up. The ticket was three hundred dollars, and she didn't even have three dollars to her name. She screamed, "Fuck you and your fuckin' ticket! I don't fuckin' care!"

The traffic cop stood there stoically. "Ma'am, your outburst is uncalled for. The ticket will just be mailed to your address."

"I don't have a fuckin' address! Can't you see? You stupid dumb-fuck! I'm homeless!" she shouted heatedly.

The man turned and tried to walk away, but Pearla chased behind him.

"Don't fuckin' walk away from me, nigga!" She wanted to hurt him so bad, she had her fists clenched. She shoved him.

He tumbled forward but quickly found his footing. "I will call nine-one-one, ma'am," he said coolly.

"Fuck nine-one-one, you bitch-ass, nigga!"

The traffic cop got on his radio and immediately called in the hostile situation to his superiors.

Pearla could hear his radio crackling and his superior on the other end. She knew she had taken things too far. She couldn't afford to get locked up. Coming to her senses, she rushed back to her vehicle, jumped inside, and sped away.

Once again, she started to cry. She'd been sleeping in her car since the eviction. The nights were becoming colder and longer. She had been trying to move her car from one inconspicuous place to another. She was trying to stay strong, but every day was more challenging than the previous one.

Pearla raced away from the area, jumping on the freeway. She felt dirty and tired. Her car looked like she had been traveling from state to state.

She made her way to a gas station near the Belt Parkway. She parked around the back and asked the attendant for the key to the bathroom. He gave it to her. She went inside carrying a small bag and locked the door.

She flicked on the lights to the grungy-looking restroom and sighed heavily. It wasn't the Grand Hyatt, but it would have to do. She had to make herself look right.

The first thing Pearla did was wash her face and then style her hair. She pulled it into a bun high on top of her head. She quickly put on a pair of tight blue jeans and a black V-neck halter-top. And last, she put on a pair of wedges. Her look wasn't perfect, but for now it was decent.

One last look at herself in the mirror, a quick hair adjustment, and she was ready to go. She stepped out of the bathroom trying to look proud and respectable. She walked back to her car and climbed inside.

The ignition started, but she lingered for a moment, staring at the gas mileage. Less than a half a tank and her stomach was growling. The two dollars on her wasn't enough for gas and food. She needed to hustle up some money to eat and fill up her gas tank.

The attractively dressed white woman sat with her husband on the serene sidewalk seats along tree-lined West 4th Street outside the restaurant in the bustling West Village. The sidewalk tables were set far back from the curb to evade the traffic fumes and tetchy pedestrians.

Pearla had her eyes on the seated woman as she walked, noticing her name-brand pocketbook dangling on the back of her chair. The woman was engaged with lunch and conversation with her husband. The prize was right there for Pearla to take; she just needed the perfect distraction.

Passing the restaurant, she walked closer behind a thick, tall man, blocking her petite frame from others. He was Pearla's cover. She saw the lady waiter attending to one of her customers. It was now or never.

The waiter had her back turned to Pearla, and the minute Pearla walked by her, she pushed her into the table, having the poor woman topple over the patrons and create some confusion, spilling dishes and drinks. For a moment, everyone had their eyes on the scene, and as that was happening, Pearla shrewdly removed the woman's pocketbook from the chair while passing by and quickly slung it over her shoulder like it was hers and hurried away.

Pearla walked briskly back to her car and got inside, both hands trembling. A year ago she could have done this sleepwalking. Now, she was rusty and second guessing herself. Whatever happened to the hustler she was born and bred to be? Where was that woman?

She closed and locked her door and dumped all the contents onto the passenger seat, spilling lipsticks and eyeliners, perfume, half-dozen credit cards, and five hundred dollars in cash.

Pearla finally exhaled. It felt like she could breathe again. She'd briefly pulled herself up from drowning in hunger and poverty. She still had a lot to do, and a long way to go.

She started her car and made her way to the nearest gas station to fill up her gas tank. And then she went to the closest Applebee's and munched on a couple entrees. She ate like the homeless person that she was and promised herself that she would never allow things to get this bad again.

Now with her hunger and gas tank taken care of, Pearla finally could think. It was time to come up with a new hustle, one that would catapult her back into her old lifestyle.

She was too hot to go inside any of her familiar department stores to boost, or to try and set up any illegal green card weddings. So for now, her new hustle was taking women's purses out of the front seat at gas stations, out the shopping cart at the supermarkets, or off the back of a chair in a restaurant or bar. She targeted mostly older Caucasian women who appeared to be distracted or multi-tasking.

Pearla knew she couldn't keep up this scheme for long. The reward wasn't worth the risk, but the money she was collecting, along with the credit cards, was helping keep her afloat.

TWELVE

Pearla slid the card key into the electronic lock, and the green light flickered, giving access to the hotel room. She walked inside and clicked on the lights.

"Yes!" she hollered excitedly.

It wasn't a luxurious suite, but it was a decent hotel room at the Hilton in downtown Brooklyn.

She sat on the comfortable queen bed and took in the room. The TV had HBO, the bathroom was spacious with lots of clean towels, there was a desk for personal business and a computer chair, and she had Internet service, though no laptop. The room was paradise to her.

Pearla fell back on the bed and stretched out. She exhaled. She gazed at the wall and smiled to herself. "I'm a survivor," she said to herself. The only thing she wanted to do tonight was relax and enjoy the fruits of her labor.

She ordered room service and ran a hot bath. She slid down into the water and let it soothe her. She closed her eyes and imagined the finer things in life, and the respect. She missed the shopping sprees, the thrill of boosting, the cars, the hustle of being a get-money bitch.

Pearla continued to keep her eyes closed and enjoy the solitude. The quietness and comfort of her room were hypnotizing.

After the bath, Pearla orders a cheeseburger and fries from room service. She watched TV for an hour and dozed off.

Pearla spent the next morning watching TV and taking notes. Tax season was approaching, the seasons were changing, and she was ready to change with it. Watching CNBC, CNN, Fox News, and other networks, Pearla brainstormed. She was ready to look for potential victims to implement various schemes.

The Brooklyn Heights library on Cadman Plaza W opened at ten, but Pearla had been waiting outside since nine thirty, eager to go inside and do her research. When the doors opened, she was the first one inside. From there, she sat at a computer and used the Internet, where she was able to find almost anyone's name, age, and address, and sometimes, their telephone number; she had to pay for additional information.

Day after day, she visited the library, and hour after hour, she meticulously jotted down all the pertinent information she needed, until she had over one thousand names, zeroing in only on the elderly, the easiest to con and scam.

Next, she went to Wal-Mart and purchased a burner phone with unlimited minutes. They were difficult to track. She chose Washington DC area code as an added bonus.

Last, she went to the local post office and acquired a post office box. She was putting the money she'd stolen to good use, investing in her scam.

After a week of preparation, Pearla was ready to start one of the many scams she had prepared. Hotel rooms became her base of operations. Doors locked and the television off, she dialed her first number, an eighty-six-year-old retired nurse named Eloise Simpson.

The phone rang, and Ms. Simpson answered. "Hello?"

"Yes, good afternoon. Can I speak to a Ms. Eloise Simpson?" Pearla asked in her professional tone.

"Speaking."

"Hello, my name is Janet Brown, and I'm calling from the IRS to inform you that you have an outstanding tax bill, and if the matter isn't settled soon, then we will be forced to freeze your bank accounts and take further action. And we can attach liens to your home or properties."

Ms. Simpson responded in a nervous voice. "Oh my! I didn't know that I owed money to the government. I'm on a fixed income."

"It's okay, ma'am. I'm here to help. There's no need to panic."

"What do I need to do?"

Pearla smiled. She had her first fish hooked and was ready to reel her in. After she asked probing questions to figure out how well-off the victim was, Pearla gave her an amount that she allegedly owed.

"Twenty-five hundred dollars."

"Oh, that's a lot," Ms. Simpson replied.

"We can make a payment arrangement for you, if necessary, but then interest and penalties will be applied."

If they didn't have savings, then Pearla planned to ask for five hundred dollars; if they did, anywhere from fifteen to twenty-five hundred.

She gave Ms. Simpson the PO box and informed her to either pay via money order or a prepaid debit card that she could purchase at any supermarket. Ms. Simpson opted to send a money order. Pearla kept the scam under three thousand dollars, knowing that if you purchased any U.S. Postal money orders over that amount, she would have to fill out federal paperwork and Pearla didn't want any trace.

Ms. Simpson assured her that the payment would be in the mail no later than Thursday. Pearla smiled, thanked the victim, and then hung up. Victim one was down.

She made the next call to a Ms. Candice Partlow, 69. Then there was Mildred Tully, 89, and Leslie Miles, 76.

Hour after hour, Pearla kept herself busy with phone call after phone call, conning her victims. Some fell for the scam, and some didn't. Some of these elderly woman pushed back, asking for her name, IRS badge number, and contact number so that one of their family members could call Pearla back. Those calls Pearla just hung up and went on to the next victim.

The first day, Pearla was exhausted, but she did good, making over ninety phone calls. Out of the ninety, thirty-five percent seemingly fell for the scam. The only way to be sure was when she actually received payments.

The next day, Pearla started her "grandparent scam." It seemed simple enough, however it proved to be quite difficult. Pearla had gone through over fifty telephone numbers and no one bit. She was just about to nix this scam when she found a victim.

She called the number in Tennessee, and after several rings, a lady answered, "Hello?"

"Hi, Grandma! Do you know who this is?" Pearla asked excitedly.

"Jennifer?"

"Yes! It's me, Grandma, Jennifer! How you been?" Pearla quickly established a bogus identity with the woman without having to do a lick of background research.

"I'm fine, chile."

"That's good to hear. I miss you, Grandma."

"I miss you too, Jennifer."

"Grandma, I need your help with something."

"What is it?"

"I'm in New York, and I need your help to get back home. I hate it here, Grandma, and I wanna come home," she cried out. "I lost my ID, and I don't have anything left."

"New York," the lady asked, skeptically. "I thought your mom said you and the kids were on vacation . . . on that island . . . I can't remember where—"

"Yeah, we were but then I came to New York, and I need you, Grandma. Promise you won't tell mom."

"Don't get upset. I'll help you. What do you need?"

"I need you to send me five hundred dollars. I need a bus ticket. And I'm so hungry, Grandma, I haven't eaten in days."

"Oh my Lord. Okay, I'll send you the money. Just come home, Jennifer."

"Thank you, Grandma! Thank you so much!"

Pearla gave the old woman a bogus name. She would be able to pick up the cash without identification as long as the person sending it gave a password or test question. The next day the cash would be sent via Western Union.

After that call Pearla was drained. No more "grandma" calls. Too time consuming.

THIRTEEN

Ray-Ray danced and sang in front of the Brooklyn liquor store like he was a contestant for *American Idol.* He was in very high spirits. The smile on his face stretched a mile, and his gregarious laughter could echo into next week.

"It's a very beautiful day, isn't it?" he hollered to people passing on the sidewalk. "God is wonderful. Life is so precious. Appreciate the day, people."

Most people ignored him, thinking he was some crazy old man, while others gave him a dollar here and a few coins there. Tilting his dingy baseball cap out, Ray-Ray was happy to take whatever folks could give him.

He continued to dance and sing, opening the door to the liquor store to allow customers inside. He greeted people with charm, jokes, and compliments. His clothes were raggedy and outdated, but his soul and character was upbeat and enjoyable.

"Hey there, beautiful lady. I didn't know Beyoncé had a twin sister," Ray-Ray said to a young woman as he opened the door for her.

She giggled and smiled, smitten by his comment. She then gave him a few dollars.

"Thank you, Ms. Beautiful. I appreciate your generosity so much."

Ray-Ray twirled in the middle of the sidewalk like he was Michael Jackson, and did a crazy split. Then he jumped up and did a moonwalk in front of everyone. His age didn't stop him from performing like a young person.

"Ray-Ray is in town, and he's at your service!" he shouted.

It was a breezy and cloudy day, but Ray-Ray didn't care.

He shouted, "The clouds are above, the sun is gone, but it's cool, because on Ray-Ray's block, the sun is always out!"

He opened the door for two males and said, "Welcome to Ray-Ray's boom-boom room. If I had the cash, the drinks would be on me."

He made them laugh, and one tipped him five dollars.

"I appreciate the generosity, kind sir."

"You crazy funny, old man," the other said to him.

Ray-Ray lit the block up with his humor, dancing and just being himself. He enjoyed people, and he enjoyed life. "Ray-Ray is here to turn anyone's frown upside down! Just come around and get ya laugh on! Kevin Hart don't have shit on me!"

Cash circled the block looking for his father and found him at his usual spot in front of the liquor store in the middle of the block. He parked and climbed out his car. He had a lot on his mind, so he went looking for his pops for some wisdom.

Cash could hear his father from half a block away. There was no mistaking Ray-Ray's voice. It was a deep baritone and a bit raspy. But it was always a delight to hear. He casually walked toward his pops.

Cash smiled. He hid his demons perfectly. No one would suspect Ray-Ray had committed a double homicide several months earlier.

"Hey, Pop."

Ray-Ray turned around, and his smile grew even larger. "There he is, my son, the prince of Brooklyn, because I'm the king, and when I die, he will get to inherit all of this."

Cash shook his head and laughed. "You ain't ever gonna change, Pop." He hugged his father.

"Why change, when it's so much fun being me? I mean, look at the envy on all of these people faces"— He pointed at the passing foot traffic. "They love me and hate me at the same time."

"Yeah, I see that, Pop," Cash replied dryly.

"Anyway, what brings you around?"

"I came to talk," Cash said in a serious tone.

"You know my ears and heart is always open, son. You can talk to me about anything. Come, let's step into my office."

Ray-Ray's office was a bench nearby in the projects. He and Cash walked that way, and father and son sat near each other. Ray-Ray sat upright, arms spread across the back of the bench, while Cash sat hunched over, elbows pressed against his knees and looking away from his pops.

The two looked like night and day. Cash was finely dressed in designer jeans, a white V-neck T-shirt underneath his leather jacket, and brand-new beige Timberlands on his feet, sporting a diamond earring and a fresh haircut. He was a pretty boy 24/7. Three ladies in passing gave him a fleeting look and a warm smile.

Cash smiled back, his eyes lingering on their backsides.

"You still showing off, I see," Ray-Ray said.

"I can't help it if the ladies love me."

"They used to love your old man. You should have seen me back in my prime. Boy, I would have made you look like Steve Urkel."

Cash managed to smile, looking at his father. "I bet."

"So, what's new in your life, or should I say who's new in your life? I see you're still looking fresh to death."

"You know me—I gotta always shine."

"How's Pearla?"

"We ain't together anymore. I left her."

"Why? She was a good woman."

"We just had our differences."

"Yeah, you done had your differences with many different women."

"Hey, I'm a chip off the old block, right?"

"And you see where that got me. So who's the new lady, and what's your new hustle?"

"There's no new hustle, Pop. I'm just shacking up with a woman twice my age. She's cool, but she can be a bit demanding. I needed a place to stay, met her by chance, and I've been dicking her down for a roof over my head."

"You know I can't cosign on that, Cash. I'd rather be homeless and panhandle than to allow a woman, any woman, to make me her bitch."

Cash was offended. "I ain't nobody's bitch!"

Ray-Ray shrugged. "It's okay. I say what I say."

"I ain't got no friends right now because niggas think I'm snitching and forgot about them, and I'm broke, Pop! This bitch I'm stayin' wit', she's been looking out for me, giving me money here and there."

"The Cash I know would be telling me a different story."

"Well, this Cash here, he got a lot going on."

"And you ready to give up? You ready to surrender all your hoes and become a one-woman man?"

"Nah, Pops. You know a nigga like me ain't meant to be domesticated."

"Well, you can either be a pimp and live off women your whole life, or you can become a boss. But both choices do have consequences, Cash."

Ray-Ray focused on his son and continued with, "Being a pimp, Cash, you leave your balls at the door each day. You can never become a real man having a woman make the money for you. Being a boss, you step into grown-man shoes and make your own money. So which one are you, Cash?"

Cash had never thought of himself as a pimp. The females loved his company and would do anything for him. But the cougar he was with was definitely running the show, telling him what to do, nagging him about a job. Should he stay with Gloria or not? He just wanted a quick answer from his father.

"I know I'm a man, Pops, and I always held my own."

Ray-Ray chuckled lightly and shook his head. "Until now." He didn't raise Cash, so he couldn't get mad at him over the decisions he was making. He was mad at Mamma Jones for making him a mama's boy. The boy was spoiled, always had been. Ray-Ray wanted Cash to be so much better than him.

"You have a cigarette?"

Cash pulled out his pack of Newport and handed his father two cigarettes.

Ray-Ray lit up then said, "Why do you think I panhandle, son?"

Cash shrugged. He thought, *Because you're a lazy bum that never worked a decent job in your life.* "I don't know. Why?"

"Because I'm my own boss."

Cash loved his pops, but in his eyes, his pops was a failure in life.

Ray-Ray took another drag from the cigarette. His lively attitude had cooled down, and he was nonchalant. He added, "I earn my own money. I provide a service for people, which is opening up the door and giving them a laugh. Whether they're laughing at me or my jokes, they're still laughing, and that's fine with me. I love to make people smile and laugh, Cash. There's too much hatred and resentment in this world, and I want people to know that when they're on this block and they see me, I'm gonna always be Ray-Ray, the front-door jester."

For a moment, Ray-Ray and Cash stared off elsewhere, temporarily diverted by their personal thoughts.

Ray-Ray finished off the cigarette and flicked it away. "Being my own boss allows me to make my own rules, what I eat, where I sleep, what time I go to work. I'm not trapped by the rules of employment, trying to keep up with the Joneses, or depending on a woman."

"But you always out here, Pops, depending on other people's kindness."

"And that's fine with me. I've been doing this for years, and I'm happy. I have my own place now. It's small, actually I'm renting a room, but it's mine, and I eat every day. And, best of all, I have a relationship with my son. It took some time, but you're here, able to sit and talk with me whenever."

Ray-Ray talked like he ran a Fortune 500 company.

"You know, if I wanted to live off a woman, then I would've stayed with Momma Jones and allowed her to prostitute herself to take care of me, but that's never been me. And you had a good one with Pearla. I liked her."

Cash sighed. "She's the reason why I'm in this jam in the first place, following and listening to her fuckin' ass.

She always thinks she knows it all, like she's smarter than me. Because of her, my niggas don't fuck wit' me, and I'm out here struggling. And now I got this bitch on my back about a job. You know I ain't built for no nine-to-five. But Pearla is bad news, Pops. I can't take this shit. This shit is fuckin' wit' me."

"Nigga, stop ya fuckin' whinin'! You're soundin' like a little bitch right now!"

Cash looked at him. "What?"

"You heard me, Cash. Either you do or you don't. But don't blame your situation on no woman. That makes you look weak. Go out there and do what you need to do—hustle. Do what you do best, but make sure you're happy doing it."

Cash nodded. "Ya right, Pop. I need to start doin' me again."

"That's my boy talking." Ray-Ray smiled. "Let me get another cigarette."

CHAPTER FOURTEEN

It was really late, and Cash hoped that Gloria was asleep and would stay that way. He was in no mood for her constant bickering. Her voice—loud and pitchy, could irritate even the most patient person. Three steps into the house and she was on him, nagging. Gloria started to lecture him like he was a kid. What was it with woman and their control issues? Cash hated to be managed.

"I'm a grown fuckin' man!"

"I hate when you do this to me, Cash!" she hollered. "I just want you to respect my fuckin' house!"

"What? I'm supposed to have a fuckin' curfew now?"

Gloria suspected he was cheating on her and lying to her about finding work. The other day, she'd smelled an unfamiliar fragrance in her bedroom. The perfume didn't belong to her, so who did it belong to?

They argued until four in the morning. Cash left and went for a quick walk to cool off, leaving her frustrated and angry.

When he came back from his walk, Gloria was apologizing profusely to him, and then she wanted to have sex. She tugged at his jeans, attempting to pull out his dick to suck it, but Cash pushed her away. He wasn't in the mood.

Cash was up early and ready to start his day, feeling his time was wearing thin with Gloria, who was getting dressed for work. She was silent, refusing to say a word to him.

"You ain't gonna say good morning to me, Gloria? It's like that now?"

"Why? You couldn't give me what I needed last night—I wanted some dick."

"I just wasn't in the mood."

"Well, I was. After all the bullshit I put up with, at least when I want to fuck, you can fuck me, Cash. You live here rent-free, with food in the fridge, cable television. I give you money, and you have a warm bed to lie in and some good pussy to fuck. Nigga, any muthafucka with some common sense would realize when he has a good thing at home. I'm a good thing, Cash!" she yelled. "Treat me like it!"

Gloria marched around the bedroom putting together her outfit for work. She was ironing her skirt, trying to do her hair, and quarreling with Cash at the same time.

Cash had heard the same spiel from different women. All women thought they had the bomb pussy and all women thought they were a good catch. Cash was so fucking bored with this conversation.

"Well, I'm sorry. I just wasn't in the mood to fuck."

"Why? Is it because you already had your fill yesterday? Huh?"

"Nah."

"Don't lie to me, Cash. You always been in the mood for sex. Since you moved in here, we've been going at it twice, maybe, three times a day. So what is fuckin' different now, huh?"

It was hard to believe Gloria was an assistant principal, with her potty mouth.

"You smothering me."

"Smothering you? Nigga, if I'm fuckin' smothering you, then you can leave my fuckin' house and breathe again!"

"I ain't tryin' to argue wit' you."

"Too late!"

Cash sighed. He still needed her.

Gloria's frown transformed into a scowl. She speedily got dressed for work, cursing at him, and stormed out of the room.

Cash knew later she would be forgiving and yearning to get fucked. This time, he was going to fuck her so good, she would develop amnesia.

With Gloria gone, and a very long day ahead of him, Cash didn't waste any time getting dressed. Before long, he was out the front door.

He opted to take public transportation, taking the local bus to a distant, quiet neighborhood, where he began his search.

The minute he stepped off the city bus in Springfield Gardens, a working-class neighborhood in Queens, he went walking, trying to look nonchalant and inconspicuous. He walked the quiet block with homes with driveways and short front yards, searching for the right vehicle to pick off. It was early afternoon, so most folks were either at work or school, or out running errands, if they weren't at home. Some car thieves found it risky to steal during the day, but Cash saw it as opportunity.

He rounded the corner toward the next street, discreetly looking in every yard. He rested his eyes on a pretty dark green Honda Accord sitting on chrome rims parked at the end of the driveway.

Cash took a deep breath and quickly checked out his surroundings. First, he walked up the front steps and rang the bell. No answer. He looked around a second time and made his move. He removed the tools he needed to swipe the car—a slim Jim, wire cutters, and more. Cash knew by the look of the car, it being an older model, that security wouldn't be too difficult; it probably just had an alarm.

He hugged the door and slipped the slim Jim between the car's window and the rubber seal and, with careful manipulation, opened the door. But the alarm sounded.

Cash hurried into the car, dived underneath the dashboard, and in less than a minute, he dismantled the alarm. Then he hot-wired the car, and the engine came to life, purring like it was ready to hit the road. It was simple with the 2001 Accord—easy to steal and easy to sell because of its parts. He backed out of the driveway and was gone.

Brooklyn was Cash's destination with the Accord. He wasn't looking to just joy-ride; he needed a new fence. He hit East New York and then Brownsville. He rounded the corners slowly, no loud music or eyes looking at every passing cutie with a big booty.

He came across Benny again. He was exiting the bodega on Sutter Avenue. Cash honked the horn, catching his attention.

Benny walked over to the car. "I see the hustle is nonstop, my nigga."

"Yo, get in. Let's go for a ride."

Benny shrugged his shoulders and jumped into the passenger seat, and Cash drove away. Cash lit a cigarette and passed one to Benny.

Benny took a few pulls from the Newport and then said, "Yo, I heard what happened the other day wit' you and Manny."

"Man, fuck them niggas!" Cash didn't want to talk about Manny and Darrell. He wanted some information. Benny was a lowlife, but he knew the streets. He always knew the right connects and who was doing what.

"Yo, I'm tryin' to make some money, and I wanna get rid of this Accord. Who can I go to? Who's the new chop shop around town?"

"What's in it for me, man?"

"I'll give you a one-time fee—five hundred dollars—if you steer me in the right direction."

Benny nodded. "A'ight. The only nigga I know about is this cat name Roberto."

"Roberto?"

"Yeah. He the same dude Manny and Darrell be goin' to. He got a shop out in Coney Island."

"A'ight, let's ride then."

"Now?"

"Yeah, now. You want your money, right?"

Benny took another pull from the cancer stick. "Yeah, cuz a nigga broke like a muthafucka."

Cash drove way across town toward Coney Island. Twenty-five minutes later, he pulled up to a quaint-looking garage right off Neptune Avenue. The area was cluttered with car-related businesses—auto repair, window repair, auto glass, collision work, and transmission maintenance and repair. It was an auto haven.

Cash and Benny climbed out of the stolen Accord. They approached a graffiti-scrawled, rolled-down metal gate. The sign above read: Coney Island Auto/Collision Repair.

Benny knocked on the gate. Above their heads a security camera monitored their movement.

The side door opened, and a slim, short man dressed in stained, greasy overalls stepped out. He was light-skinned, curly hair, and clean-shaven. "What do y'all want?" he asked the duo roughly.

"We lookin' for Roberto. Y'all closed?"

"Yeah, for the day," the man replied. "And what y'all want with Roberto?"

"I came here to do business wit' the man," Cash chimed.

The man looked skeptical. "Business?" he replied dryly.

Cash said, "I hear he's in the market for a good car."

"Look, the only thing we're in business for is auto repair. That's it."

Cash knew the man was being cautious. It was hard to trust a complete stranger when criminal activities came into play. He thought he had to prove he wasn't an undercover cop.

"Look, I'm Cash, and I'm one of the best car thieves in the fuckin' city. I been stealing cars before I even learned how to ride a bicycle. I just copped this Accord from Queens. I need some extra cash. I heard Roberto's the man to go to. I heard he's fair."

The man looked at the Accord. He walked toward it and gazed inside. He then turned around and stared at Cash and Benny intensely. Though he was short and slim, he had a strong, intimidating presence.

"Bring it inside," he said.

The metal gate started to lift.

Cash got behind the wheel and drove the Accord into the garage, and the gate came down behind him.

Inside the garage was clean and well organized. The concrete floor wasn't littered with empty oil cans or worn tires. There was a car lift, diagnostic tools, toolboxes, and a workbench. A few auto parts were on the ground, and a mechanic was working on a classic BMW.

Cash followed the man into a private office.

The man sat behind a cluttered desk and asked, "What you want for it?"

"Two grand."

"Two grand?"

"It's worth it. I'm worth it. You tell Roberto I can get him any car he needs. I'm nice when it comes to stealing cars. I know the technique, and I got the right tools to work with."

The man leaned back in his chair, his eyes on Cash. "I need a twenty fourteen Honda Accord sedan, black. If you can deliver that car to me within a week, then maybe we can talk some business."

"Not a problem. I'll have that car before the week's end. And tell Roberto I won't let him down."

The man opened the drawer to the desk, reached inside, and counted out two thousand dollars. He handed it to Cash.

Cash smiled widely. He stood up and walked out of the office.

Unbeknownst to him, he was already talking and doing business with Roberto.

FIFTEEN

Pearla climbed out of her car and walked into the Brooklyn post office. She looked around cautiously, because, you never know. She went straight for the PO box and opened it. Inside were several money orders, all from different parts of the country. She smiled and removed them from the box, and left out of the post office feeling excited.

Inside her car she looked at who sent them. One was for $600 from Candice Bratcher, 67, living in Mississippi. Another money order was for $900, from Tiffany Pideda, from Orlando, Florida, and another for $500, from Michelle Godfrey of Port St. Lucie, Florida.

Pearla's scam was raking in the dough. She was keeping track of all her victims, and as payment came in, she noted the payer and the amount in her ledger. For her tax scheme, if her victims didn't send out their payment, she made it her business to call and threaten them with jail, land seizure, evictions—the whole gamut of federal punishment.

In total, she'd collected $14,000 from her victims so far. The country was big, and there were so many gullible and elderly victims out there. She constantly switched burner phones and moved from one hotel room to the next. With the money orders, she needed and untraceable way to cash them that didn't link directly back to her. For a fee, Jimmy, who owned the local check cashing store, helped liquidate. Jimmy was a trusted dude who liked Pearla's ability to come up off a new hustle.

She opened several bank accounts with various banks, and had close to five thousand dollars on her personally. With money coming in, and her lifestyle coming back, this time she planned on being careful, wiser, and stingy. No more doling out thousands of dollars to those who didn't earn it or deserve it. She had to learn the hard way that people only love you when you're paying them to.

Pearla pulled into the parking garage at Kings Plaza mall, stepped out of her car in her new heels, and marched into the mall. With her Gucci purse slung over her shoulder, she went into one store after the other. She purchased a wool coat, a pair of knee-high boots, a pair of diamond earrings, expensive jeans, and a few comfortable tops to parade around in.

Afterwards, she got her hair done, styling it into loose, beachy Victoria's Secret curls. It was a sophisticated and relaxed, but yet a very sexy look.

Walking out of the beauty salon on Flatbush Avenue, Pearla felt rejuvenated. As she walked toward her car, she heard a car horn blow.

"Excuse me, gorgeous!" a man shouted from the driver's window of his 750 BMW. "You caught my attention from afar!"

Pearla turned and saw an older, distinguished-looking gentleman slowing down, pulling closer to the curb. She kept on walking.

The man parked his Beamer, climbed out, and hurried her way.

Pearla, car keys in her hand, hit the alarm to her vehicle, and as she was about to climb inside, he slid toward her slickly and opened her car door for her.

"You know I can get my own door, right?" she said.

"What fun would that be? And what kind of man would I be, if I allowed for you to do that?"

Pearla simply looked at him.

"Let me properly introduce myself. My name is Thomas." He spoke with a baritone voice and had kind eyes.

"Thomas?"

"Yes, Thomas Gram."

He smiled, revealing perfect white teeth. He was tall and handsome, and he was dressed sharply in a dark blue three-piece suit with a red tie. He was close-shaven with cropped, dark, and grayish hair. He looked to be in his late forties, early fifties.

"Can I get a beautiful woman's name?"

"I'm Pearla," she said.

"It's a pleasure to meet you, Pearla."

He extended his hand, which she took into hers. His grip was firm, and his hand was soft.

"Can I have the pleasure of taking you out to lunch?"

"We just met."

"Does it matter? I find it remarkable when strangers become friends. Lunch is on me; you can pick the place."

Pearla was famished, and he seemed nice. She hadn't been with anyone since Cash and she wasn't looking to get up with anybody. She had only been focused on pulling herself out of poverty and getting her former life back.

"I get to choose?"

"Yes." He smiled.

"Then lunch it is."

Avra Estiatorio was a notable restaurant located on 48th Street in midtown Manhattan. Patrons were treated to an authentic Mediterranean ambiance with imported limestone and distressed wood floors, stone walls, exposed wood beams, and French doors that opened to a flowered courtyard.

Though she was offered to pick the spot, Thomas had suggested the place.

Thomas pulled out Pearla's chair from the table, allowing her to sit. He was the perfect gentleman. He sat across from her and ordered an expensive wine. The waiter nodded and went to fulfill his order.

"It's so beautiful here," Pearla said.

"I'm glad you love the place. I come here often," he said.

Pearla raised her eyebrow. "So you bring all your female strangers here?"

He laughed. "No, I don't. I bring my clients here to eat for a business lunch."

"Clients? So what do you do?"

"I'm a management consultant."

"Oh, I see. Great career choice. What do you consult?"

"Well, basically, I help identify issues and form hypotheses and solutions. I present findings and recommendations for clients, which help them manage their projects," he said. "There's much more to my job, but I don't want to bore you with the details so soon."

Pearla chuckled. He was intelligent. He was successful. He was paid.

"And, may I ask, what do you do?" he said, focusing on her.

Pearla could have slapped her own face for not being prepared. She looked him in the eyes and replied, "I'm very private about my personal life."

"I see. You aren't crazy?"

She laughed. "No, I'm not crazy. I'm just trying to finish up school."

"School . . . that's lovely. And attaining what degree? Bachelor's, master's, PhD?"

"You sure ask a lot of questions."

"Excuse me for prying into your life so soon. It's just, when I see a beautiful woman, I simply want to know everything about her. We just met today, so let's just enjoy each other's company," he said politely, backing off.

"Let's just do that."

The waiter came to take down their meal orders. Pearla ordered the grilled fillet of organic king salmon served with marinated grilled vegetables, and Thomas ordered the charcoal grilled boneless halibut fillet over spanakorizo—spinach, rice, and dill.

Thomas seemed to have many layers. He was humorous, said he spoke three languages fluently, and was childless.

Pearla downed her wine and tried to enjoy his company. He looked like he had everything a woman would want—great looks, great personality, money, and intelligence. So why wasn't she smitten or infatuated by him?

"So can I ask you a question, Pearla?" Thomas spoke coyly.

"You can ask any question. Depends on the question if I'll answer."

"Fair enough." He grinned and then got serious. "I've noticed no wedding or engagement ring on your finger, so is it safe to assume, no boyfriend?"

She smiled. "I'm single," she told him.

He smiled. It was the answer he wanted to hear.

"How about you? No girlfriend? Have you ever been married?"

"As of the moment, I'm single too. I was once engaged . . . three years ago, but it didn't work out. She kept the ring. It was costly."

"We ladies always are," she quipped.

He laughed.

They continued to converse. Pearla looked at him and everything about him seemed legit, almost perfect. But there was something off about the whole situation, and it nagged at her.

Pearla downed her umpteenth glass of wine and sighed.

"Is everything okay?" he asked.

"I'm fine."

"You sure? Are you not having a good time with me?"

"I'm having a great time with you, Thomas."

So why wasn't she attracted to him? Why did she feel so guilty, so gloomy? Why was she ready to leave? Pearla knew that if she played her cards right, she could have a handsome, rich man tricking on her. Maybe she wouldn't need to scheme any more. Maybe he was the one. He looked like the type of man to take care of his lady. He'd come into her life so suddenly, out of the blue, like some fairy godfather, there to grant her wishes.

"I'm a complicated woman."

"Complicated, huh? What woman isn't?"

She laughed again. Was the wine getting to her?

An hour went by, and they were still laughing and talking. He was ready to order dessert and more expensive wine. He told Pearla she could have whatever she wanted on the menu, or maybe in her life.

Pearla soon figured out the problem with Thomas Gram. He wasn't Cash. He didn't come from her world. Though educated, it seemed that he was out of touch and wasn't street-smart. He talked theory and finances, something Pearla was familiar with, but he wasn't making her pussy wet. Cash had that effect on her when they'd first met. Cash was her bad-boy—a man who mirrored her hustle.

"I would definitely like to continue this, Pearla."

Pearla was haunted with the memory of seeing Cash driving by with some bitch in the car. It was obvious he wasn't thinking about her.

Fuck it! Think rational. Think smart.

"You know what? I would like to continue this too," she said.

SIXTEEN

Cash took a pull from his cigarette, flicked it into the street, and quickly glanced around. He was cool and ready to commit his next caper. He had his eyes set on the red 2015 Lexus RC 350 idling at the red light.

The female driver seemed preoccupied with everything, from her cell phone to applying makeup while looking in the rearview mirror. For three days, he had been watching her. He knew her routine and was just waiting for the right moment. Cash had always been conniving when it came to stealing cars. His stint in Miami had taught him well. He needed that car, but they were difficult to steal. It was on Roberto's list. Roberto had plans to ship the car overseas.

When the victim took her car to the dealership to be serviced several days earlier, Cash paid one of the workers at the shop to help him out. They used a key-programmer to create a duplicate key to the Lexus. Cash slipped the dirty mechanic three hundred dollars for the extra key.

He watched the Lexus round the corner and park inside the garage nearby the newly built condos on

Ocean Avenue in Sheepshead Bay, Brooklyn. The woman stepped out looking sexy in her short skirt and top. Cash was aware that she was having an affair on her husband. She was there to see her Latin lover. The last time he'd followed her, she spent nearly six hours at his place.

When she walked into the condo, Cash walked toward the garage, the duplicate key already in his hand. An ignorant car thief would have probably jacked the woman at gunpoint for the Lexus. Cash wasn't that stupid. With OnStar, LoJack, and other anti-theft devices, the owner had the power to stop their stolen car in its tracks and alert police or locate the stolen car via GPS with one phone call.

Cash casually strolled into the garage and pushed the button to the alarm system. The Lexus sounded off, alerting him to where it was parked. He unlocked the doors, started the engine, and effortlessly drove away like he owned it. It would be hours before the woman would find out that her car had been stolen. By that time, it would be too late.

"Ooooweeee! I can get used to a ride like this!" Cash hollered as he steered the Lexus through Brooklyn on his way toward Coney Island.

The enhanced bolstered sports seats were engineered to grip the driver through every turn. The dynamic coupe style was captivating. The engine sounded too sweet. It was music to Cash's ears. He was falling in love with the car. He was tempted to joyride in it a little longer, but he had to stay focused. It was about making money.

No radio, no showing off, Cash drove to Coney Island quietly, keeping a low profile. When he pulled up to Roberto's garage, the men inside were shocked.

Roberto shook his head in disbelief. "You never let me down, Cash."

"I told you, I'm the messiah of car theft. Who's better than me?"

Roberto handed Cash his payment in an envelope.

Quickly, Cash was becoming Roberto's number-one guy. On average, he was stealing ten cars a week for Roberto with no signs of slowing down, taking mass transit to quiet neighborhoods and snatching up low-end, highly sought after vehicles like the Accord, Camry, Civic, and Corolla. The Lexus was a special order.

"What you need next?" Cash asked him.

"I need a Ford Fusion," Roberto said.

"What color?"

"Color is no issue."

"A'ight, give me three days to deliver."

Cash turned around and made his exit from the garage. Five grand richer, he was feeling alive again. He stepped outside into the cool air night and lit a cigarette. For the first time in his life, he didn't have to split the profits with a crew or a bitch. The money was all his to spend.

It was dusk when Cash walked a few blocks to the nearest train station and got on the F train to Queens. The nights were becoming colder. His relationship with Gloria was still happening, but she had been complaining more often, bickering and fighting with him. He was tired and frustrated. He was hungry to get out of her house and breathe again. Dealing with her had him sometimes thinking about Pearla.

The F train roared through the underground, snaking through the tunnels. Cash sat quietly in the partially empty car. Tomorrow, he would start searching for that Ford Fusion Roberto requested.

Back in Queens, Cash lingered outside Gloria's home. It was late, really late. He could see the bedroom light on from where he stood. He saw her silhouette moving around in the bedroom, pacing back and forward, probably concerned where her lover was. It looked like she was ready to beef with him.

Cash wasn't in the mood for her bullshit. He climbed into his car and drove off with no destination in mind.

A half-hour later, he was in Jamaica Estates, pulling in front of the home he used to share with Pearla. It was dark and looked abandoned. There was a "for sale" sign placed in the front yard. She was finally gone. Cash knew he was wrong for completely abandoning her when she needed him the most. He had gotten upset, couldn't take the pressure anymore, and did what he knew best; moved on to something easier.

His nostalgia passed, and he drove off.

The alarm blared to the Ford Fusion, but that didn't discourage Cash. He quickly jumped into the front seat and disabled it, and then used the slide hammers to remove the ignition lock with one quick blow. He worked his charm, and the car started.

Cash smiled and propped himself up into the front seat, placing his hands around the steering wheel.

Suddenly the passenger door opened, and a young woman slid into the seat next to Cash, startling him completely.

"What the fuck!" he shouted.

"You trying to steal my father's car!" she hollered.

Cash looked at her. She had long black hair and high cheekbones, and her brown eyes were framed by long lashes. Her long, beautiful legs were dressed in tight dark jeans. What was his next move? Knock her out? Take her hostage? He had to do something. He couldn't sit there like a fool, looking dumbfounded. What she said next totally surprised him.

"What are you waiting for? Just go!"

"What?"

"You stealing my father's car, then steal it!"

"You serious? You gonna let me take your pops' car?"

"Yes, and he's really not my father, but my stepfather. I can't stand his ass."

Cash was flabbergasted. She didn't have to say it again. He peeled out of the driveway and headed for the freeway with her in the front seat.

The girl laughed, excited about the adventure.

"So how long you been stealing cars?" she asked him.

"Damn! You all in my business."

"And you all in my stepfather's car, so call it equal."

"A'ight, shorty, you got that."

"So where are we going?"

"*We*?"

"Yes, we!"

"You a trip, shorty."

"You don't know the half of it."

"I guess I don't." Cash was amused by her personality. He shook his head at the young girl. She was too cute.

"So what's your name, sexy?" Cash asked her.

"What's your name?" she asked him back.

"Cash."

"Ooh, *Cash*, so you about that money, huh." She laughed.

"You know it."

"Ain't anything wrong with a man about his paper. Well, my name is Sophie."

"Sophie—I like that name."

"You better," she replied. "I'm one of a kind."

"I already see that. Nice to meet you."

"Same here."

They shook hands while Cash merged onto the nearest freeway and pushed the Fusion to sixty miles per hour.

Sophie dared to ask him, "You know how to drive this thing?"

Cash laughed. "Yo, you obviously don't know who you're in the car with."

"Oh, so what? You *The Fast and the Furious*? You Vin Diesel?"

Cash laughed. "More like Paul Walker—the pretty boy with the swag."

"Okay. I dare you to do a hundred right now on this highway."

"What?"

"Show me your wild side, nigga!"

"In a stolen car?"

"It's not stolen yet. Remember, this is my stepfather's car, and he's at work right now."

"A'ight, shorty. You better fasten your seat belt."

Cash pressed down on the accelerator and started to zigzag through traffic. He hit the Cross Island Parkway toward the Belt Parkway doing close to one hundred. The faster he drove, the more turned-on Sophie looked.

Not wanting to push his luck, five miles down the road, he slowed down the car. Sophie looked like she was about to have an orgasm.

Cash laughed. "You like that," he said.

"And you dangerous," she replied.

"You like bad boys?"

"I don't like boring men."

Cash continued to laugh. "Well, I never been boring in my life."

"We'll see," she said.

"You know you could have gotten yourself killed."

She smirked. "I thought you said you know how to handle a whip."

"Not my driving skills. I meant when I was stealing the car and you jumped in. You could have gotten yourself murked or seriously hurt."

Sophie shook her head. "You're a car thief, not a carjacker."

Cash wanted to be schooled. "And the difference is?"

"Carjackers use guns. Car thieves just Slim Jims. What were you gonna do? Slim Jim my eyes out?"

She was right. Cash didn't have a pistol tucked in his waistband. He was harmless, unless pushed.

As he drove into Brooklyn, it was hard to take his eyes off Sophie and focus on the road. She was so beautiful and so outgoing. He had known the girl all but ten minutes, but there was something unique about her.

"So, what's the deal wit' your father?"

"My *step*father. We never got along. He's a fuckin' asshole. I keep telling my mother the man's a lowlife. You know how many times he's put his hands on her? But my mother don't want to believe it ain't ever gonna stop. She thinks her husband is some saint because he runs his own business and he preaches in the church. The nigga is a fuckin' fraud, always talking about redemption and forgiveness. I swear, one day I'm gonna stab his pussy ass up. What type of man puts his hands on a woman?"

"Damn! It's that's serious?"

"Hells yeah!"

"Well, you're in good hands."

"Like I said, we'll see."

They arrived in Coney Island where the exchange with Roberto went smoothly like always. Cash got his money and met with Sophie outside the shop.

"Ooh, can I get some of that?" she said.

"What?"

"My cut, of course."

"Your cut?"

"Yes. It was my father's car I allowed for you to steal."

"Your *step*father, and you never liked him."

"I want ten percent." She stuck out her hand and waited for her cut.

"Ten percent?" he repeated.

"Ten percent."

What the heck, he thought. It was only two hundred dollars. And she was cute. Cash pulled out his payment and put two fresh hundred-dollar bills into her hand.

Sophie smiled. "Now I really like you."

"You better."

They walked off and continued to converse. They went and got something to eat at Nathan's in Coney Island. Over three chili hot dogs, fries and sodas, they both kept each other entertained.

Sophie got Cash excited. She was funny. She was a spark of energy, not having one dull moment.

"You got a boyfriend?"

"No. And, you? Any special bitches in your life?"

"Nah."

"You probably would lie about it anyway," she said.

"Nah, ain't no need to lie."

"That's what all liars said when they tryin' to fuck a bitch they like."

"What makes you think I like you?"

"You do, so don't even front, nigga. Everybody likes Sophie."

Cash chuckled. "Yeah, you is somethin' other."

"One of a kind."

Cash wanted her. He wanted to know more about her. If he got his way, then he would be between her legs by the next night.

SEVENTEEN

"Yo Manny, let's go! Hurry the fuck up, nigga!" Darrell whispered. He kept looking out, swinging his head back and forth, making sure things were clear on the street.

"Nigga, I'm goin' as fast I can."

"You need to go faster. I thought I heard somethin'."

Manny was trying to hot-wire a 2012 Honda Accord parked on the residential street. The body was clean, with no dents or scratches, and the inside was mint. He worked the wires together, and the Accord came to life.

"Finally!" Darrell said.

Manny shut the door to the Accord. Darrell got behind the wheel of their truck, and they took off into the night, heading toward Coney Island to meet with Roberto. The streets were thin, with no sign of police anywhere.

Twenty minutes later, they were pulling up to Roberto's garage and asking to see him. They kept the Honda Accord idling outside the garage.

Roberto walked out onto the sidewalk and looked at the vehicle.

"We came through for you, Roberto," Manny said.

"There she is."

"Yeah, but the problem is, I already have a 2012 Accord. I don't need that shit."

"What the fuck you talkin' about, Roberto?" Darrell chimed.

Roberto told them, "Y'all niggas is late. I already had one delivered earlier."

"By who?" Manny asked.

"By someone quicker than y'all."

Manny and Darrell frowned.

"So what we supposed to do wit' this car?" Darrell asked.

"I don't know, and I don't care, but get it away from my shop. Y'all attracting too much attention."

"Roberto, we've been doin' business wit' you for months, and you doin' us like this?" Manny griped.

"Like I said, I don't need it, so get it away from here."

"Seriously, you do us like this?" Darrell said.

"What the fuck I said? Nigga, get it the fuck outta here!" Roberto told them through his clenched teeth.

"A'ight, man, you ain't gotta get hostile," Manny said. "We out."

Manny and Darrell frowned heavily. They had no choice but to get back into their cars and leave.

It was the fourth time Roberto had turned them away. Previously, he told them that business was slow. Manny and Darrell were upset and becoming suspicious. Business had never been slow, and Roberto never turned away a stolen car.

The changes in their business had all been because of Cash. He was stealing cars at a record rate, not knowing he was undercutting his rivals. Roberto wanted to do business with Cash only, placing larger orders on him. And Cash was cheaper; he wanted two grand per vehicle, while Manny and Darrell had been asking for three.

Roberto was going to ask the twosome to lower their price and still cop from them, but he was filled with resentment because Cash had told him that Perez used to pay two grand per car. Roberto felt cheated and played by Manny and Darrell. It felt good to play games with the pair. He never did like them. Roberto felt Manny was a wannabe; cocky for no reason. And Darrell was a straight up bitch. His panties were always on display.

Overnight, Manny and Darrell would have to find another trustworthy fence for their stolen cars. Which was a hard thing to do. Not everyone had the connections to sell parts from stolen cars, or stolen cars whole. It was an underground business that took lots of knowledge to run, and Roberto was one of the best in the city. He'd built up a reliable network from New York to Miami, and overseas in Germany, France, and Africa.

As they drove away from the chop shop, Manny picked up his cell phone and dialed Darrell.

"Yo, somethin' ain't right," Manny said.

"What you mean?"

"Roberto ain't ever been flaking on us like this. This the fourth time! Yo, pull over."

Darrell pulled the truck to the curb, and Manny did

too.

Manny jumped out of the Accord and got into the Escalade. "Yo, drive back to the shop," he told Darrell.

"You gonna leave the Accord here?"

"She good," Manny said. "Who gonna fuck wit' her? Just drive, nigga. I got this feeling."

Darrell shrugged. He did a U-turn on Neptune Avenue, leaving the Accord parked on the street. They went back to the shop. Darrell parked across the street and turned off the headlights. They decided to stake out the garage and see who was coming and going.

Ten minutes later, the side door to the garage opened, and Cash stepped outside, clutching his payment and smiling. They observed Cash get into a waiting livery cab, and he was off. Manny and Darrell immediately knew they'd been played.

"Muthafucka!"

Darrell scowled. "I see why Roberto is flaking on us. This nigga is taking away our business."

"Ya think, Einstein! How did you ever put two and two together?"

"Be easy, nigga! We both stressed out."

Manny thought for a moment, and in a low voice he replied, "Yo, I'm gonna kill this muthafucka fo' real now."

"I'm wit' you, nigga. He gotta go."

Now Cash had two more people wanting him dead, and he still didn't know who originally wanted him murdered.

EIGHTEEN

The driver's door to Pearla's Bentley opened, and her new Louboutins hit the pavement in Canarsie, Brooklyn. She was looking young, sexy and beautiful. Pearla was back on her A-game and looking for a new home.

The place on Seaview Avenue, a private three-family home, looked nice from the outside. She was there to check out the main floor, which was two bedrooms and one and a half bathrooms. There was a park and baseball field across the street. The traffic looked light, and the neighbors looked nice. She hoped it looked nicer on the inside.

The owner of the building, a tall, busty blonde woman with a pearly white smile, was waiting for her on the porch, dressed smartly in a business skirt and blazer.

Pearla strutted toward the entrance. She smiled at the lady.

"Pearla?" the woman greeted.

"Yes."

"Hey, I'm Cindy. I'm glad you could make it."

Pearla followed Cindy into the apartment and walked into a spacious living room with wood flooring.

The windows brought in lots of sunlight. The kitchen had been updated with stainless steel appliances, granite countertops, and semi-custom cabinets.

"How much?" Pearla asked.

"Eighteen hundred a month, and that's a bargain. This place could easily go for over two grand."

"I like it. I want it. I can give you three months' rent in advance, plus a security deposit," she told the woman.

Pearla knew that money talks. She didn't want the lady asking any questions about a job, her income, or her previous residence. She didn't have any legal income, but she had her credit, which would certainly slip soon since that real estate fiasco a few months earlier. However, she didn't think the foreclosure posted yet so she was still in good condition.

"Three months' rent, huh?" Cindy said.

Pearla nodded.

"Make it two months' rent and four months' security, and I won't ask you any questions."

"Why so much in security?" Pearla had the money but didn't necessarily want to give it to this bitch.

"If for any reason I have to start eviction proceedings, I'll have a cushion until I can legally get you out."

"Eviction? You saying I can't pay my rent?" Pearla felt insulted. Did this bitch know about the foreclosure? It was like a scarlet letter on her forehead which deeply embarrassed Pearla.

The homeowner cleared her throat so she could be heard loud and clearly. "I'm saying you can either accept my terms or not. Period."

Pearla's smile fought through all her anger and appeared. She pulled out a checkbook and gave up the money.

"Okay then, the place is yours," Cindy said, cheerfully. "I'll have all the paperwork and lease ready for you next week."

"Okay."

Pearla walked out of the apartment and went to her car. She turned around and took one last look at the place and smiled. It felt like making her first hundred thousand all over again. Finally, she was back to her old self. She climbed into her car and started it. Her next two stops would be the post office and Western Union. She had a few more payments to collect.

Day by day, she was getting back on her feet, becoming whole again. It was a good feeling. This time, she would be on her own, no live-in boyfriend, no extra drama. The apartment was going to be her temporary safe haven.

As she continued looking around the place, her cell phone rang. The caller ID told her it was Thomas calling. She answered. "Hey!"

"Hey, lovely, what are you doing tonight?" he asked.

"Nothing much."

"I want to see you."

She smiled. "You do, huh?"

"Yes. I want to take you out tonight, someplace special. I enjoyed our last encounter."

She still wasn't too much into him, but in a way, Thomas was the distraction she needed. They hadn't had sex yet, but being wined and dined was a welcoming feeling, especially after everything she'd been through. Pearla didn't plan to get into anything serious with him. He was okay, kind of fun to hang out with.

"Okay, I'll meet you. Just text me the location," she said.

"I'll do that right now." He hung up.

A minute later, the text came through: KATRA LOUNGE, 217 BOWERY. MEET ME AT 8PM, AND WEAR SOMETHING NICE.

NINETEEN

Flight 989 from LAX, California landed on the tarmac at JFK Airport in Queens smoothly and taxied into the terminal. It was a breezy fall day in New York, a sudden change from the warm, sunny California weather for the passengers exiting the plane and walking into the terminal.

Hassan grabbed his carry-on luggage from the overhead compartment and made his exit from first class. His business in L.A. had been concluded.

He was dressed sharply in Tom Ford, moving through the jet bridge coolly and walking into the terminal with his small bag. Inside the terminal, he collected his small roll-on luggage from the conveyor belt and made his way toward the exit.

Outside sat a black 2014 Rolls-Royce Phantom. James, his driver, and Bimmy, his right-hand man and natural-born killer, were standing next to it.

James smiled, took Hassan's luggage, and opened the suicide door to the Phantom. "How was your trip, sir?" he asked.

"It went fine," Hassan replied tersely. He slid into the backseat of the luxurious automobile and was ready to move. He sat back and chilled.

Bimmy climbed inside too.

James hurried behind the wheel and drove off slowly, merging into the airport traffic, trying to make it toward the Van Wyck Expressway.

"How was L.A.?" Bimmy asked.

"Fuckin' hot, cramped, and pretentious."

"I got what you need." Bimmy passed him a Cuban cigar.

It was what Hassan needed. He cut off the tip with one chop and lit it with a cigar lighter. He held the cigar to his mouth and drew in the smoke. He held the smoke in for a few seconds to taste it and then he let it go.

"So L.A. is out?" Bimmy asked.

"No, but muthafuckas in that town are fuckin' arrogant."

"You should've sent me."

"Nah, I was able to handle it."

L.A. wasn't the town for Hassan. He simply had business with a drug connect out there, a major player in the Crip organization. Hassan's business had expanded, and he had a solid relationship with the Gulf Cartel. He had come up significantly in the drug game and was a major distributor—nobody to fuck with. He was smart and motivated, and he knew how to launder his money into legitimate businesses and surround himself with good lawyers and corrupt cops, judges, and senators. The game wasn't just about the streets, but how to invest and build a wall around oneself.

"There was a minor problem while you were away," Bimmy said.

"With what and who?"

"Not with the streets, but with your music label," Bimmy said. "That idiot Santana, he still don't want to let Heaven out of her contract. He's holding out. I think he needs a little more persuasion to make things go our way."

"I agree."

James merged onto the Van Wyck. The traffic was thick, looking like a parking lot, with brake lights stretching for miles. He sighed heavily. "Fuck!"

Hassan rolled down the partition.

James quickly said, "We're in a lot of traffic, sir."

"Change of plans, James. I want you to take me to the city, not Brooklyn."

"Yes, sir. I'll try and get you there as quickly as possible."

The partition went back up, giving Hassan and Bimmy their privacy.

The Phantom came to a stop in front of a six-story building on the corner of 129th Street and Lennox Avenue. Hassan and Bimmy climbed out and marched inside the lobby. There, they took the elevator to the fourth floor and stepped out into the narrow hallway. They strode toward suite 4k and barged into the private office.

"Excuse me!" Santana Boyd's personal assistant was minding the front desk when Hassan and Bimmy stormed inside.

"Don't mind us," Bimmy said. "We're here to see your boss."

She shouted, "But y'all can't just barge into this office!"

They ignored her and stormed into the next room, Santana's office. It was a small place and in bad shape. Old take-out bags filled the trash can in the corner, and files and paper coated the desk in thick files. There was a flat-screen mounted on the wall playing music videos on MTV Jams.

Santana used to deejay for a popular hip-hop group in the nineties. Then he became an A&R for an up and coming record company. There he discovered some major superstars and worked on a few hit records, subsequently catapulting his reputation in the music industry as the man to work with. Then a few years later, his career took a major nosedive when he caught charges on gun possession, drunk driving, assault with a deadly weapon, and drug possession. His first few offenses got him on two-year probation. He did six months on Rikers Island for his other offenses.

Santana then started his own record label, but his streak had run out, and he wasn't the same go-to guy like back in the day. He'd burned a lot of bridges, and things continued to spiral downhill for Santana.

Heaven was one of his female artists. The promises he'd made to her had fallen through. She looked toward

Hassan to free her from her contract and sign her to his artist management company.

"Hassan, you're back in New York," Santana said, shocked by his presence. He was sitting behind his desk, busy on his laptop.

"What's this I hear about Heaven not being freed from her contract?" Hassan asked.

He and Bimmy moved closer to Santana, who removed himself from his chair looking back and forth at each man. He tried to look fierce in front of the two notorious street thugs, but it wasn't working.

"You know how much I invested in that bitch? And she thinks she can just leave this company, and I don't get what's owed to me?" Santana shouted.

"I don't care what is owed to you, Santana," Hassan replied. "I told you, she's out."

"And I'm supposed to take the loss? I set up a show for her tonight. I'm doing what I can."

"Well, now it's my time to do what I can for her," Hassan replied coldly.

"So you think you can just come in here and bully me? Take away one of the first artists I signed, put money in, helped build the little career she got now? Fuck y'all!" Santana shouted. "You're a fuckin' drug dealer, Hassan! What the fuck do you know about the music industry!"

Scowling, Bimmy approached Santana, who tried to reach for a pistol. Bimmy was on him before the gun could appear in his hand. A hard right to the face caused Santana to wobble and howl. That was followed by an uppercut to his chin, which lifted Santana off his feet, and then another staggering left hook.

Santana dropped to his knees and hunched over on his hands and knees, coughing.

Bimmy grabbed him by his collar roughly, pulled him off the floor, and then slammed him against the wall. Bimmy exclaimed into his face, "Listen, muthafucka! You think you got a choice in this shit? This ain't a democracy. It's a fuckin' dictatorship!"

"This ain't right, man. It ain't right. S-s-she's my artist," Santana stammered.

Hassan chimed, "Life is never fair, Santana. You win some, and you lose this one. And if you ever call me a drug dealer again, I will personally rip your fuckin' balls off and make you choke on them. Now Heaven is off your label and no longer your responsibility. *Capisce*?"

Bimmy flashed the Glock 17 holstered on his side for reassurance on his end, and Santana reluctantly nodded.

"Now sign the fuckin' paperwork, and let's move on with our lives," Hassan said.

Santana signed.

Hassan and Bimmy walked out of Santana's office laughing.

Hassan said, "We got a listening party to attend tonight at Katra Lounge. Let's make Heaven a star."

TWENTY

Pearla walked toward the entrance to Katra Lounge and saw a few people lingering outside. The people were staring, admiring her beauty and outfit. She walked on the sidewalk feeling incredibly upbeat. She was in a very happy space. It felt good to attend events in Manhattan, rubbing elbows with classy people and feeling important.

She spotted Thomas standing outside near the doorway. He was dressed sharp in a gray-and-white suit and hard bottom shoes. He smiled and waved her over.

"Hey, I'm glad you could make it. You look beautiful tonight," he said.

"Thank you."

They hugged. His masculinity gripped her. He smelled good; his cologne filled her nostrils with an engaging scent. He was starry-eyed over Pearla's arrival.

"What is this place? What did you invite me to?"

"It's a listening party for this singer," he said.

"Oh really? What's her name?"

"Heaven," he said. "And she's a talented singer. Certain people are invited out to listen to her."

"I can't wait to hear her."

Thomas stepped aside and allowed her to walk into the lounge. Security was checking for people's invitation. Pearla slid through easily, since she was with Thomas.

Inside the Moroccan-themed duplex lounge were well-dressed folks mingling and drinking cocktails. Dozens of people lined the entranceway all the way toward the VIP section in the rear. The DJ was spinning Daley's "Look Up." The place also offered hookahs. A few people were seated in the pillow-filled sections enjoying the flavored tobacco in the fashionable lounge.

Pearla followed behind Thomas, and they took their seats in the lofty VIP section. He called over one of the hostesses and ordered their own personal hookah, two large Voss waters, and a bottle of Moët. He tipped the lady with a twenty-dollar bill.

"Are you having a good time yet?" he asked Pearla.

"Yes, I am."

"Good. It's only going to get better."

She smiled.

Throughout the night, Thomas introduced Pearla to some associates of his, friends, and business partners. A quintessential prep, Thomas was well-known and well-liked. In a way, he reminded Pearla of Carlton Banks. He had an incomparable laugh, and his dancing was almost "white." Pearla knew the goons from her hood would call him an Oreo—black on the outside, but white inside.

The DJ made an announcement about Heaven, who was in the building, and started to play some of her music. Some of her songs were upbeat and made people want to dance, while others were measured and melodic, reminiscent of Mary J. Blige. The crowd in the place couldn't wait to hear her sing.

Heaven appeared in front of everyone with a bright smile. She had long sensuous black hair, dark eyeliner, high cheekbones, hazel contacts, and was dressed in edgy lace leggings with a wet look that highlighted her thick curves and butt, a stretchy hooded bikini top showing off her flat stomach, and six-inch stilettos.

The minute she gripped the microphone and opened her mouth to sing, everyone was captivated. She danced like Janet Jackson and sang like Beyoncé, and she wrote her own material.

After performing eight songs, Heaven smiled, addressing the audience, "Thank you all for coming out tonight to show me the support and love. God bless! I have my CD selling at the front entrance. So feel free to grab a copy and continue the movement. Heaven is fo' real."

The crowd shouted and cheered.

Throughout the night, Pearla received extended stares from different men in the lounge, and a few ladies too. Heaven wasn't the only star in the place. Some of the men looking her way were so fine, Pearla was crossing and uncrossing her legs back and forth and taking a drink. She smiled at the attention. Thomas was busied with a business partner on the other side of the room. It was a mistake leaving her with the wolves in the party.

Pearla continued to flirt with some of the men with her eyes, and then she saw him sitting across from her in the VIP section, regal and handsome. She was stunned. She'd thought she was never going to see him again. But there he was, looking too fine. They locked eyes, and she was speechless.

TWENTY-ONE

Hassan climbed out of his Phantom Rolls-Royce on Bowery in his black tuxedo and white bowtie, along with his alligator shoes and diamond Rolex peeking from underneath his sleeve. And he was clutching a cane. He looked at the front entrance of Katra and nodded his head. He couldn't wait to see Heaven perform.

Bimmy climbed out of the Phantom behind Hassan. He was dressed more casually in black slacks and black silk shirt unbuttoned at the neck and looked a bit intimidating with his dark scowl and strong physique. His body was in top physical condition. He rocked a low haircut and dark goatee. His eyes were always black and ominous.

Hassan entered the crowded lounge with Bimmy, his pit bull on a leash, his bite more vicious than his bark. The place was lively, music playing, people laughing and talking, hookahs being smoked, and drinks being consumed. Hassan had people's attention.

They were seated in VIP. Hassan ordered three bottles of Cristal. He conversed with a few people, while Bimmy stayed quiet and observant. No matter where he was, how casual or relaxing the environment, he always kept his guard up, never trusting anyone or anything.

Heaven came up to Hassan with her catching smile, and they hugged. She thanked him for helping her out. Hassan said a few encouraging words in her ear before she sang.

Hassan was impressed by her performance. She was going to become a star. She was the total package and had what it took to succeed—beauty, talent, and personality. Now that she was officially signed to his management company, Hassan had major plans for her.

He leaned over and whispered in Bimmy's ear, "She's the one, my nigga. She's gonna take us to the next level."

Bimmy nodded in agreement.

The listening party was going well. Heaven was speaking to a few media folks and selling her CD at the front entrance.

Hassan took a sip of champagne and looked around. He was shocked to see Pearla staring at him from across the room. *What is she doing here? And who is she with?* he thought. He remembered she used to be with that prick, Cash. He wondered if he was in the building. He hoped not.

Hassan didn't hesitate to get up and walk toward her. Bimmy remained seated. Hassan had to say something to her. She was his dream girl.

Pearla sat like she was glued to the chair, her eyes on Hassan approaching.

"Pearla, you look truly beautiful tonight," he said.

She smiled. "Thank you. And you look really good. I didn't expect to see you here."

"The same here. What brings you to Heaven's event?"

"I heard about it. Do you know her?"

"She's signed to my new management company."

"Management company? I'm impressed. You're coming up, Hassan. I'm happy for you."

"Thank you. And you, you're still gorgeous, take a man's breath away and imprison his heart."

She smiled and giggled.

He sat down next to her and looked at her directly. He had a lot of questions and wasn't shy in asking them.

"You still with Cash?" Hassan couldn't hold the question in any longer.

"We broke up."

"Well, I'm not sorry to hear about that. He was a fool to let you go. So you're here alone?"

"No. I came with a friend." She pointed to where Thomas was, engaged in conversation, laughing and sipping his drink.

"A friend? So you're with him, huh?"

"Do you know him?"

"I don't. So you're single?"

"Yes, Hassan."

"You know I always wanted you. When you decided to be with Cash, it broke my heart."

"I'm sorry."

"Don't be. I feel this is fate, you being here tonight."

"You do, huh?"

"I do. When you left me for him, I couldn't stop thinking about you. I wanted to give you the world, Pearla. And I still do," he said seriously. "Whatever you want or need, I can provide it right now."

"Hassan, you were always an overwhelming person."

"Why hesitate on giving the woman you're in love with everything? I lost you once, and I don't want to lose you again. I'm willing to do whatever it takes."

Pearla was floored by it all. He was extra handsome and extra sharp in his clothes. The tuxedo and bowtie did him justice. It was working for him from head to toe. It made him look significant. She knew his background in drug dealing and the streets, but tonight, he looked like some kind of music mogul.

"Hello," Thomas said. "Who's your friend?"

Hassan looked at him and smirked. The man's presence and tone was no threat to him. Hassan bluntly said to Thomas, "Excuse us and leave. We're talking."

"Um, I think you're confused, mister. She's my date tonight," Thomas shot back.

"She *was* your date," Hassan said.

"Who do you think you are?" Thomas got loud, his face tight.

Hassan stood up and glared at him. "You don't know me, so for your health, walk away and don't look back."

"Fuck you!" Thomas shouted. "Do you know who I am?"

Hassan managed to laugh.

Bimmy stood up from his seat and zoned in on the quarrel between his boss and some square patron. It wasn't an intense threat, but still, Bimmy wasn't the one to take things lightly. He marched over, ready to react with force.

Pearla sat there looking dumbfounded by the two men having words over her. Thomas wasn't ready to back down from Hassan, and they were starting to create a scene.

"Pearla, tell this man that you're with me and that he needs to leave right now!" Thomas exclaimed.

Pearla didn't say a word. She just sat there, still looking thunderstruck. In honesty, she didn't want Hassan to leave. Him standing there, his words, his conversation, it stirred some kind of fire inside her belly, and she was deeply attracted and hypnotized by him. She thought that if Cash wasn't in her life, then she would have been with Hassan. He did have everything she needed.

"Pearla, what are you waiting for? Tell this goon to leave."

"Yeah, Pearla," Hassan teased, "tell me to leave."

She looked at Hassan and then her eyes shot up at Thomas. "I can't."

Thomas shouted, "What? This is absurd!"

To everyone watching, it was like a scene out of a soap opera.

"I'm sorry, Thomas," she said softly, averting her look from his.

"Pearla!"

Hassan said to him, "Yo, can you kindly leave my

event. The woman made her choice."

Bimmy positioned himself closer to Thomas. He was ready to lay his paws on the man, nothing deadly, but give him a severe beating if he didn't back off.

"I see," Thomas said sadly. "It was nice knowing you, Pearla."

Embarrassed, he turned around and marched away. He knew when he was defeated. Hassan and Bimmy were giving him a look, and he read between the lines. These thugs would kill him.

Hassan looked at Pearla and smiled. "Like I said, beautiful, this was meant to be."

TWENTY-TWO

Ooooh shit, Cash! Work that dick, nigga! Yes! Ooooh, yes!" Sophie cried out. "You feel so good, nigga! Oh, you feel so fuckin' good."

Cash had her doggy-style in the backseat of a stolen Denali. The windows were fogged, the heat inside the vehicle a contrast to the November cold. The backseat of the SUV gave them plenty of room to stretch out and fuck their brains out. Sophie was on all fours, with Cash holding on to her sides, his chest flexing with every thrust.

"I know you love it, nigga! Love this pussy! Yes, love this pussy! Love it, nigga!" Sophie chanted.

The freak and dog that he was, Cash pulled her hair and spanked her ass, and then rubbed her clit. He was super hard inside of her, and she was super wet.

Sophie was daring and spontaneous, and though it wasn't official, she was definitely his boo thang.

"I'm gonna come!" he announced.

"Come, baby, come for me. Ooooh, you feel great, muthafucka!"

He hooked his arm around Sophie's waist, lowering her shoulders, and continued to penetrate her roughly and hit her G-spot. Her feverish cries echoed through the truck. She shuddered and gripped the back of the headrest firmly, feeling her body about to come.

And then they both howled and exploded quickly. Afterwards, he peeled the condom from his dick and tossed it out the window. They sat back against the leather and exhaled.

Sophie pulled out a cigarette and lit it. After a few drags, she passed it to Cash. He took a smoke.

She looked at him. "You falling in love with me yet?"

He laughed. He knew she was joking.

"What? You think I'm joking?"

"I love how my dick be filling up that good pussy of yours. And I love the way you make me come."

She put on her panties and then straddled him in the backseat. "You better love it, nigga."

"You know I do."

They passed the cigarette back and forth inside the vehicle.

Cash had been seeing Sophie on the regular. Everything about her was fun and risky. She wasn't scared to help steal cars with him and go joy riding. Though she came up in a middle-class neighborhood, she had this wild side to her. She was untamed and fanatical. Her passion for fun and living life turned him on.

"What now?" Sophie asked, thumping the cigarette ashes on the floor.

"What now? I get paid for this truck."

"And then what?"

"What do you wanna do?"

"Let's go to Coney Island the park," she suggested.

"Coney Island park? Why?"

"Yes! Let's go to the beach, walk around."

"Yo, it's like forty degrees outside."

"So? You scared of the cold?"

"I ain't tryin' to catch a cold."

"You'll be a'ight. I'll suck your dick on the sand."

"Yo, you a trip, Sophie."

"I know. That's why you love me."

Cash simply shook his head and put the rest of his clothes back on. He climbed into the front seat. Sophie remained in the backseat topless and in her panties.

"You not gonna get dressed?"

"For what? I like being naked."

"But I'm 'bout to head to the shop."

"So? Give them niggas at the shop a little bonus."

"Yo, get dressed, Sophie. I can't be riding around wit' a naked chick in the back."

"Who says you can't? The windows are tinted."

Cash sighed. Sometimes she could play a too much. "I'm not driving off until you get dressed and sit your ass in the front seat," he said. "You tryin' to fuck up my money?"

Sophie waited a second, but no smile came across his face. "Fine!"

She got dressed and positioned herself in the front seat with her arms crossed over her chest tightly.

Cash started the ignition.

Sophie looked at him and asked, "So we still going to Coney Island?"

"If you behave yourself."

"Oh fuck you!"

He drove off to take care of his business with Roberto.

Cash collected another two thousand dollars. He was on a roll. Roughly, he was stealing two cars a day, making close to twenty thousand a week. He wanted to become his own boss. He was saving his money so he could move out of Gloria's house. He'd saved almost a hundred thousand and had it hidden somewhere safe. This time he wouldn't be stupid enough to give it away to friend, foe, family, or any freak bitches.

Cash kept his word, and the couple caught a taxi to Coney Island's amusement park, which was less than a mile from Roberto's shop. The beach was deserted and cold. The park had shut down due to the winter season. It was a ghostly looking place, despite occasional stragglers on the boardwalk. Cash and Sophie walked the boardwalk and peered at the ocean.

Sophie walked toward the beach. The minute her feet touched the sand, she removed her sneakers and started running away from him.

"Come and catch me," she hollered at Cash.

"C'mon, Sophie, stop playin'. It's too cold for this shit!" Cash shouted.

"Who's playin'? If you want your blowjob under the boardwalk, you gotta come get it first."

Cash shook his head. "Fuck it!" He refused to take off his sneakers, but he went chasing after her.

She ran toward the ocean, and Cash sprinted her way. Sophie looked back and saw him steaming her way. She laughed and then zigzagged into different directions, trying to shake him off.

When he got close, he stumbled and fell face first into the sand. Cash had sand in his mouth. He spat it out. "Fuck!"

Sophie laughed.

"All this for a fuckin' blowjob?"

"Yup! I gotta make it fun, right?"

He picked himself up, dusted the sand off his clothes, and continued to chase after her.

Finally, he caught up with her and wrapped his arms around her waist, picking her up and spinning her around. Then they both fell against the sand, laughing.

He tickled her, saying, "Why you got me chasing pussy?"

She laughed. "Because you need the exercise."

They kissed passionately and then disappeared underneath the boardwalk, where Sophie proved she was a woman of her word.

Cash parked in front of the house and sighed. It was late, and he wasn't in the mood to put up with Gloria's mouth and her bickering. It was about time for him to pack his things and move out. The sex was good still, but he was just tired of her attitude. He got out of his car and walked toward the house.

He walked in to dim lights and candles burning throughout the house. Rose petals were all over the floor, leading to the stairs and up the bedroom. R. Kelly's "Honey Love" played in the background.

"What the fuck!" Cash stood in the living room and looked around in awe. There definitely wasn't about to be any bickering with Gloria tonight. The sensual atmosphere was proof of that.

Gloria loomed into view in a pair of stripper heels and a lace baby doll PJ set with a G-string underneath. She posed and seductively smiled at Cash.

"I'm glad you're home, baby. I have everything set up for you," she said.

She walked toward Cash, wrapped her arms around him, and pressed her lips against his, kissing him passionately. Then she took him by his hands and led him farther into the living room. She pushed him into the chair and straddled him. Her kisses were wet and all over.

"I missed you, baby," she said.

Cash was still silent. One day she was pissed off and threatening to kick him out if he didn't oblige by her rules, and the next day, she was forgiving and loving, ready to please him and be with him. Now it was a loving moment, but tomorrow, he might wake up to the same ol' bullshit.

Gloria grinded her pussy into his lap and sucked on his earlobe. She had him growing hard. She fondled his chest and his private area, and said into his ear, "I wanna have your baby inside of me, Cash."

Cash pushed her off his lap and stood up abruptly.

Gloria looked up at him. "What is wrong with you?" she shouted.

"What is wrong wit' you? Lately, you all nice and shit."

"What? A woman can't be nice and sexual to the man she loves?"

"You got issues," he said.

"I got issues? Baby, I just want to please you. I want to suck your dick. I want to have your baby. I want us to be a family."

"Family?" he spat, like it was the ultimate sin.

"Yes, Cash. You don't want a family?"

"You got shit twisted, Gloria."

Gloria looked at Cash and could sense something was going on. He had stopped asking her for money. He was dressed expensively, always wearing something new, and sporting new jewelry. They weren't fucking regularly, like they used to. She knew there were other women in his life.

One day she found a pair of pink lace panties underneath her bed. They didn't belong to her. But she refused to kick him out. Her threats were nothing but idle. Cash's strong back and thick, big, black dick had her open.

Gloria assumed Cash had another sugar mama taking care of him. She was ready to do anything to keep him, even if it meant having his baby.

"Baby, just relax and let me take care of you tonight," she said. "I have a hot bath waiting for you upstairs. And I'm gonna give you the best massage from head to toe. And then I'm gonna give you all mama's treats."

Cash looked at Gloria, almost shamefully. "Look at you. You lookin' too thirsty for this dick. It makes you look like a fool."

"A fool? What are you saying, Cash? You don't want me? You don't want this anymore?"

"You know what? I'm out."

"What! After all this I planned for you, you just gonna leave?" Gloria hollered.

Cash marched toward the door, but Gloria chased behind him and grabbed his arm.

Cash spun around and shouted, "Yo, don't fuckin' touch me!"

Her eyes watered, and the look on her face was crushing. "I love you," she said.

"Yo, I don't love you, a'ight? You be on some trippin' shit most time. I ain't got time for your mood swings."

"Oh, so you just gonna leave me?"

"I'm just gonna go for a walk. Just get the fuck away from me, Gloria! Go blow out your fuckin' candles and go masturbate!" Cash pushed away from Gloria and stormed out of the house, leaving her truly hurt and dumbfounded.

TWENTY-THREE

Flight 1979 landed at McCarran International Airport, Las Vegas smoothly and on schedule. As the plane taxied toward the terminal, Pearla looked out the window wide-eyed. She had never been to Vegas. She was excited.

Hassan took her hand into his and held it. He smiled.

"You okay?" Hassan asked.

"Yes! I can't believe we're in Vegas," she said.

"This is only the beginning, baby. Wait until you see what I have planned for you."

Pearla was filled with zeal. She and Hassan walked off the plane and into the terminal. They both looked relaxed but beautiful. Pearla was wearing a white drop-waist skirt, white mini crop-top, and wedge heels. Hassan looked comfortable in a pair of beige cargo shorts, sneakers, and a V-neck T-shirt. His diamond Rolex was shining around his wrist.

They retrieved their luggage from the conveyor belt and walked toward the terminal exit and out into the Vegas heat, which hit them like a ton of bricks. It was a searing 99 degrees with high humidity.

While the other people were waiting on line for taxi cabs, Hassan had already arranged a private pickup for them. The minute they were outside, they saw a black Maybach idling, the waiting driver dressed in a black suit, standing by the passenger door.

Quickly, the man greeted them, "Welcome to Vegas!" and then relieved them of their luggage. He opened the back door and placed their luggage in the spacious trunk. Pearla sat snugly against Hassan in the backseat of pure luxury. They had first-class leather airplane seats, TV screens embedded into the headrests, champagne, and a panoramic sunroof.

"Damn!" Pearla said. "I can get so used to this."

"Well, get used to it."

She smiled. The two kissed. The vehicle drove away from the terminal and headed toward the big signs, astonishing scenery, and a massive crowd of tourists. Pearla couldn't take her eyes away from the city. There were so many wonderful things to see driving on Las Vegas Boulevard—the lavish hotels, casinos, and the mega signs. It was hard to believe that a city so grand was built in the middle of the desert.

The driver proceeded toward the Venetian, an Italian-themed all-suite casino hotel that towered over the Las Vegas strip. The Maybach headed toward the front entrance of the five-diamond hotel. It all looked like a glorified carnival and circus, with everything showy and grand.

The Maybach stopped, and they climbed out. Pearla's gaze lifted upwards toward the size of the 36-story hotel.

"Wow! This is crazy!"

"You haven't seen anything yet," Hassan said.

The bellhop took their bags and rolled them into the lobby. Hassan and Pearla followed behind him. They walked into the lobby, the grand gallery, and its opulence and design was overwhelming, almost over the top. Pearla was transfixed by it all, from top to bottom.

Hassan took care of business and checked them into the Piazza suite, where they were escorted.

When Pearla stepped inside the room, she was even more overwhelmed. "Oh my God!"

The impeccable suite featured a king-sized bed with body-soothing Egyptian cotton sheets, a 46-inch LCD HD TV, a living room with a dining table, and wet bar. The bathroom had a jetted tub with separate glass-enclosed shower. The picturesque view they had of the Vegas strip and beyond from their floor was breathtaking.

"Hassan, this is so beautiful."

"Like I said, nothing but the best for you, Pearla. Enjoy your room. I'll be next door."

"What? Next door?"

"Yes, I'll be next door."

"Why?"

"Because I'm a gentleman, Pearla. I didn't bring you out here for sex. I want to give you a memorable experience. You deserve it."

His statement threw her completely off, leaving her speechless. *Damn! What kind of man is he?* she wondered. She'd underestimated him.

Hassan knew he could have sex with her. He saw it in her eyes. She was hungry for him. But he wanted more than sex; he wanted her heart absolutely.

Pearla couldn't believe it. She had gone from sugar to shit, and now she was back to sugar. Just a few months ago, she was broke and homeless. Now she was living like a queen, flying first class, dressing in the best, and staying in luxury suites.

Hassan tipped the bellhop a fifty-dollar bill, and the young boy was very grateful. He exited the room to give them their privacy.

Hassan went to the wet bar and removed a pricy bottle of champagne and two flute glasses. He popped opened the bottle, and poured the gold-looking liquid into the glasses. He handed one to Pearla. He raised his glass for a toast. She did too.

"This is to us, Pearla. I'm glad to have you in my life. You are a very beautiful woman, and all I ask from you is your loyalty. So let's enjoy our lives together."

"Together," she repeated.

They clinked glassed and downed the champagne.

"So what do you want to do first?" he asked her.

"Where do we start? There's so much going on here."

"I know. How about we change clothes and go get something to eat?"

"That sounds good."

Pearla and Hassan sat down in B&B Ristorante in the hotel to enjoy some fine dining. They both looked elegant, Pearla in a blush geometric lace halter dress, and Hassan in a stylish collared shirt and slacks.

Pearla told Hassan her story. She was honest about Cash. She didn't hold anything back as she berated him.

"I never liked him, Pearla. I know him. I grew up with him. He was never for you."

"You're right," she replied sadly. "He wasn't."

"Cash is a little boy trying to play a grown man. He's the type of man who will never succeed because his thinking isn't right."

Pearla nodded, agreeing with Hassan.

"For that nigga to leave you high and dry like that, what kind of man is that?" He growled angrily, "I could kill him for that."

"Don't!" Pearla uttered. "Just let him be. I'm with you now." For a moment, her eyes were sad and nostalgic.

Hassan could see that faraway look in her eyes. "Get that nigga out your head and enjoy me, baby. Okay?"

She nodded. "Okay."

Their three days in Vegas together was spent gambling almost a hundred thousand dollars away, shopping, eating lobster, extravagant pool parties, drinking the finest champagne, and enjoying the Vegas nightlife. They even visited the theater and wax museum.

By the end of their trip, Pearla was on cloud nine and definitely feeling Hassan. He was pulling out all the stops and going extra hard wining and dining Pearla.

TWENTY-FOUR

Manny and Darrell stepped off the public bus at Rikers Island and followed behind the group of mostly women and children entering the visiting center. They went through a rigorous degree of body searches at several metal detectors before they were able to walk into the visiting hall. The place was crowded with inmates and loved ones, mostly girlfriends, wives, mothers, and children sitting across from the men at their designated tables and filled with chatter. Correction officers were strategically placed around the room, watching inmates and visitors closely.

Manny and Darrell sat at the round table, waiting for Petey Jay to walk out. Both men were nervous. They hadn't visited their friend since his incarceration. They didn't know what his attitude toward them would be.

After ten minutes of waiting, Petey Jay was escorted into the visiting room behind several other inmates, all lined up single file. Manny and Darrell hooked their eyes on Petey Jay dressed in an official Rikers Island gray jumpsuit, his hair in cornrows, and he was growing a beard. He looked their way and walked over, looking expressionless.

Both men stood up to greet their friend with a quick dap and hug.

Petey Jay sat opposite of them. "What's good, my niggas?" he asked coolly. "It's been a while. Y'all niggas just come to visit me now?"

"Yo, we sorry 'bout that," Manny said. "But I can't stand to see you in a cage."

"Yeah, I feel you on that."

"What your lawyer sayin'?" Darrell asked.

"Nothin' good. He talkin' about takin' a plea deal. I feel I should take this to trial, take my chances wit' a jury, ya feel me?"

"Yeah, well, the nigga responsible for you being in here—we gonna make that muthafucka pay," Manny said.

"Cash gotta go," Darrell chimed.

"That nigga is out there tryin' to shit on us," Manny said. "Look where he put you."

Petey Jaw scowled. "Hells yeah, he gotta go."

"Snitchin'-ass muthafucka," Manny said in a low tone. "Good news, though. We gonna post your bail."

Petey Jay looked at them. Why had they taken so long to post his bail? Rikers Island wasn't the place for him. He wanted out. He wanted his revenge on Cash, but not for reasons Manny and Darrell thought. He owed Cash a lot of money, and if he didn't take care of Cash, he believed Cash was going to take care of him. Three hundred thousand dollars was a lot of money. He would kill someone if they owed him that much.

The men continued to talk, with Cash being the main focus.

Manny and Darrell believed that once Petey Jay was freed from Rikers then he would go hunting for Cash, and with Cash dead, they would be free to continue their business enterprise without any interference from him. If Petey Jay got knocked for Cash's murder in the interim, nobody was going to cry a river. Petey Jay was going to blow trial whether he wanted to believe that or not.

Their visit was short, but they felt they'd gotten something accomplished. Both men stood up and said their goodbyes to Petey Jay. It was sad to see him go back inside, but with their help, he was going to be home really soon.

TWENTY-FIVE

Cash invited Sophie over to Gloria's place to help him move. He was parked outside the house with his trunk open, and he and Sophie were going back and forth from the house to his car moving his belongings on a chilly, cloudy day.

He could have easily made his move in the morning after Gloria went to work and disappeared from her life without her knowing what went down. But he wanted to parade his new bitch in front of Gloria. So he purposely waited until late afternoon so she could get the shock of her life.

"So you used to live here?" Sophie asked, looking around the house.

"Yeah, don't remind me," Cash replied dryly.

"This bitch don't have any style. Her place is so whack."

"Well, I was homeless for a minute."

"You should have stayed homeless then," she joked.

Sophie went through the woman's house, going through her drawers and closet, invading the woman's privacy. She even went looking inside Gloria's medicine cabinet.

Cash and Sophie were smiling and laughing, looking all booed up when Gloria pulled into her driveway, arriving from work.

Seeing Cash with another woman on her porch caused Gloria to frown. She noticed his car trunk open and all of his things protruding out from it. She climbed out of her car with urgency and stormed their way.

"What is this?" she hollered. "What are you doing, Cash?"

"What the fuck it look like? I'm moving the fuck out."

Sophie looked at Gloria. "Cash, you was fuckin' this old lookin' bitch? Nigga, I know you got better taste than this."

"Excuse me!"

"Bitch, you heard me!" She turned to Cash and bluntly asked him, "How you gonna put your dick in this bitch's dried-up pussy?"

"Bitch, you need to watch your mouth in my house!"

"I don't need to do shit, bitch! My nigga don't want you anymore. He found better."

"Don't you disrespect me at my own house. You don't know me, bitch!"

Cash said, "And you don't fuckin' know me."

Sophie was in Gloria's face with her hands, screaming and yelling. It got to the point where Sophie spit in Gloria's face. It was as if it was happening in slow motion. You could visibly see the spit spew from Sophie's mouth, fly through the air, and just as it was landing on Gloria's face, the left hook came.

Gloria assaulted Sophie with a left punch to her face, knocking her back. She continued to pound on the young girl like she was Laila Ali. The girl's face went right to left from the combination of blows.

Cash, caught off guard by her punches, stood there looking dumbfounded.

"Bitch, don't you ever spit in my fuckin' face and disrespect me!" Gloria shouted.

Sophie's face was bloody, and her eye was black.

Cash ran toward Sophie and took the poor girl into her arms and looked at Gloria like she was crazy.

"How could you?" Gloria whined. "I took you in, and I helped you out, Cash. And you do this to me?" The tears leaked from her eyes and trickled down her face.

Cash looked at Gloria like she was the one who did wrong. As an assistant principal at a high school, she should have been mature enough to walk away, but Cash and his new girlfriend pushed her buttons.

It didn't take long for a squad car to stop in front of Gloria's house, and two uniformed officers climbed out of their vehicle and approached the situation with caution. One of Gloria's neighbors had dialed nine-one-one and complained.

They took one look at Sophie's face and knew they were going to take someone to jail.

"I'm pressing charges, officers!" Sophie blurted out quickly.

"What happened here?" one of the cops asked.

"She assaulted me! Look at my fuckin' face."

Gloria couldn't explain herself. The second officer approached her, removing his handcuffs, ready to arrest her.

"You're under arrest, ma'am," the cop said to Gloria as he folded her arms behind her and placed the iron bracelets around her wrists. He read her the Miranda rights.

Sophie smirked.

Gloria's tears continued to fall even more. She felt like such an ass. She'd got open off some young dick, lost her cool, and now she could ultimately lose her good-paying job.

Sophie lay naked against Cash in the motel room as the two shared a nice-size blunt and a bottle of 1800. They had just finished a steamy session of sex and were chilling out between rounds. She needed to recuperate from the ass-whipping Gloria had put on her.

"I should go back over there and kill that bitch. She thinks she can put hands on me and live," Sophie griped.

"Just let that bitch be."

"Look at what she did to my face, Cash," Sophie replied, pointing to her black eye.

"Hey, love hurts," Cash joked.

"Yeah, and I'm ready to make that bitch hurt a lot more."

"You gotta admit that shit was funny. I didn't think she had it in her." As the words tumbled from his mouth, Cash relived the moment and burst out into laughter. That shit was so funny after the fact.

"I know you ain't taking up for that bitch!" Sophie exclaimed.

"Nah, baby, you my one and only female. I got love for you, baby."

She smiled. "You better. I had your back. And you need to make it up to me, because I was trying to help you out. And now look at my eye."

"What you want me to do?"

"Get creative with me."

"Creative?"

"Yes, creative," she said with a mischievous grin. "My pussy is getting bored down there. She needs to be entertained."

"Entertained, huh?"

"Yes, entertained. You do me nice, I do you nice."

Sophie was a serious freak. She pushed herself away from him and spread her legs, showing the landing strip to her pussy.

Cash finished the blunt then positioned himself and went to work below, licking her pussy from top to bottom.

Sophie moaned, "I love you, baby." She wrapped her legs around him and thrust.

Cash didn't miss a beat dining between her legs.

An hour later, she was back in his arms, enjoying another blunt and sipping on some more liquor. Sophie had come tremendously from Cash's head game, and their sex was amazing. It felt like their bodies were meant to be together.

"Baby, what's your plan?" Sophie asked him out of the blue.

"What you mean, plan?"

"I mean, do you plan on stealing cars forever? Because, if so, then that plan is so fuckin' lame. I know you got better sense than that."

"I love what I do, and I'm good at it. And I'm gettin' that money! Paid."

"Yeah, you gettin' paid, but you do take a lot of risks doing it. I might know a way where you can still get paid and don't have to take so many risks," she suggested into his ear. "You have money saved up, right, so why not invest it into something worthwhile?"

"And what is this something? Is it illegal?"

"Do you care if it is? I thought you were a bad boy that loves to take risks."

Cash chuckled. "You right about that."

"So be my bad boy and let's take this risk." She snuggled against him and fondled his flaccid penis. "I want you to meet my brother."

"I didn't know that you even had a brother."

"I do on my dad's side. He's my older brother and his name is Kwan."

"Kwan?"

"Yes, and he's the man you need to link up with if you want to make some serious money."

"How much money we talkin' about?"

"He can make you rich."

Cash liked the idea. He wanted to step his game up and take things to the next level. He knew she was right. He couldn't steal cars forever, though he would try.

"You know what, let's meet your brother and talk. He cool peoples, right?"

Sophie smiled. "My brother is definitely cool peoples. You can trust him. Let's get this money, baby. You and me."

They kissed passionately, and Sophie was ready to fuck again. She couldn't get enough of Cash and his loving.

TWENTY-SIX

Pearla rotated in front of the full-length mirror in the Manhattan clothing store on 5th Avenue, loving the dress she was trying on. It was gorgeous. It fit her body just right, and the material was soft and comfortable against her skin.

"You look beautiful in it," Hassan said. "So sexy."

"Thank you."

He couldn't take his eyes off his woman. He sat in the chair near the dressing room watching her try on different outfits, each one more extraordinary than the next. The price tags were high, but money wasn't an issue when it came to pleasing Pearla.

"I'll take this one too," Pearla said to the woman helping her out in the changing room.

She tried on several more outfits and was ready to take them all.

Hassan stood up and passed the saleswoman a credit card and said, "She'll take them all."

Pearla smiled. The total was over nine-thousand dollars.

"Thank you, baby," Pearla said.

"Anything my lady wants, she gets."

The saleswoman smiled at their love. She wanted the same thing; the look on her face was evident.

Pearla walked toward her man, threw her arms around him, and kissed him. She appreciated everything he was doing for her. Their trip to Vegas was great. The shopping sprees were wonderful, and the attention he was giving her felt great. She couldn't ask for anything more.

"I want you to look lovely tonight," Hassan said. "We're going out with Bimmy and his girl."

"To where?"

"Someplace special."

"I know the perfect outfit to wear," she beamed. "You're gonna love me in it."

"I know I will. You look remarkable in anything you wear."

Pearla walked out of the 5th Avenue store with shopping bags and a large smile. "You're spoiling me."

"It's my plan."

They both climbed into the Rolls-Royce Phantom and were off to their next destination.

Hassan surprised Pearla when the car pulled in front of Neiman Marcus in the city.

Twenty minutes later, she walked out of the store with a $70,000 mink coat. She couldn't believe Hassan was so generous. She wondered just how rich he was. Riding around in the city in the luxurious Phantom, Pearla felt like a queen.

It was hard to believe she was on Cash's dick once. Cash wasn't half the man that Hassan was. He didn't abandon her, he treated her special, and he adored the ground she walked on.

But, still, throughout this fairytale, whimsical day she couldn't stop thinking about Cash, for some reason. He lingered in her mind like a bad taste she couldn't wash out of her mouth. It seemed like he had a spell over her. Pearla shook it off and smiled Hassan's way.

"Everything's okay?" he asked.

"I'm fine."

"What's on your mind?"

"Just random things," she replied.

"Random things, huh? Are you enjoying your day?"

"I am. This has been one of the best days ever."

"I'm glad."

It was taking a lot of wining and dining for Hassan to feel that he had finally captured Pearla's heart and mind. He didn't want any woman but her, and he didn't want any man to have her. Something about Pearla drove him crazy. Although she tried to act as if she hated Cash, always bad-mouthing him and bashing him, Hassan was smart enough to know that hate was truly some sort of twisted love. He felt Cash was a bird-ass nigga, and he was confident that if he kept going hard, kept on showing Pearla what type of man he was, then eventually he would totally win over her heart. Hassan knew that she couldn't shake Cash because there wasn't any closure. The way Cash had left her like that would fuck up any woman's mind. Hassan knew there had to be unresolved issues, things left unsaid, and accountability to be discussed.

Hassan was firm believer that you only live once, and he'd trained his mind to be in the moment. When conversing with someone, he made that person think they were the only person on earth. He paid complete attention to their every word. That's how he came up in the drug game—having complete focus, paying attention to detail, and using common sense. When handling his business, he had laser focus. Too many people multitasked, and that's how they ended up murdered or incarcerated. It was always important for him to pay attention to every minute aspect. One slip-up could cause a man to fall and crumble and possibly never get back up again.

Pearla stepped out of the Phantom behind Hassan, and he took her by the hand and escorted her to the front entrance of Shot Call, a club on the East Side of Manhattan. It was a chilly night, but Pearla was looking cozy in her new mink coat.

The crowd outside was thick. The line to get inside was a block long, and it wrapped around the corner.

Hassan skated toward the entrance and walked inside the place with no hassle. Security, recognizing who he was, unhooked the velvet rope, and Pearla was right by his side.

Shot Call could accommodate 1,100 people and boasted three VIP areas above the main floor. The club also displayed 40-foot-high ceilings, techno lights, a long, full bar and flat-screen TVs mounted everywhere.

The second Hassan walked inside the dim and loud club, he and Pearla were ushered toward the VIP section, where Bimmy, his crew, and his baby mama, April, were chilling with six-hundred-dollar bottles of champagne and taking top-notch ecstasy.

Bimmy stood up and greeted his friend with dap and a hug. "My nigga," he said, grinning. He planted a kiss on Pearla's right cheek, happy to see her with Hassan. He felt that they made a cute couple, and his friend seemed happy.

Bimmy was dressed in his usual club wear—a dark silk shirt and dark slacks, his crisp haircut and goatee trimmed neatly. He said, "Pearla, I want you to meet my baby mama, April."

April was a beautiful, shapely woman dressed in a hot pink body-hugging dress. She had on bamboo earrings and long blonde hair with blue contacts. Pearla immediately picked up that she was hood.

"Hey, girl!" April said loudly. "I love your dress and those shoes."

"Thank you. And I love your hair," Pearla returned.

"Thanks."

The two sat next to each other and started drinking champagne while the fellows talked. April was from Brooklyn, like Pearla, and she ran the streets like Pearla. They had a lot in common, from shoplifting to knowing how to fight and handle their own. April was from Brownsville, and she'd grown up with drug-dealing brothers, thug cousins, and a crackhead mother. She was the only girl and was rough. She'd done some jail time on Rikers.

The DJ played some Jay Z, and April got hyped. "Brooklyn in the house!" she shouted.

"Brooklyn!" the others repeated behind her, making their presence known.

"Brooklyn!" Pearla shouted too, grinning.

Pearla and April were connecting like Legos. The two ladies danced together on the dance floor and continued to down champagne while their mates talked minor business on the side. The club was packed, and the DJ was spinning one hit song after the other.

"Yo, Hassan, I like her," April said. "Your girl is cool peoples."

"That's why I'm with her," Hassan replied. "She's beautiful and cool."

Pearla blushed a little bit.

Bimmy had seen April in action a few times. When she didn't like a bitch, she was rude and frank. They continued to talk and party like it was New Year's Eve 1999.

April and Pearla went into the ladies' room to smoke a blunt. In the bathroom stall Pearla continued talking and let a few secrets known about herself. April shared some of her dirty little secrets as well.

"Pearla, what you doing tomorrow?" April asked.

"Nothing much. Why?"

"Let's go hang out and do us, go spend some of our niggas' money and have some fun. I know a place you'll like."

"I'm down with that," Pearla replied.

They finished off the blunt and joined the fellows back in the VIP.

The partying went on for another two hours, and then both couples left the club together and went to the local diner for a late night/early morning breakfast.

Pearla had found herself a new friend, who looked like she was about that life and then some.

Dawn was barely breaking open the sky when Pearla walked into Hassan's lavish condo on the East Side of Manhattan. The liquor had her feeling right and horny. She'd had a wonderful time with Hassan; her night couldn't have been any better. Since their reunion he had been the perfect gentleman to her. Now it was time to show him the love back.

Before they walked into his 3,972-square-foot, five-bedroom condo, she threw herself into his arms, and he caught her. Pearla straddled him as he held her in his grip, and they kissed passionately.

"Thank you for everything," she said.

"I'm always gonna look out for you, baby."

Pearla looked deeply into his eyes. Hassan had an aura about him that turned her on.

They kissed again, and he carried her into the bedroom, where he peeled away her dress. Touching her, kissing her, Hassan could feel his male instincts taking over. His hands roamed freely over her smooth curves, and he caressed gently her small waist and sexy bottom.

Pearla could feel the wetness between her legs increasing. She buried her hand into his pants and felt for his dick. He wasn't completely hung and thick like Cash, but she wasn't disappointed either.

Stroking him, Pearla whispered into his ear, "I want you." She guided him toward the bed, holding both his hands, and eased herself back on the blue down comforter on the king-size bed.

Hassan positioned himself between her legs and pushed himself into her soft temple. He grunted, feeling her tightness and wetness. "Damn, you feel so good!" he said. He started to rotate between her legs, thrusting.

Pearla kissed his neck and ear, as he moved inside her.

Switching positions, she got on her hands and knees and presented Hassan with a view of perfection—her pussy from the back.

Hassan knelt behind her and guided his hard dick to her sweet opening and penetrated her doggy-style. Soon they both reached the peak of their arousal.

TWENTY-SEVEN

Petey Jay stepped off the Rikers Island bus and out into the public parking lot a free man, his belongings in a plastic bag. It was a cold day, but it felt like summer. He couldn't wait to get his life back in order. He looked around and grinned. He exhaled and walked away from the bus stop. He wanted to get away from the jail quickly. He didn't have an exact location in mind, but the first thing he wanted to do was get something to eat and then go see his girl.

But he wasn't out of hot water yet. Out on bail, he still had Cash to deal with. Once close friends, they were now deadly enemies.

Manny and Darrell were waiting for him, their SUV idling at the end of the parking lot. When they saw him walking toward the street, Manny honked the horn. He looked their way and managed to smile. They'd come through for him, and he felt that he owed them.

Petey Jay climbed into the backseat and greeted his friends with dap. "My niggas, good lookin' out."

"Yo, we couldn't leave you rottin' in that piece-of-shit place," Manny said.

"I appreciate y'all lookin' out for a nigga. I owe y'all, fo' real."

"No doubt," Darrell said. "We family, my dude."

"I know somebody got a cigarette. I need some fuckin' nicotine right now, stress and shit, my niggas."

Darrell went into his coat pocket and pulled out two Newports and handed them to Petey Jay, who lit up.

Petey Jay sat back in the seat and gazed at the entrance to the jail. "Yo, get me as far away from this place as possible. I don't even want to look back at that hell."

Manny put the vehicle in drive and drove away, allowing the jail entrance to fade away in the distance.

Petey Jay refused to look back. He'd had a few issues in Rikers with haters, but nothing too big to handle. He came from the streets and handled himself like a thorough-ass nigga. There wasn't anything bitch about him.

Petey Jay continued to smoke his cigarette, his mind going a hundred miles an hour. He was out, but life wasn't sweet at all, not yet. "Yo, y'all seen that nigga Cash anywhere around?" he asked.

"Nah, not in a minute," Manny said. "He's been out of the loop for a few weeks. I heard he fuckin' wit some new bitch. You know that nigga ain't wit' Pearla anymore. That bitch fuckin' wit' Hassan now."

"Oh word?" Petey Jay uttered.

"Yeah, that nigga done came up, fo' real," Darrell said. "I heard he a boss nigga now."

Manny said, "You know Hassan always been that get-money nigga since back in the days. I heard he got connects wit' some Mexican cartel now. He ain't nobody to fuck wit'."

"Well, I hope he gets Pearla pregnant and they have many babies. Fuck that nigga Cash! He ain't deserved her anyway. Yo, that nigga gonna get got, son, fo' real," Petey Jay hollered.

"Ho-ass nigga!" Darrell said. "He probably walkin' around wit' AIDS and shit."

They all laughed.

Manny made his way toward Grand Central Parkway and merged onto the busy parkway. He nodded toward Darrell.

Darrell said, "Oh yeah, I almost forgot. We got you a li'l welcome-home gift."

"Oh word, my niggas?"

Darrell reached under his seat and removed a 9mm Beretta. He passed it to Petey Jay. "It's for you, my nigga. Some protection you gonna need for snitchin'-ass niggas."

Petey Jay gripped the cold steel in his hand, admiring its beauty. He smiled and nodded. "I love this gun."

"We know how you feel about nine millimeters," Manny said.

"Yeah, y'all niggas know."

"You gonna get a little payback on Cash for snitchin' on you?" Darrell asked.

"Y'all niggas already know. He's a dead man walkin'."

Manny and Darrell looked at each other and smiled. Their plan was going well.

TWENTY-EIGHT

Cash and Sophie came to a stop in front of the Howard Houses projects on East New York Avenue. The area was bustling with activity from residents, drug dealers, and fiends. The cold December weather didn't slow anything down. It was a ghetto haven where dope and coke flowed 24/7. There were a few local thugs lingering in front of one of the building lobbies, where a dice game was taking place and beer and liquor were being consumed.

Cash sat behind the wheel of his car staring at the activity. The men were in a circle gambling, their winter coats masking the small artillery, crack vials, and alcohol.

"And which one is your brother?" he asked.

Sophie gazed at the men, trying to find Kwan. "I don't see him. He must be inside the apartment."

"So we gotta go in and meet this nigga?"

She nodded.

"And your brother is cool, right? He ain't on no foul shit? Cuz I ain't tryin' to fuck a nigga up."

"Cash, relax. He's really cool peoples. You good with me, and he good with you. I'm vouching for you, baby.

He's gonna like you, trust me. We all about getting this money, right?"

"A'ight, let's go then."

Before Cash exited the car, he opened the glove compartment, took out a .45 automatic, and stuffed it into his waistband, concealing it with his coat and shirt. He looked at Sophie. "Now I'm ready to go."

Sophie shook her head. "You really don't need that."

"Hey, you never know. I'm not tryin' to get caught slippin'."

Cash and Sophie stepped out of the car and headed toward the lobby entrance, crowded with a half-dozen thugs. Cash fixed his eyes on each one and walked coolly. The closer they approached the more they caught the men's attention. Gambling stopped for a moment, all eyes on him and her, and Cash found himself in the hornets' nest.

"Yo, shorty," one of the men said, his attention on Sophie. "What's good? You wit' this nigga?"

"What the fuck it look like to you, nigga? Don't you fuckin' see us walkin' together? You stupid or blind?"

The man spat back, "Damn, shorty! Ya mouth is reckless. Yo, you in the wrong place wit' that tongue."

"Yo, maybe she need someone to teach her some manners," another towering thug chimed. "And her nigga here lookin' scared and shit."

Cash didn't reply. He kept silent and cool.

The goons stared at Cash. Sophie's reckless mouth and nasty attitude had thrust him into a very bad situation.

They were blocking the entrance into the lobby and scowling his way, but Cash had his hand near his pistol, ready to react if things went bad.

"No, I'm in the right place because I'm looking for my brother," Sophie shot back. "I'm looking for Kwan, my brother."

Hearing Kwan's name cooled down the hot tempers that were flaring. "You Kwan's sister?"

"Yes."

"I ain't never seen you around."

"Because I don't live in the area, stupid!"

"Yo, shorty, you wild wit' that mouth. Ya moms ain't teach you no manners?"

"And your moms ain't train you how to suck dick correctly."

"Yo, you a bitch that's about to get fucked up out here." The thug stepped toward Sophie.

Cash stepped in between the goons and Sophie, doing his best to protect her. "Yo, we didn't come around for any trouble."

"You need to tell ya fuckin' bitch that shit, cuz she gonna get fucked up."

"We here to see Kwan, that's all," Cash said.

"If you have a problem with me, then you gonna have a serious problem with my brother Kwan. I know y'all niggas know what he's about."

"You really his sister?"

"Call and find out. I know one of y'all niggas have his cell phone number. And if one of y'all niggas put your hands on me or my man, then there's gonna be trouble, trouble, trouble."

"A'ight, shorty, we take ya word for it," one said.

Sophie smirked.

The goons stepped aside and made a way for them to walk into the lobby. Once inside and pressing for the elevators, Cash looked at Sophie and said, "Damn! Ya brother got weight and pull like that around here?"

"You don't even know the half of it. My brother ain't no joke. He gets mad respect."

They walked into the elevator and took it to the fourth floor. They stepped out into the narrow hallway and approached apartment 4D. Sophie knocked twice and waited. Cash stood behind her and kept his reach near his pistol. He was cautious and nervous, but he trusted Sophie.

"Yo, who the fuck is that?" a deep and rough voice asked from behind the door.

"It's me, Sophie, Kwan. Open the fuckin' door!" she hollered.

Immediately the door opened, and a man appeared in front of them. He smiled at Sophie but frowned at Cash. "Yo, who this nigga wit' you?"

"I told you about him, Kwan. This is my boyfriend, Cash."

He and Cash locked eyes. Kwan still didn't change his foul look on Cash, but he gave Cash dap and invited them inside the apartment.

Right away, they were hit with lingering weed smoke. The place was sparsely furnished and a mess with takeout food, guns on the table, and drug paraphernalia everywhere. The muted TV was on ESPN, showing highlights of the Knicks' loss to Miami.

Kwan was a physically intimidating character. Black and slim, but muscular, he stood six one, with a mane of short dreadlocks and tattoos up and down his tank-topped arms. He was black and ugly and looked like he had lived nine hard lives and wasn't going to make it to his tenth.

Flashing a gold grill, Kwan said, "Have a seat. Make yaselves at home."

Cash sat opposite of Kwan, and Sophie sat on her man's lap, crowding him. In an ordinary situation, Cash would have told Sophie to plop her round ass in her own chair. But today, she almost felt like a security blanket. Cash knew that as long as she was on his lap no bullets would go flying. At least, he hoped that was the case.

Kwan removed a half-smoked joint from the ashtray and lit up. He took a strong pull and looked at the happy couple.

"Can I get some of that, bro?" Sophie asked.

Kwan leaned forward and handed Sophie the blunt. She took a few pulls and then shared it with Cash. The weed was potent. It created a quick buzz for everyone.

Cash tried to relax, but he couldn't get too relaxed. He was in a strange environment, and though he was there to talk business, he was on edge.

"So my sister tells me that you might be the man I need to go into business wit," Kwan said.

"Yeah, we talked."

"Well, that's my little sister, and if she vouches for a nigga, I trust her. She tells me that you get money stealing cars, that you really good at it."

"I do me," Cash replied, being terse.

"I do me too, nigga. But I'm tryin' to step my game up and take things to the next level. You feel me?"

"Yeah, I feel you."

"Did my sister tell you what I do?"

"Vaguely."

"I'm a drug dealer."

"I don't judge or knock a nigga for their hustle, or what they do. We all gotta eat, right?"

"My nigga, I'm fuckin' hungry right now," Kwan said. "But here's the thing—I need some seed money for this certain connect upstate. He got seven kilos of pure cocaine for me for fourteen grand apiece. He only fucks wit' heavyweight niggas. Seven kilos or more will get him to do business wit' you. That's close to hundred thousand up front, and the return on that investment, close to three hundred *K*, easy. Listen, I got the clientele and the real estate, and I got the soldiers ready to work. I'm just short on the cash right now."

"This is where we need you, baby. I know you have money to invest in my brother," Sophie said. "Think about it, us three working together, we can be a strong team."

Cash was skeptical. His last business partner in the game was Petey Jay, and his best friend had backstabbed him, taken his money, and run. So it was hard for him to trust a complete stranger.

"How much do you need from me?" Cash asked.

"Seventy thousand."

"That's a lot to invest into someone I just met."

"Believe me, my nigga, I'm legit. I'm a man of my word. You fuck wit' me and we gonna get rich together," Kwan assured him.

"My brother ain't gonna cheat you or lie to you, Cash. He real wit' his, and he about that life. Both of y'all are real muthafuckas. Together, I know y'all can make shit happen."

Cash took one final pull from the blunt, lingering on his decision. The drug game was nothing to play with. It was profitable, but it was risky and deadly.

He tried to read Kwan. He didn't want to make the same mistake twice. He'd lost once and wasn't about to lose again.

Sophie picked up on his hesitation. "What do we need to do to convince you this is a good thing?"

Cash said, "Sixty-forty split."

Kwan didn't look too pleased with the forty split.

"I'm putting a lot of money into this, so it should be fair, right?" he said.

"But it's my connect."

"I understand, but without my seventy grand, you don't have this connect," Cash replied.

Kwan looked at Sophie, who nodded slightly, telling him to take the deal. Kwan stood up, and so did Cash and Sophie. They quickly shook hands, with Kwan saying, "Sixty-forty split for now."

Sophie smiled. "Two of my favorite men combined. This is gonna be so sweet."

They continued to share the blunt and talk.

Cash then said, "You know what, I'll make it a fifty-fifty split if you do me a strong favor."

"What's the favor?" Kwan asked.

"I need somebody got. I know a man wit' your caliber and position knows someone that can execute this favor."

Sophie was unaware who Cash wanted murdered.

"I might," Kwan replied nonchalantly. "Who's the unlucky nigga?"

Cash was aware that Petey Jay had been released from Rikers Island and that Manny and Darrell went to pick him up. Cash didn't want to bump heads with him again. They already thought he was a snitch, and he wanted the threat gone. It was either him dying or Petey Jay, and Cash planned on living for a long time.

Cash had killed too, but only in self-defense and to avenge his pops, but he wasn't a thoroughbred killer like Kwan—a kill-just-to-kill type of nigga wasn't who Cash was at all.

Kwan gazed at Cash with his black eyes and said, "Your enemy is my enemy too. I'll ride wit' you, my nigga."

TWENTY-NINE

It was exactly three a.m. when several gunshots went off, piercing the cold air. The gunfire echoed for blocks, waking the neighbors. When the smoke cleared, a young man was dead behind the wheel of a Lexus, shot eight times. The body was slumped against the steering wheel and his brains on the dashboard, five bullets to the chest and three to the head.

The first responders to the gruesome scene were two uniformed cops, who called it in. No need for an ambulance; they needed a coroner. Soon, the area was roped off with yellow crime scene tape, and numerous officers and detectives were on the scene trying to catch a clue. The looky-loos in the neighborhood stood behind the crime scene tape, striving to get a look at what was going on, wondering who the victim was.

The coroner removed the body from the car and placed it onto the asphalt. Many pictures were taken, detectives talked amongst each other and then tried to get a statement from onlookers, who didn't see a thing or hardly knew the victim.

The victim didn't have any ID on him, and the police found a loaded 9mm Berretta inside the car.

As they were investigating the crime scene, suddenly a young woman in her early twenties came running to the car dressed in a long white T-shirt under a winter coat. She was barefoot, looking panicky and screamed, "No! No! No! No! No, that's my boyfriend in that car! Is he dead?! He can't be dead!"

"Ma'am, you can't pass," the cop said.

"Get off me!" she screamed. "I need to go to him!" She was ready to fight the cop and run to the car.

She was quickly restrained by cops posted near the crime scene.

"He can't be dead. No!" she screamed, engulfed in tears and grief. "Why? He just got out!"

She was quickly consoled by a few neighbors.

As she cried her eyes out, folded down on her knees in complete grief, two white suit-and-tie detectives approached her.

One of them stared at her impersonally and asked, "The victim was your boyfriend?"

"Yes," she shouted.

"What was his name?"

"Petey Jay!"

Petey Jay's gruesome murder brought the hood to a standstill. Many were in tears, knowing he would be missed.

Manny and Darrell heard about their friend's murder, and grief and guilt quickly consumed them. If they hadn't bailed him out and sent him looking for Cash, they figured he would still be alive. The two knew it had to be Cash behind the murder. Cash was a sneaky motherfucker and the only one who wanted him dead.

Manny and Darrell were both absolutely shook. They both feared that they would be next. They began packing their bags, leaving town to lay low for a while.

"Where we gonna go?" Darrell asked.

"I don't know," Manny said. "Down south, somewhere far away from here. Shit is too hot everywhere to try anything."

"You really think Cash will come after us?"

"I don't know what Cash is gonna do. But why take any chances?"

"This shit is fucked up! Everything is fucked up! If you didn't get that nigga amped up by pulling out that burner and waving it in his face we all could have gotten along."

"What, nigga? So this is my fault? This wasn't my beef. This shit had everything to do with him and Petey Jay!"

They argued continuously, pointing fingers back and forth until they were exhausted. Both went back to preparing to leave town.

Now the two were running around town scared like chickens with their heads cut off. Manny and Darrell packed up everything they owned, tossed it into the back of the Escalade, and headed for South Carolina.

As they crossed the Verrazano Bridge, Manny said, "I got a cousin in Spartanburg. We can chill at his place for a moment, until this shit cools off."

Darrell sighed. "All I know is New York, yo."

"Well, you better know someplace else, because it's too dangerous to stick around. I promise you we ain't gonna be OT for long. Somebody's gonna push that bitch-ass nigga's wig back, and then we heading back north when the fire dies out. But I'm not taking any chances. I'm gone!"

THIRTY

The money on the living room table overall was in the hundreds of thousands. Cash and Sophie stared at the cash, smiling. Kwan lit a blunt and smiled too. The seven kilos purchased from Tank in upstate Albany was a goldmine. The quality of coke on the street sold itself. It was stamped "24/7 Bedrock," and the fiends couldn't get enough of it. Brooklyn was on fire with 24/7 Bedrock. Product so pure, it almost came with a halo. Another re-up of seven kilos was in the kitchen and ready to be cut and processed by a few of Kwan's goons.

Because of Kwan, they had acquired some of the best real estate in the area to push their product, with some minor gunplay, of course. A few lives had to be snuffed out in order for their business to thrive. And a steady drug connect coming from Albany kept them all paid like a Rockefeller. Once cut correctly, the street valued tripled what they'd put into it.

Stealing cars gave Cash a thrill and was fun, but drug dealing was a lot more profitable.

"What I tell you, baby? It looks good, don't it?" Sophie said.

"Yeah, it do," Cash replied.

"I owe you, my nigga," Kwan said, "cuz wit'out you, I couldn't do this."

Cash was on cloud nine. He was paid, and it felt good. There were so many things he wanted to do with his money. He went from making twenty thousand a week stealing cars to collecting close to half a million dollars dealing coke.

Sophie sat near the money and played with it, looking like she was about to have an orgasm. She smoked the blunt and started counting.

Cash looked at Kwan and said, "Yo, let me holla at you fo' a minute."

Kwan and Cash went into the master bedroom to talk.

"What's good, my nigga?" Kwan asked.

"Yo, thanks for doin' me that favor. I heard about it on the news."

"What favor?"

"That thing I asked you to do."

"Yo, that wasn't me," Kwan said.

"What you mean, it wasn't you?"

"It wasn't me. Somebody else got to him before my peoples did. It seemed like your boy had enemies elsewhere too," Kwan said.

Cash was shocked.

Kwan added, "People think you had somethin' to do wit' it. Everyone know y'all was beefin'."

"Fuck it! Let them think it. It ain't no sweat to me."

"C'mon, nigga, let's finish counting this money and get this next shipment street-ready. Murder is murder, so get used to it, my nigga."

Cash nodded.

With Petey Jay out of the way and the streets thinking Cash was behind it, his street credentials got a big boost. He was a rising star in the NYC. With 24/7 Bedrock becoming the popular coke out there and the group also dealing in heroin, their world was about to change radically. Cash was stepping into a different ball game, where the stakes were a lot higher and one slip-up could lead to either death or life in prison.

Kwan walked out of the bedroom, and Cash followed. Sophie was still on the couch counting money and enjoying herself with her newfound riches. Her pussy was wet; her new lifestyle was making her horny.

When Cash walked back into the living room, she smiled his way and then threw a handful of hundred-dollar bills at him, making it rain everywhere. She laughed, falling back on the couch, her feet up in the air.

Kwan yelled, "Yo, why the fuck you tossin' money around like that, like you in the fuckin' strip club? I just fuckin' counted that shit, Sophie."

"Relax, big bro. I'm just having fun. I know y'all drug-dealing niggas didn't lose y'all sense of humor. C'mon, light up another blunt and break out the good liquor and let's have some fun! Let's celebrate in this bitch!" Sophie stared at Cash and licked her lips, making it very clear to him that she wanted to fuck.

Kwan walked her way, frowning, and picked up the money from the floor. He continued to curse at Sophie.

"We got a second re-up in the kitchen that we need to get street-ready. I ain't got time for games or a celebration. I got time to make this fuckin' money."

Sophie sucked her teeth. "All work and no play makes you look like—"

"A rich fuckin' nigga!" Kwan interrupted her saying.

"Boo-hoo, nigga, you borin'! But I know my man is ready to have some fun with me. Right, baby?" Sophie removed herself from the couch with a naughty smile and approached Cash.

She wrapped her arms around him and proceeded to kiss him. She didn't care who was watching. Her hand slid down to his crotch, where she fondled his manhood and then dropped to her knees, unzipping his jeans, and was ready to suck his dick in front of everyone.

Kwan's goons in the kitchen were caught off guard by her boldness.

One said, "Yo, shorty is wildin'."

Cash felt very uncomfortable, especially in front of her brother.

Kwan glared at her. "Yo, what the fuck you doin', Sophie? You out ya fuckin' mind?"

"I'm just trying to have fuckin' fun with my man."

"Yo, take that freaky shit somewhere else! Not here!"

Sophie sucked her teeth noisily and quipped, "You just mad because you don't have anyone to suck your dick right now."

Kwan shook his head. "A'ight. Whatever! You and him get ya knocks off somewhere else, but not in here."

Cash said, "Yo, Kwan, no disrespect to you, but I'll be out in the hallway. Ya sister is too high right now."

Sophie said, "Nigga, I'm fine. I just want some dick."

Cash shook his head and laughed. Sophie was something else.

Cash went up to the rooftop to smoke a cigarette and catch some quick solitude. It was cold, but he looked impervious to it, wrapped snugly in his winter coat. He gazed at Brooklyn, stretching for miles from where he stood, and almost looked transfixed by it.

It didn't take long for Sophie to follow him on the rooftop and wrap her arms around him again.

Cash turned around and asked her, "Yo, what was that down there at your brother's place?"

"What? I was just tryin' to please my man because I'm happy."

"Yeah, you was getting a little too happy down there."

"So! If I wanna suck your dick in front of people, what's wrong with that?"

"But that's your brother, Sophie."

"And he got his whores too. I like to please and take care of my man. I don't care who's watching. I love you, baby. Look at us! Look at what we're doin'! We gettin' that money, and when my man gets money with me, I get super horny and sometimes I can't control myself."

"I feel you. But no more tryin' to do freaky shit in front of your brother, okay?"

Sophie smiled. "Okay."

What the fuck kinda relationship y'all got? Cash thought.

After their business with Kwan concluded, Cash and Sophie left for home. They took Rockaway Avenue toward the Belt Parkway to the place they shared in Sheepshead Bay, a three-bedroom condo with a view of the ocean from a distance.

Cash parked on the block, and as he and Sophie were walking toward the entrance of their building, two detectives came toward them out of the blue.

One of them said, "Are you Cash?"

Cash scowled and replied sharply, "Who askin'?"

"I'm Detective Garcia, and this is my partner, Detective Saab. We would like for you to come in for questioning."

Hispanic and black detectives, both men had ten years in homicide, and were major veterans on the police force. They were serious about their job and looked like they weren't taking no for an answer.

"For what?" Cash said.

"It's about the murder of Petey Jay. You remember him. Y'all used to steal cars together and run the streets," Detective Saab chimed.

Cash looked reluctant. Both cops were playing him closely.

Sophie spat, "Y'all muthafuckas got a warrant to be pressin' my man like this?"

"Look, we can do this the easy way and you come with us willingly for questioning, or we can do this the hard way, and turn your life upside down," Garcia said sternly.

Cash continued to frown. He looked both detectives in the eyes and said, "A'ight, whatever. I ain't got shit to hide."

They quickly escorted him toward their unmarked Impala parked across the street. Sophie chased behind them, cursing out the cops. Then she said, "Baby, I'm gonna call my brother."

Cash shouted back, "No need, baby. I'll be home soon. You ain't gotta involve your brother. I ain't do shit."

He was guided into the backseat of their car, and they drove off, leaving Sophie scowling like a mean pit bull. She wanted to throw a rock at the car and shatter the back glass. She screamed out, "Fuck y'all pigs!"

Cash sat in the windowless interrogation room looking smug. He wasn't worried about anything. Petey Jay's death wasn't on his hands.

Both detectives entered the room and immediately started to question him heavily about the homicide. They tried to coerce him into a confession. But Cash had a solid alibi, one that Sophie could confirm. They continued to press him, but with no hard evidence, the detectives had no choice but to let him go.

Cash knew his rights. He glared at both men and sternly said, "I had nothing to do with that man's demise. It wasn't me, so can I fuckin' go now?"

With reluctance in his tone, Detective Garcia looked at Cash with major contempt and growled, "Yeah, get the fuck out my face!"

Cash smiled, pushed his chair back and stood up proudly, carrying the same smirk he'd walked into the precinct with. He marched toward the door, but before he could exit the room, Garcia turned toward him and said, "Hey, Cash . . . catch you later."

"Whatever!" Cash waved him off and walked out.

THIRTY-ONE

"So, do you ever want to get married and have kids?" Pearla asked Hassan.

"Of course. Have some kids, live in a nice house in the suburbs surrounded by a picket fence and have a few dogs."

"Are you mocking me, Hassan?"

"No, I'm not." He laughed. "I do wanna get married one day, maybe one day soon, and I'm looking directly at the woman I want to marry right now."

"I always thought about having a family. This life we live, do you think we can live on forever like this? I believe that everything comes to an end, even the good life."

"Hopefully, you and me, we will never end. But this business I'm in, sometimes there's no way in getting out. Especially if you're tied in with the cartels. If so, then you gotta do it gradually and subtly."

"Is that why you're trying to invest into the music business, put your money behind that girl, what's her name, Heaven?"

"Yeah."

"Did you fuck her?"

"Aren't we straightforward this morning?"

"We're just talking, right?"

He smiled. "Yes."

"So you fucked her."

"No, I didn't fuck her. I was saying yes to we're just talking."

"She is attractive."

"She is, but she doesn't have shit on you, beautiful. You're the one that caught my eye, not her," he replied smoothly.

Pearla smiled.

The pair was having a delicious breakfast in the kitchen at his condo in the city—stacks of pancakes, scrambled eggs, bacon, and freshly squeezed orange juice across the long glass kitchen table. Hassan was no slouch when it came to cooking. His grandmother had taught him well.

Pearla dined on the stack of pancakes and downed the orange juice. Her morning was starting out splendidly. Though it was a cold day, their relationship was starting to heat up like a Jamaican summer. She was exactly what Hassan needed in his life—a strong hustler like himself.

"So between you and me, how much is everything worth, your empire? I can keep a secret."

Hassan leaned back in his chair and stared at Pearla deadpan. He looked somewhat offended. His looked worried Pearla. She didn't mean to offend him.

Then Hassan burst into a smile and said, "She's worth a pretty penny, roughly close to a hundred million."

"Damn!" Pearla blurted out in shock. "And I thought I was a hustler."

"I've earned it one dollar, one block, one life at a time," Hassan said chillingly.

"Yes, you did. You definitely came up, Hassan. I'm happy for you."

"Don't be happy for me, just be happy with me."

Pearla smiled. What girl could walk away from a fortune so large? He was the king, and he wanted her to be his queen.

Hassan knew Pearla was a hustler, and that she was attracted to a nigga who could hustle hard like herself. A broke nigga couldn't do anything for her. She came up, from the bottom to the top, and was getting it on her own before he'd stepped into her life.

"You're a survivor like me, Pearla. I can see it in your eyes. That hunger you have in you, it's good. It's that same hunger that will feed you. It will continue to feed us both."

Hassan had to keep expanding his organization. He had a crew of loyal soldiers distributing coke and dope throughout the tri-state area, most likely expanding to the West Coast. He strongly felt that with Pearla by his side, offering her thoughts and counsel, he could expand his business into something legitimate, help launder his drug money, and even expand distribution into the South, to states like North Carolina, Georgia, and Florida.

"So what's on your agenda for today?" Hassan asked her.

"Me and April supposed to link up, go shopping."

"And spend some more of my money."

"Yes, spend some of your money, Hassan, if you don't mind."

"Baby, you know I don't mind. I want you to be happy and to look good."

"Oh, I'm gonna look fantastic for you."

He smiled again. "You and April are becoming pretty close, I see."

"She's cool. We have a lot in common. She can be a bit on the wild side, but she's real. I like that."

"Yeah, April can be something else. Bimmy loves her."

Looking at Hassan, his style, his speech, his intelligence, Pearla was mesmerized. If he wasn't running a criminal drug empire and killing people, maybe in an alternate universe, he could have been running a Fortune 500 company. He was that smart. Coming from the world they came from, the only way to come up was the illegal way.

Pearla stood up and walked toward Hassan with an impish smile that indicated breakfast was over, and it was time for an early dessert. Hassan fixed his eyes on her; he could never control his smile around her. A good woman should be able to make the most dangerous man smile if she was doing her job right.

She straddled him while he was seated in the chair, no panties underneath the long T-shirt she wore. The two kissed passionately. Hassan felt up her womanly figure, and just as things started getting hot and heavy, Bimmy appeared in the kitchen suddenly, throwing yesterday's paper on the kitchen table and startling Pearla.

"Damn! Does he ever knock?"

Bimmy looked at Hassan and said, "We need to talk."

"About what?"

Bimmy motioned toward the newspaper on the kitchen table. It was open to a headline that read: "Rikers Island Inmate brutally murdered a week after his release."

"What does that have to do with us?" Hassan asked.

Bimmy didn't want to talk in front of Pearla.

"I'll let y'all boys talk. I'll be getting dressed," Pearla said, removing herself from the kitchen.

Hassan stood up to talk with Bimmy. "What do that nigga's murder gotta do with me?"

"He was once friends with Cash, and then the two had a falling-out."

"And this involves me how, Bimmy?"

"It don't. But Cash do. He linked up with some nigga named Kwan, and together, they're moving some weight in our areas, some shit they callin' twenty-four/seven Bedrock."

"What?"

"Cash has gotten into the drug-dealing business. This product of theirs, they're wholesaling it too. It's reaching some of our customers, cutting into our clienteles with lower numbers per brick. These two muthafuckas are bad for business, Hassan, and they gotta go."

Hassan walked toward the window and gazed out at the city. He chuckled inwardly at the murder, thinking about Cash being a killer and becoming his competition. "Cash is no threat to me," he said.

"I can handle these two, Hassan. Just give me the word."

"No, don't do anything. Not yet anyway."

"What you mean, not yet?" Bimmy said. "Kill the seed before it can spread its roots—ain't that what you used to say?"

Hassan knew how Pearla felt about Cash, or used to. It would have been too easy to eliminate him, but he wanted to have some fun. He wanted Cash to see for himself that when it came to Pearla, he was the better man.

He and Pearla were pushing strong, and Cash was nobody to him; a bug hanging onto the bottom of his shoe. When it came time to put his foot down and squash Cash, he would. But for now, it was more fun watching the insect squirm and wiggle, trying to become something he wasn't meant to be—a drug dealer calling shots.

"Don't worry about them niggas, Bimmy, because when the time comes, we'll handle Cash and this Kwan character. Two young boys trying to wear grown man's shoes."

Bimmy nodded, hoping that the seed his boss allowed to stay planted wouldn't develop into a hardening root and wrap around them.

Pearla and April walked out of the Manhattan mall with a handful of shopping bags. They'd hit up a lot of stores inside, and between the two of them, they had spent over five thousand dollars. The city was busy, congested and cold. But snuggled warmly in their nice winter coats, they were impervious to the winter weather. Together, they looked like long-time friends enjoying the city.

"Let's get something to eat," April suggested.

"Girl, you read my mind."

They crossed Broadway and went into the Martinique Café, sat opposite of each other, and ordered a light lunch.

"So how long you and Bimmy been together?" Pearla asked.

"A long time now. We got three beautiful kids together, and that's my boo. He would kill for me, and I would kill for him. Bimmy ain't no joke in these streets."

"I heard."

"He and Hassan are like this"—April crossed her middle finger over her index finger.

Pearla nodded.

"So you and Hassan, is it that serious?" April asked.

"It's something special."

"I know it is. He really likes you. I can tell. I couldn't stand the last bitch he was with. Bitch thought she was too cute and uppity. I hated that wannabe model skinny bitch. That's why I had to beat her down. I broke her nose and fucked her up so bad, that bitch had to get plastic surgery on her shit."

"Damn! That bad, huh?"

"You know Hassan didn't give a fuck about that stupid bitch. She couldn't hang wit' the team, but I know you can. We come from the same world, Pearla."

"I know we do."

Both girls downed the Cîroc they'd ordered and ate their lunches.

Pearla could relate to April in so many ways; it felt like they could be sisters. April also had a foul mouth and uncompassionate mother who whored herself out to different men. They both hardly knew their fathers and did what they needed to do to survive, coming up in rough neighborhoods.

"Hey, let me show you something," April said, displaying a sinful grin.

"Girl, what you about to do? Or what you done did?"

April went into one of her shopping bags and removed a purse with the price tag still on it. She showed it to Pearla.

"April, you stole that?"

"You know I did. I just wanted to have some fun."

Pearla smiled and said, "I feel you on that. Girl, you are bringing back memories."

The two started to talk about shoplifting and the streets. Pearla told her new best friend that she once ran an underground shoplifting ring that netted her thousands and thousands of dollars of month.

Pearla went on to tell April about the various scams she used to get tons of money from. She talked about the stores and the malls she used to hit, and went on talking about her crew, explaining how good they once were.

"So what happened? You didn't get caught, right?"

"It just fell apart. Bitches that I trusted stabbed me in the back. One bitch, she fucked my man, and the other girl, she simply turned her back on me. And I'm the one that started her in this business and had her getting money when she used to be a broke bitch."

"You see, I can't stand that shit. Disloyalty. I can't stand a disloyal bitch, especially when you look out for a bitch too. Bitches like that need to get got," April said, not caring who heard her.

"They do."

Pearla was still upset that Roark had not only turned her back on her, but that she and Chica had partnered together with boosting and setting up the illegal marriages. The grudge inside her was so strong, it almost protruded out like a pregnancy. Roark was running around town trying to fill her shoes, thinking she was the shit. Pearla felt it was about that time to put the bitch back in her place.

"So what you gonna do about these disrespectful bitches, Pearla? I'm ready to ride wit' you and help you handle your fuckin' business. If you wanna teach these bitches a lesson, then let's do this. I'm definitely down, and I know my cousins are too. You know where these bitches live?"

"I do."

"Then let me make a phone call."

April was true to her word. It took her no time to call up a few of her hood gangstress cousins. First they rode to Roark's apartment but she wasn't home so they all converged outside of Chica's place in Brooklyn. Pearla sat in the passenger seat of April's white Benz, and three of her cousins were in a second Benz parked behind them. Pearla was itching to see Chica and Roark again. She had revenge in her mind and heart. She couldn't wait to see the look on their faces when she came charging inside with April and her cousins.

While they sat outside the building and waited for Roark to arrive, they smoked a blunt and had some more girl talk.

Pearla asked April if Bimmy was her first.

April replied, "Oh hell nah. I lost my virginity when I was twelve. He was eighteen and mean, but the nigga was fuckin' fine."

"I lost my virginity when I was sixteen."

"Sixteen. Why so late?" April asked.

"I just did. I thought boys were immature," Pearla said.

"They still are," April joked.

They shared a good laugh and continued getting high.

Finally, Pearla pointed out Roark walking into Chica's building. It was go time. Pearla couldn't believe that Chica had the audacity to go into business with the bitch she trained on how to get money.

Pearla knocked on Chica's apartment door and Roark swung the door open without vetting who was there. It gave Pearla, April, and her cousins an opportunity to push their way into Chica's apartment, knocking Roark to the ground. Chica was a bitch that was hard to catch slipping.

She was always on her game. Today she was caught completely off guard.

"What the fuck y'all bitches doing?" she screamed. She went running to retrieve a weapon to protect herself and her investment, but one of April's cousins knocked her to the floor with a baseball bat. Chica quickly regained her composure just in time to fight back. Her long, strong arms began swinging, wildly landing meaningful blows against the bitches who were jumping her.

Pearla and April beat down Roark, who cried out for mercy. Once the crew got a handle on Chica and Roark, they went ransacking Chica's place, while she cursed them out from the floor.

"I'ma fuck y'all bitches up!" she screamed. "Fuck you, Pearla!"

"Shut the fuck up, she-man!" April screamed, taking up for Pearla. "I'm not gonna tell ya ass again."

"Bitch, who you?" Chica was still reckless with her mouth. "You're a ugly, punk bitch who had to jump me! You real tough with five bitches holding you down, but I promise you I'ma see you again!"

"See me now! Freak-ass bitch!" April pulled out her burner and pistol whipped Chica with a .45 handgun.

Chica hit the floor again and curled into the fetal position. April wasn't showing her any mercy.

Pearla got in on the action too. She kicked and punched Roark repeatedly, taking out her rage and anger on Roark's face.

Roark found herself being dragged roughly across the

wood floors by many hands, her eyes black and blue and swollen, and her bloody split lip drooling. With each blow raining down on her, she looked more grotesque.

"Fuck these bitches up!" April screamed.

Pearla wanted to leave scars on Roark's face that would last forever. The beat-down on Roark from Pearla was because she'd fucked Cash, and Pearla never had gotten past that.

As Pearla and the cousins beat them down with fists, bats, and guns, April continued to go through Chica's apartment and rob her, taking jewelry, clothing, and cash from the bedroom.

Chica found herself glued to the floor, her clothing torn, and her dignity torn apart. They ridiculed her as they beat her. As the baseball bat went across Chica's back and her legs multiple times, she had the chance to lock eyes with Pearla.

"Yo, that's enough. Let's go!" April commanded.

Chica and Roark were sprawled across the apartment floor, both of them looking like they had gotten ran over by a Mack truck and dragged for blocks. Pearla and April's cousins were preparing to make their exit, but Chica had to have the last word.

She glared at Pearla and shouted heatedly, "You're a dead fuckin' bitch, Pearla!"

April stopped dead in her tracks and glared at Chica. She marched toward her with the .45 gripped in her hand and trained the weapon at her face. She was ready to kill Roark and Chica without any hesitation at all.

April was ready to blast the freak bitch in her face and leave her body to rot.

"No!" Pearla said to April. "Not here."

"Just let me do this corny-lookin' faggot nigga," April growled, itching to pull the trigger.

April withdrew the gun from Chica's face. "You lucky, bitch," she said. "But next time, you won't be."

April and her cousins ran from the apartment, while Pearla lingered momentarily, looking at Chica.

"What?" Chica hissed. "You expect me to say thank you?"

Pearla smirked. The only reason she'd spared Chica's life was because she didn't want to be an accomplice to murder. If April had killed Chica and Roark, then they all could've ended up in jail for murder. April and her cousins didn't hold any allegiance to Pearla, and if either one of them got arrested in the future, then there was nothing to stop them from snitching on her.

She and Cash had discussed this months earlier—you either do your dirt on your own, or with the one you love. She and Cash still held that secret together.

Pearla knew it wasn't over between them. Like herself, Chica was a bitch to hold a long grudge and would come looking for revenge. For all she knew, it could have been Chica who sent men to kill her and Cash inside their home. Or Roark. Or maybe Poochie.

Pearla knew one thing for sure. She was going to get Hassan to kill them all.

THIRTY-TWO

"Perez, you got a visitor!" the correction officer shouted out. "On the tier!"

Perez quickly removed himself from his bunk and walked toward the end of his cell. He wasn't expecting any visitors today. Rikers Island had been his home for over a year now. Being incarcerated didn't stop him from going after the people he felt had betrayed him and destroyed everything he had worked so hard to build.

Perez followed the correction officer toward the processing room, where he was about to go through a rigorous strip search and put on a jumpsuit before he could meet with his visitor.

Perez had a lot on his mind. So far, things hadn't been going his way. He was the one who'd sent the goons to kill Cash and Pearla. They'd stiffed him for that insurance money when they implemented the insurance scam together. Seven thousand dollars wasn't a lot compared to what Perez was used to bringing in, but it was the principle that mattered. If he allowed one person to get away with stealing from him, then other people would have the audacity to steal from him too. He wanted to put a choke on the situation before it started to breathe life. But things didn't work out the way he had planned.

Perez was locked up with the two goons he'd befriended and then hired. Wild and Mercy were notorious gangsters who would do anything for a reasonable buck. He talked to them and persuaded them to kill Cash and Pearla for ten grand, half now and half when both of them were dead.

Now Perez had a problem. Cash and Pearla weren't dead, and Wild and Mercy were never heard from again. How did Cash get the drop on them? How did he survive? What did he do with their bodies? These were puzzling questions for Perez.

Perez felt he got his second chance to kill Cash and his young bitch when he'd encountered Petey Jay, who was in Rikers on a drug charge. When word came to him that Petey was about to be bailed out, Perez had a word with him before his release. He offered Petey Jay the contract for $7,500 to murder Cash. Petey Jay needed the money, and he wanted to kill Cash.

A week had passed, and Perez wasn't seeing any results. He felt hiring Petey Jay was a mistake. When he called Petey Jay collect to find out what was happening, the man was giving him the runaround. Then, on the tenth day, Petey Jay stopped answering Perez's collect calls from

Rikers. Perez was so infuriated that he paid another goon to kill Petey Jay. Twenty-four hours after Perez put out the contract, Petey Jay was gunned down in a car. He had finally gotten results.

Perez walked behind the guard toward the visiting center. From the hallway, he could hear the chatter of inmates with their families and loved ones. The sizable room was crammed, and the guards and cameras above monitored all activity in there. It looked like every chair and table was taken.

Perez waited behind the red line painted on the floor, an area that was off-limits to visitors. The guard pointed to his visitor seated in the back, right underneath the ceiling vent and near the brick wall.

Perez coolly walked their way, avoiding eye contact with other inmates with their families, strictly focused on who was there to see him. When he got close, he managed to smile. He wasn't expecting to see Spike until the following week. He and Spike greeted each other quickly with glad hands and a bro hug, and the two men then took a seat opposite each other.

Spike was a pretty boy dressed sharply in an expensive suit. He had pale bronze skin that exaggerated the depth of his ink-black eyes, a neatly trimmed moustache, and his head was bald as a baby's bum. Nothing about him looked intimidating or evil. He looked like a regular Wall

Street guy that knew math and liked numbers, but he was well connected, linked to some very powerful, dangerous people.

"You're early," Perez said.

"You're complaining about that?"

"No. Just delighted to see an old friend. It's just been rough lately."

"I heard you're in trouble."

"Nothing I can't handle on my own."

"Whatever I can do to help, let me know."

"Yeah, I need your help with this one situation. It feels like the people I had hired to do this job are fuckin' inept, and I'm losing money. I should have come to you in the first place. I remember you always had the best people on deck for any job and any situation."

"And I still do."

"It's the reason why I'm reaching out," Perez said almost in a whisper. "I wish I reached out earlier. Now I'm out almost thirty grand for fuckin' with amateurs."

"I just need the names and pictures, and it's ten grand a head—no mistakes."

Perez nodded. "That's cool. I'm willing to pay whatever to finally have this nigga and his bitch dead. I'll get my bitch Amanda to give you pictures and more information on them. I just want them fuckin' gone."

"Don't fret, my friend. I'll have two of my best men on the job, and before you can blink, they'll be dealt with."

The two men continued to speak in a low tone. Perez steadily watched his surroundings as he was talking business. He didn't want anyone ear-hustling his conversation.

With their meeting concluded, Perez departed from the visiting center with a good feeling that things were going to be done correctly this time around.

THIRTY-THREE

Damn! Cash thought the stripper dancing butt naked on the dimmed stage in Legs and Diamonds gentlemen's club in the city favored Pearla. He sat back in the club chair with a fist full of hundreds and fifties transfixed by the resemblance to his ex-girlfriend. The dancer was cute, nice body, bigger tits and ass than Pearla, but Pearla was prettier. She moved gracefully and on beat to R. Kelly's "Naked."

Cash tipped her a few hundred-dollar bills, and the girl smiled and continued to put on what appeared to be a private show for him, even though there were other patrons inside the place watching her too.

Life was good, so Cash and Kwan went to this high-end strip club in Manhattan to celebrate. Kwan was getting a costly private dance in one of the back rooms from a curvy, Latino dancer, while Cash chose to sit by the stage and just watch the show. He kept his eyes on the dancer who called herself Dream.

It was hard to look at her and not think about Pearla, whom he hadn't seen or heard from in months. He had heard that she had gotten with Hassan and was parading herself all around the city like she was this queen-bee bitch. It honestly made Cash feel some type of way. Out of all people, why did she have to get with a man he seriously loathed?

He figured she got with Hassan to get back at him. It worked for a moment, but then he realized he was better off without her in his life.

Cash had convinced himself that Pearla was bad luck. Thinking back, he realized that the moment he got into a relationship with her, his pops got shot, then he got locked up twice, Petey Jay took him for over three hundred thousand, and someone tried to kill him. Cash was done with Pearla. *Fuck her!* She was no good. Good riddance. Hassan could have the trouble.

Lounging in the club chair, he threw back his shot of Patrón. He continued to make it rain on the dancer and get his drink on.

The club was alive with sexily dressed women, good music, liquor, and paying customers. Cash was in the mix, conversing with the stripper that looked like Pearla, trying to fuck her, when Kwan walked up behind him and tapped him on the shoulder. He quickly got Cash's attention and said into his ear, "We gotta run, my nigga. Something came up."

Cash nodded and curtailed his conversation with the stripper and walked out of the club with Kwan. They climbed into Kwan's newly purchased Audi S3 and headed back to Brooklyn.

During the ride, Kwan ran down the four-one-one to Cash, bringing him up to speed on what had happened. One of their spots was hit by stickup kids, a shootout ensued, and one of their soldiers got hit a few times. He was rushed to the nearest hospital, and it looked like he wasn't going to make it.

Kwan sped across the Brooklyn Bridge and raced toward Brownsville via Atlantic Avenue. He was livid. He was constantly on the phone communicating with his goons, trying to find out some answers, eager to learn the identity of the men behind the daring robbery.

"Niggas tryin' to rob me," he shouted, racing down the avenue, swerving in and out of traffic.

Cash was silent. This was an inevitable part of the game. No doubt, more bloodshed was about to follow. He was a boss now and had to make decisions that involved life and death.

The moment they turned the corner to Rockaway Avenue, they were face to face with the chaos that had taken place earlier. Almost the entire block was roped off with yellow crime scene tape, and police lights were shining brightly in the night, lighting up the urban block with law enforcement from corner to corner.

Kwan sprang from his car and immediately started searching for one of his goons to talk to. Cash was right behind him. The area was like a zoo, hot with police and locals everywhere.

Kwan quickly spotted his little nigga Keybo and went his way, moving with a sense of urgency. "Yo, Keybo!"

Keybo turned and quickly went Kwan's way. Kwan was frowning as he stood in front of Keybo. "Yo, what the fuck happened?"

"Four niggas just came outta nowhere and started poppin' off. Soup got lit up, three to his chest. They sayin' he ain't gonna make it."

"You know who it was?" Kwan asked.

"I'm not sure, but to me, it looked like them 6-9 Bloods over from Dumont," Keybo said.

"You sure, my nigga?" Kwan looked like he was ready to explode with violence.

"Yeah, cuz one of 'em spoke, and it sounded like that nigga Obey. That muthafucka got that distinctive fuckin' voice."

"You sure it was the 6-9 Bloods?" Cash asked, breaking his silence.

Keybo nodded.

Kwan tapped Cash on the back and said, "Let's ride, my nigga."

They both got back into the Audi and drove away from the area. Kwan was ready for war—a reaction was a must.

Cash saw a slight dilemma with striking against the 6-9 Bloods. They were heavily connected, seriously crazy, and they were getting their drug supply from Hassan and a wild, murderous gangster named Bimmy. Bimmy was no joke.

Kwan decided to cruise around enemy territory, near Dumont Avenue and Mother Gaston Boulevard.

He wasn't scared or worried. Underneath his seat was a loaded Glock 17, and in the trunk of his car was a sawed-off shotgun.

"Yo, we gonna find these niggas and take care of them, Cash. They fucked wit' the wrong muthafuckas!"

Cash nodded.

The next day, Kwan received some intel on Obey's whereabouts. Supposedly, he had a bitch out in East Flatbush and was staying in one of the tenement buildings on Foster Avenue.

Kwan and Cash hurried out that way in a stolen Accord and reached the corner of Foster and New York Avenues late in the evening. Kwan was heavily armed, itching for revenge, and anticipating Obey's exit from the building in Flatbush Gardens. The area wasn't too populated with people because of the cold weather and late hour, but traffic was flowing.

Cash and Kwan sat and waited. They shared a cigarette and made small talk. The only thing on Kwan's mind was murder.

An hour passed, and Cash was becoming antsy. The nicotine wasn't helping him too much. "Maybe he ain't here," he said to Kwan.

"Nah, that nigga here. Him and his niggas wanna take from me," Kwan said, upset. "I'ma see this nigga, even if I have to wait all fuckin' night for his ass."

The car was becoming cold, and Cash feared that

sitting parked on the street too long would leave them too exposed. But Kwan was determined to carry out deadly retribution. Soup had died early that morning, and Kwan strongly believed in an eye for an eye.

Finally, their patience paid off. Kwan spotted Obey leaving his girlfriend's building, but he was with another male. The two men were conversing.

Kwan sparked like a firework ready to go off. He cocked back the Glock he was carrying and threw on the black ski mask. He looked at Cash and said, "Yo, I got this. You stay wit' the car and keep it running. I'ma go toe-tag this muthafucka!" He left the car and hurried their way.

Cash looked at the event unfolding like it was a B horror movie. He slid behind the wheel of the Accord and was ready to leave.

Kwan marched toward both men unwavering, and he immediately caught their attention. "Steal from me, muthafucka!" he shouted, his hand outstretched with the Glock at the end of it.

Obey and his friend became wide-eyed and tried to flee in a panic, but it was too late.

Kwan had the man in his sights, and he was dead to rights. He opened fire. *Bam! Bam! Bam! Bam! Bam!*

Obey caught three in the back as he tried to run, and another bullet tore into the back of his skull. He fell face down against the cold concrete. Kwan wasn't done yet.

The friend tried to escape the carnage by running back into the building, but Kwan chased after him. The man was screaming.

Cash couldn't believe Kwan was so bold. It was getting too risky. Cash had the urge to drive off, knowing gunshots would bring the police soon.

Obey's friend made it toward the stairway entrance, but he was stumbling. He had been shot in the leg, and he tripped and fell.

Kwan was right there, the gun aimed at his head.

The man lifted his hands in self-defense, begging for his life, his eyes wide with fear. He screamed, "C'mon, man, don't do this. Please! Don't do this! Don't kill me!"

"Fuck you and ya life," Kwan replied. *Bam! Bam!*

Kwan blew his brains out execution-style and fled from the scene. He dove into the idling Accord, and Cash didn't wait one second before speeding off.

"Yo, what the fuck was that?"

"I ain't leavin' behind any witnesses," Kwan said, trying to justify his actions.

"You coulda gotten us caught doin' that dumb shit."

"Nigga, we ain't caught, though, so chill."

Cash frowned and hurried back to the hood. Kwan was a maniac. Cash had killed before, because he had to, but Kwan looked like he had come in his pants when murdering those two men.

Kwan quickly settled into the front seat, removing the ski mask. "I love this shit!"

That statement proved Cash's suspicion. Sophie's brother, Cash's partner in crime, was a complete psychopath. Cash had now seen another side of Kwan, and honestly, it made him a little nervous.

THIRTY-FOUR

"I swear to God, that bitch is fuckin' dead!" Chica screamed. "I'm gonna kill that bitch. Ooh, she don't fuckin' know. She fucked up coming in here and violating me like that. I'm gonna fuck Pearla up and that other stupid bitch!"

It had been a week since the incident, and Chica was still on fire. Every time she saw herself in the mirror, it fueled her rage. They'd really done some damage to her face. Her doctor was saying that she might need surgery on her right eye. Chica cursed Pearla and the other bitches who assaulted her and then stole from her. She was running her mouth all over, talking shit about Pearla, and letting everyone know she was a foul, grimy bitch. She was slandering Pearla's name, telling her secrets, and making up some rumors.

"That bitch had to get me jumped, because she know she is pussy. That bitch is fake. She a scared bitch. She know she had to sneak up in my place with an army to come at me because, if she came by herself, I would have stomped that fuckin' bitch out with my stilettos and put a fuckin' hole in her head!" Chica's voice had some bass to it.

Chica was serious about retaliating against Pearla and her newfound friends. She made phone calls all over Brooklyn, trying to pull together an army to go against Pearla. Chica wanted a round two with these bitches, and this time, she planned on being ready for her and April.

It was out there. Chica and Pearla had serious beef between them. But not so many people were quick to jump on Chica's side, knowing that Pearla was seeing Hassan, one of the most feared men in the city.

"Roark, I'm gonna kill that bitch. You know where she be at now?" Chica asked.

Roark had no idea. Roark wasn't talkative like Chica. After that beat-down, she started to have second thoughts about going against Pearla and shunning her the way she did. It was a mistake. Things had gone too far, and she didn't want any part of it.

Roark should have known that Pearla wasn't going to stay down and out for too long.

"Roark, I know you're ready to kill that bitch too. Look at what she did to your face," Chica said.

"Maybe we just need to chill, Chica. Pearla is a different person, and she has support in some very strong places."

"What! Hell no! That bitch made a mistake coming at me like that. I'm supposed to just fuckin' forget about what that bitch did to me? Fuck no!" Chica said, sounding a lot more like a man than a woman. Her anger and rage was gradually bringing that testosterone out of her.

Roark knew there was no talking any sense into her. She didn't want any part of Chica's suicidal plans. The only thing she wanted to do was make some money and become her own boss. Maybe partnering with Chica was a bad idea. Roark was ready to lick her wounds and move on.

She removed herself from the couch and left Chica's apartment. She was scared of Pearla, and she felt the only safe and reasonable thing to do was find Pearla, apologize for her actions, and ask for her forgiveness.

It didn't take too long for Roark to find Pearla. She'd gotten word that Pearla sometimes frequented a lounge on E. Houston Street called Kindle Lime. Roark made it her business to travel into the city and stand in front of the lounge, hoping to run into Pearla either coming or going.

On the fourth day in the city, she caught a break and ran into Pearla and April getting out of a silver Bentley. They were about to step into the lounge for a few drinks and the see the poets perform.

"Pearla!" Roark called out from a short distance.

Pearla and April both turned around, and when they saw Roark standing not too far from them, both ladies became nervous and immediately thought Roark was there to carry out revenge.

"Is this bitch following us? I'ma fuckin' hurt this bitch!" April shouted. She was ready to charge Roark.

Roark shouted, "I'm just here to talk. I didn't come here for anything else, Pearla. I swear to you, I'm not here for that."

"April, chill. Let her talk and hear what she gotta say. If she doesn't come right, then we'll fuck her up."

Roark had only a few seconds to convince Pearla not to have her killed.

"Can I talk to you in private?" she begged. "I just need a few minutes of your time."

At first, Pearla looked reluctant, but what harm could Roark do? If she moved wrong with April around, then she would regret it, if she left alive at all. Pearla gave Roark the privacy they needed by them both sliding into the backseat of the Bentley and closing the door. April stood outside like Pearla's guard dog.

Pearla looked fiercely at Roark and said, "You got one minute, so talk, bitch."

With her tail between her legs, Roark said, "I'm so sorry, Pearla, I am. Please, I didn't know what I was thinking when I went against you. It was stupid. I got carried away. I'm so sorry. I should have never doubted you. You took me under your wing and helped me out. Please forgive me. Chica is ready to go to war with you, but I'm not."

"I'm not worried about Chica; she's nothing to me. When the time comes, she, or shall I say, that faggot-ass queen will be dealt with."

"I don't want anything to do with her. I'm done."

Pearla still wasn't moved by Roark's speech. The damage had already been done. Pearla knew Roark was scared. She could see it in her face and almost smell the fear on her.

"And tell me why I shouldn't have you killed the minute you step out of this car. You think it's that easy? Come here with your rhetoric, and your betrayal should simply be forgiven afterwards?"

Roark, shame and trepidation written all over her face, couldn't even look Pearla in the face directly.

"I'll do whatever you want or need, Pearla. I don't want any beef with you. I'm not Chica. She's crazy. She's talking about going after you with guns and her own crew."

"I'll handle Chica," Pearla repeated.

Pearla came up with the perfect plan to punish Roark's foulness and insubordination. She decided to pimp her.

"You want my forgiveness, Roark," Pearla started, "then I'll give you it, but under one condition. From here on, I want fifteen percent of everything you make, whether it's from the marriage scheme or selling the clothes you boost. I don't care if you sell candy bars to kids. I want my fuckin' cut. You wanna be a boss, then you pay your taxes like a boss."

Roark thought it over quickly. She agreed reluctantly. It wasn't like she had a choice.

Pearla wasn't done yet. She looked at Roark closely and went on to say, "Bitch, you better come correct with the right amount of money all the time. Because if you screw or cheat me, if I hear I'm getting shorted in any kind of way, Roark, then it's on and I'm coming after you. And that ass-whipping you got the first time from me will be nothing compared to what I'm gonna do to if you lie or cheat me. You understand?"

Roark nodded.

"Like I said, if there's a nickel bag of crack being sold, I want in. Now get the fuck out my car and go get my money, bitch."

Roark hastily removed herself from the Bentley, averted her eyes from April's, and walked away like a scared mouse scurrying away from a cat's wrath.

"Stupid bitch! I don't like or trust that bitch," April said.

"I trust her fear," Pearla replied. She felt proud and satisfied, seeing Roark humbled and belittled like that.

THIRTY-FIVE

Cash held Sophie in his arms and relaxed in their king-size bed inside their new apartment with high-end furniture, 60-inch TV, and cream-of-the-crop stereo system. Their bodies were contorted sexually underneath the silk sheets.

They'd just had an intense second round of sex. Cash looked somewhat pensive. He was thinking about Kwan. He'd told his girlfriend about the murders that her brother had committed the other day.

Sophie said, "Why you think these niggas fear my brother out here like that? He ain't no joke. His gunplay is fuckin' real. And these niggas don't play around with him. He'll kill you in a heartbeat if he feels you disrespected him or his family."

"He takes too many risks with his, Sophie. Shit could have been thought through and handled differently."

"You see, in a world like this and the business we're in, I trust my brother because we gonna need him when shit gets really heavy in these streets. Kwan won't hesitate to show strength. He got your back as long as you got his."

Cash looked a little worried.

"You ain't gotta worry about Kwan, Cash. When my brother is with you, he's with you, and he got your back. He likes you."

Cash thought, *And what happens when he's suddenly against you? Then what?*

Cash wasn't a slouch when it came to guns and handling his own, but he'd seen men like Kwan before—off the hook and fueled by borderline insanity. Bloodshed and violence got their blood going, got them extremely excited, probably more so than sex.

"We can't be weak out there, baby."

Cash nodded. "We gotta be smart too."

THIRTY-SIX

Hassan was having dinner in the living room of his apartment when Bimmy walked in to give him the grim news.

"Obey is dead," he said.

Hassan continued eating his meal, remaining cool. It was sad news to hear. "When and where?"

"Flatbush Gardens last night. One crazy individual gunned him and his cousin down while leaving his girl's building. He was one of our best customers, Hassan."

"You know who did it?"

"Word on the street, that nigga named Kwan. He blamed Obey for hitting one of his spots and killing one of his men. It was a revenge hit."

"Did Obey do it?" Hassan asked.

"It don't matter if he did it or not. He was connected to us. He made millions for us every year. Now that profit and loyalty is gone in the wind like yesteryear because of this muthafucka named Kwan."

Hassan still looked hesitant in green-lighting the hit on Cash and Kwan. A drug war was the last thing he wanted. That would bring the cops, even the feds, into the mix when bodies start dropping left and right, slowing up profits and making things hot on the streets. A drug war was never good for business.

Hassan knew that the matter needed to be dealt with accordingly. He couldn't slack on reacting or underestimate Cash and Kwan. Hassan could see that the seed Cash and Kwan had planted had started to grow quickly and spread roots throughout Brooklyn.

Hassan removed himself from the table and prepared one of his Cuban cigars. He walked toward the window and lit the cigar. For a moment, he gazed out the window, savoring the flavor, staring at the city.

Bimmy stood behind Hassan. His pressure was slowly rising at Hassan's slow to simmer attitude. He was itching to respond with violence. He felt they needed to make a statement right now. Obey was an important factor in the cash flow of their organization. If the streets even hinted that Hassan was weakening, not ready to fight fire with fire, then how would they look?

"Is everything okay, baby?" Pearla asked.

Hassan turned around and saw his beauty gazing at him, looking sexy in a silk robe.

Hassan smiled. "Everything's fine, baby." He looked at Bimmy and said, "We'll finish talking about this tomorrow."

Bimmy didn't look like he wanted to talk about it tomorrow. He wanted a response from his boss now. "Tomorrow then," he replied dryly. He pivoted and left the room, leaving Hassan with his girl.

Pearla walked toward Hassan and slid her slim figure between his arms and lay her head against his chest.

Hassan held her close and tight. He thought about Cash. Hassan was a very jealous man. He wondered if she knew about her ex-boyfriend's new career change? Did she still have feelings for him?

"Do you still think about him?" he asked her.

"Think about who?"

"Your ex, that clown."

"I don't. And why bring his name up during a moment like this? He means nothing to me."

"It just crossed my mind. Do you love me more than him?"

Pearla locked eyes with him. "I love you, Hassan, no one else but you. Cash was my mistake; you're my future."

Hassan had a habit of wanting to test people's loyalty. It was nice to hear, but did she really mean it? He loved Pearla deeply. He was giving her the world, but in the end, where did her heart truly belong? If Cash came back to her asking for her forgiveness and talking that sweet talk, would she fall for it and go running back to him?

Hassan wanted a woman completely true to him. It was one of the reasons why he was hesitant in having Cash killed. If he killed Cash, then he would never know where her true loyalty lay, so keeping him alive for now gave him the chance to put her through that test. If she passed, he would be the happiest man alive, if she failed, then he might pay for her funeral—if he decided not to dispose of her body himself.

"Baby, come to bed with me," Pearla said, taking Hassan by his hands and pulling him toward the bedroom. She led the way and he followed. Pearla had something special planned for him in the bedroom.

Hassan walked into a candlelit room with some The Weeknd playing. He was slightly impressed. Pearla grinned his way and slowly undid her robe. Her perky tits were calling out to him.

He reached for her, his dick hardening from her sight then her touch. She pushed him against the bed, where he landed on his back. She quickly straddled him and unfastened his pants, and Hassan quickly became a submissive little boy underneath her.

She worked her kisses down from his chest to his erection, slowly kissing and tasting him everywhere. His hard dick was the perfect fit in her hand. She stroked him gently, up and down, and then took him into her mouth, her saliva becoming the perfect lubrication. She licked the head, circling it slowly, and then she moved her mouth farther down his shaft.

Pearla could hear her man groaning as she sucked his dick all the way down to his balls. Her king needed to relax and enjoy her—from her lips to her body. Pearla wasn't holding back, fucking his dick with her mouth.

With Hassan super hard and swelling, she jumped on his dick and started to milk him nice and slow with her pussy. She pressed her hands against his chest and gyrated her hips into him, eliciting a strong, gratifying sound from her mate. He was fully inside of her, thrusting in and out with rhythm and grace. Passion consumed them deeply, their bodies hot and sweaty with love.

They both were on a mission to make each other come. Their bodies moving in union, they danced sexually until they both exploded.

Pearla collapsed against her man and lay there. As Hassan held her in his arms, he knew that she held his heart in her hands. He was hoping he wouldn't ever be forced to have her killed for cheating, especially with Cash.

THIRTY-SEVEN

The American Airlines flight from Miami landed at JFK Airport early in the evening, and two serious-looking men stepped off the plane dressed in dark suits, mirrored shades, and a Florida tan. They walked through the terminal with their carry-ons and hard-looking faces, moving along with the other passengers like two robots, showing no emotion.

Fifteen minutes later, both men were met by Spike near the exit. Spike greeted them with a matching stone stare and handshake. "Welcome to New York," he said.

There was no such thing as small talk with these two men. For years, they'd only been about murder for hire, with over twenty kills between them. From politicians to drug kingpins and family men, they didn't discriminate. Their motto was to kill them now and let heaven and hell sort them out later.

The two men followed Spike out of the terminal, crossed the busy street, and headed into the parking garage. All three climbed into a Lincoln Navigator, and Spike proceeded to drive away from the airport.

The men drove in silence as Spike made his way toward the expressway. They stared out the window taking in the little scenery Queens had to offer. The traffic wasn't heavy, but the New York cold and snow was a direct contrast from Miami's warm sun, blue sky, and sprawling, sandy beaches.

Spike decided to start the job right away. He removed a manila folder from the passenger seat and handed it to the two killers, Elliott and Jarrett, who'd decided to sit together in the backseat.

Both men were in their early forties, well groomed, and highly intelligent with photographic memories. They were skilled marksmen, good with knives, worked well with poison, and were deadly with their hands.

"The first picture is of Cash," Spike informed them. "Early twenties, a car thief and womanizer."

The men studied his picture, and Spike continued to give them the rundown. He had enough information on Cash to predict his next move.

Next, Spike moved on to Pearla's photo. He gave them her age, pedigree, and last known address.

They studied her photo.

"A reminder, these two are tricky. They escaped being murdered twice. My employer doesn't want it to happen a third time. This bitch can be very resourceful, and she's connected. She's involved with a heavyweight in this town named Hassan. So she might be an issue."

Elliot swatted the air dismissively. "We'll handle this issue," Elliot said unworriedly.

Spike continued driving toward the city, where he had reserved a large, two-bedroom suite for them at the Marriott in midtown Manhattan, rolling out the red carpet for these two killers.

Inside the hotel room, Spike presented them with a suitcase filled with automatics, knives, and cash.

"If y'all need anything else, I left my contact information on the cell phone on the bed," Spike said.

The men started to settle into the room. They only planned on staying a few days, four at most. They worked quickly and efficiently. New York wasn't one of their favorite cities.

Before Spike left the room, he turned and smiled. "Oh, I left something else special inside the bathrooms. Enjoy!"

Spike walked out of the hotel and climbed back into his Navigator feeling confident about these killers. Perez wouldn't have to worry anymore. He was right to come to him.

THIRTY-EIGHT

Cash lit up a Newport, inhaled deeply then exhaled. He had a lot on his mind. He lingered outside his building, trying to cool off. If he didn't, then he probably would kill his bitch in a fit of rage. He'd just had a serious argument and fistfight with Sophie, who had gone through his phone and found an old picture of Pearla in the mix.

She'd confronted him. "Why is this bitch's picture still in your phone?"

"Yo, I don't know. I forgot it was even in there," he said, dumbfounded that it was still in his cell phone.

"You ain't forget, nigga! You fuckin' lyin'! You kept it in your fuckin' phone for a reason! You tryin' to go back to that bitch, huh, Cash? You want your fuckin' ex?"

"I want you! I don't want her, Sophie. Why the fuck you trippin' for?"

"I'm trippin' because I think you trying to play me, muthafucka!"

Sophie loved to move her hands as she talked. She had gotten so angry at Cash, she repeatedly mushed him in the head and punched him in the chest.

Cash had to restrain his anger and control himself. He didn't want to hit her back. Sophie was a violent person like her older brother. She was in his face, not backing down.

The picture of Pearla in his phone caused her to slap him and then punch him just thinking about it. She felt disrespected. She was in love with Cash, and the last thing she wanted was a broken heart from him.

"Yo, baby, you need to really fuckin' chill out right now," he warned her through clenched teeth.

"Or what, nigga? What the fuck you gonna do?"

Sophie was a jealous female, especially when it came to Cash. She was secretly jealous of Pearla, and felt Cash and Pearla weren't done with each other. Cash could see the jealousy in her eyes. Sophie was extremely crazy over him. She would kill for him, even die for him.

Cash didn't talk about Pearla, not openly anyway, but there was something about Pearla that bothered her greatly. Maybe it was because her name rang out around town, and she knew how strongly he once felt about her.

And Sophie was well aware of Cash past with women. He was a pretty boy, a playboy, and he was a wild boy—a major male whore. But wild boy or not, she wasn't about to tolerate any foolishness. She felt that she should be the only woman he needed. She did everything to please him, from sucking his dick, to fucking him regularly. She was the only freak he needed in his life.

Cash and Sophie continued to argue. It got really loud between them. She threatened violence and death if he ever cheated on her.

Cash hated to be threatened. He screamed at her, "You ain't gonna do shit, bitch!"

After she punched him, Cash quickly lost control and backhanded her, knocking her against the wall and to the floor. With a bloody lip, she sprang up and charged at him in a frenzy, her eyes red with rage. She wanted to tear his balls off and break him apart. Cash pushed her off of him and cursed her out. When she attempted to stab him with a knife, he punched her so hard, she went flying off her feet. Things between them had gotten out of hand.

"Crazy fuckin' bitch!" he screamed.

"I'm gonna get my fuckin' brother to fuck you up!"

It was the last thing he wanted to hear. He wasn't afraid of Kwan, but he wasn't itching to go against him.

"Sophie, I ain't got time for your shit. I gotta head to Albany wit' ya brother tomorrow. You tryin' to get a nigga locked up!"

"I don't give a fuck! Why you got that bitch's picture in your phone? Why her?"

"I'll delete the shit, okay! I don't give a fuck about that bitch!"

Cash snatched his phone from her and deleted Pearla's picture. Before things escalated between them and he or she did or said something they would regret, Cash hurriedly left the apartment, slamming the door behind him, and fuming, feeling like a volcano ready to erupt.

Cash loitered outside, finishing off his cigarette. He hadn't thought about Pearla in a long time. He still felt she was nothing but trouble in his life.

It started to snow, but he didn't care. The feel of the cold snow coming down in the night was helping him to cool off. The flakes were settling everywhere, blanketing the streets, the cars, trees, and the buildings with whiteness.

Cash took a deep breath. He knew he needed to apologize to Sophie. She did help him a whole lot. And, besides, now wasn't the time to beef with her or her brother, now that they were making money hand over fist.

He marched back inside, took the stairs, and went back into the apartment. He stormed into the bedroom to find Sophie on the phone, probably telling a friend or her brother about their recent fight. She turned and looked at him. She was still upset. She still wanted to fight him.

"I'm sorry, baby! I fuckin' love you, and I want you in my life, nobody else!" he said with ferocity that nearly shook the bedroom.

Cash moved toward her with a burning hunger in his eyes, scooped her into his arms, not trying to tolerate any resistance from her

She said into the phone, "Let me call you back."

He pushed her onto the bed, against her stomach, tore off the panties she was wearing, and dove into her pussy, eating her out from the back. She had her knees up and out, with a pillow under her stomach while Cash was kneeled behind her and between her legs.

Sophie was face down on the bed, moaning and groaning, already forgiving Cash for all of his wrongdoings. "I love you, Cash," she cried out.

Their fight earlier—what fight?

Cash and Kwan were loaded up with their umpteenth re-up from Tank in Albany. They were ready to hit the road and drive back to the city. It was a three-hour drive back to Brooklyn via I-87. This was their biggest re-up yet—twenty kilos of yayo and heroin with an estimated street value of 1.8 million concealed within the wall panels and seats of the minivan they drove. It was going to be another big payday for the duo.

It was getting late. Albany was a city they didn't want to linger too long in. It was the state's capital, and state troopers were known to be a bitch when it came to pulling over drug traffickers.

The sky was dark, and the highway was clear from there to the city. It was Cash's turn to drive back. Both men said good-bye to Tank and got inside the minivan that was loaded up with a fortune of drugs.

Kwan was smiling heavily. He felt great. Their re-ups were increasing, and their money was continually growing. Kwan wanted to expand their operations elsewhere, feeling like he was untouchable.

Cash steered the vehicle toward the tollbooths, going to I-87. As he drove, Kwan was in his ear, trying to convince him that they needed to get rid of their competition, Hassan and Bimmy.

"It can be done, Cash. We can do this, take over this shit and become gods, nigga."

"Gods?" Cash chuckled.

"Fuck, yeah. Hassan and Bimmy—fuck them niggas—they bleed red just like everybody else. Niggas ain't invincible. I want that shit. Power, nigga! John Gotti did it, Scarface too."

"Scarface, that nigga was a fictional character," Cash replied.

"So what? He built his empire from scratch, killed anyone that got in his way."

"At the end of that movie he got shot the fuck up."

"Peep how he went out, though. If I gotta die, I wanna go out the same fuckin' way, bussing off my gun and takin' muthafuckas to hell wit' me," Kwan said.

Cash shook his head. "Nigga, you watch too many fuckin' movies."

"I wanna be a legend in my fuckin' hood."

"Well, you on your way, nigga," Cash said.

"Nah, *we* on our way, nigga," Kwan corrected. "And, besides, I know you wanna body that nigga Hassan. Ain't he fuckin' ya ex-bitch?"

"I don't give a fuck about that ho anymore."

"Pussy was that bad, huh?" Kwan joked.

Actually, it was some of the best he'd ever had, but he didn't want to think about Pearla.

"That bitch is just dead to me."

"She shouldn't be. Maybe we can use her to get to Hassan. Once he's out of the way, who gonna stop us?"

There was a burning sensation in Cash's stomach. He hated Hassan when growing up, and it had been hard to outstunt and outshine him. Now that he had some substantial amount of power in the streets, it felt like the perfect opportunity to follow up on what Kwan was talking about. However, he knew it wasn't going to be easy. Going after a kingpin like Hassan and killing him always came with repercussions.

Cash did sixty-five on the highway, making sure to keep the car at a moderate speed limit, not wanting to catch the attention of state troopers and risk receiving a twenty-five years to life sentence for drug trafficking.

Cash and Kwan continued to talk. His partner was good company; they shared their last cigarette and talked about the future.

They passed Poughkeepsie and were halfway home. Ten miles outside of that town, bright blue police lights started to blare behind them.

"Shit! Muthafucka! I ain't goin' back to jail," Kwan shouted.

"Just chill, Kwan. We don't even know what he's pulling us over for."

"I ain't goin' back to jail, Cash."

Cash slowed the car down and was about to pull to the side of the highway, but Kwan instructed him to pull off at the approaching exit. The state trooper was directly behind them; there was no mistaking it, he was after them.

It was after midnight, and the highway was dark and wintry. Cash steered the minivan off the highway and toward the approaching exit.

Kwan was animated, frowning heavily and looking back at the police car closing in behind them.

Cash tried to keep cool, but he was nervous. The drugs were hidden very well inside the car, but what if there was a snitch? And what if they decided to do a thorough search of the vehicle and bring in drug-sniffing dogs? Then he and Kwan would be fucked! There was a lot of weight inside the minivan to give them enough hard time until they were in their late forties, if not life.

Cash pulled to the side and stopped the vehicle on some dark, backwoods road not too far from the highway. The state trooper came to a stop directly behind them. The bright blue lights and the headlights made it difficult to see the occupant inside the cop car.

"Yo, I ain't about to get caught up wit' all this shit inside the car, Cash. How the fuck they know? We need to do somethin'. Fuck this redneck cracker muthafucka! I hate police, nigga! Yo, I'm 'bout to body this cracker-ass pig!" Kwan growled.

"Yo, just chill, Kwan," Cash said calmly.

"Nah, fuck chillin', nigga! He gotta fuckin' go! It's him or us, muthafucka!" Kwan pulled out a 9mm Beretta and cocked it back. He was itching to stir up some chaos. The look on his face was twisted and almost demonic. He rocked back and forth in the passenger seat, looking like he was losing his mind.

Both men kept their eyes fixated on the state trooper's car, looking through the rearview.

Both doors to the police car opened up, and two state troopers cautiously stepped out and approached the car.

Cash uttered to Kwan, "Yo, something ain't right."

Usually, there was one state trooper inside the car patrolling the highways alone, and most likely, they would have backup come to watch their backs, meaning two state trooper cars on the side of the road. As an expert car thief, Cash knew the routine.

When did state troopers ever pair up? And why were they stopping them in the middle of nowhere?

"Fuck this!" Kwan yelled. He leaped from the minivan and opened fire on both troopers. *Boc! Boc! Boc!* His 9mm lit up the night with a barrage of bullets.

One trooper immediately got hit in the chest and was pushed back to the ground. The second pulled out an Uzi with a silencer at the end of the barrel and returned fire.

Poot! Poot! Poot! Poot! Poot! Poot! Poot! Poot! Poot! Poot!

The hail of bullets tore into the van, shattering glass, and ripping through the seats.

When did state troopers start carrying Uzis with silencers? Cash took immediate cover, feeling the bullets whizzing by his ear.

Kwan fired back at the trooper relentlessly. "Fuck you! Fuck you!" he screamed.

"They ain't cops!" Cash yelled. He jumped up from his hiding spot and shot back in haste.

One shot from Cash's 9mm tore through the side of one cop's neck, temporary crippling him. He was shot, but he wasn't out.

His partner was picking himself up from the ground and ready to aid his injured friend. The Kevlar vest had saved his life.

"We gotta go!" Cash hollered.

Cash jumped back behind the wheel of the van and was shifting into drive. Kwan came to his senses and followed suit, dipping inside the van as his ammunition ran out. They had a small window of escape and took advantage of it. Cash drove like a bat out of hell, pushing the ride to eighty, never looking back.

Kwan's paranoia had saved their lives. If he hadn't gotten the jump on the killer troopers before they got closer to the van, then they would've opened fire on both passengers without them seeing it coming.

Cash exhaled. He was sweaty and nervous. Everywhere he looked, people were trying to kill him. The minivan was shot up to pieces, and it was hard for them to look inconspicuous with a vehicle full of bullet holes, shot out windows, and two disheveled black men in the front seat.

"We need to get off the road and get us a new ride," Cash said.

Kwan shouted, "It was Hassan and that nigga Bimmy who set up that hit on us! They're fuckin' dead! I'ma kill them niggas wit' my bare fuckin' hands if I have to! Yo, they want a war, I'ma give them niggas a fuckin' war!"

Elsewhere, Elliot and Jarrett had failed the contract. They'd missed their mark. They never missed. Their plan was to pretend to be cops, make a routine stop, and then exterminate both men, even though Cash was their intended target.

Jarrett was clutching the side of his neck, angered by being shot. He was bleeding badly, the bullet went straight through, and Elliot was still recouping from when Kwan had shot him in the chest. They both would live, but they were extremely disappointed with themselves.

THIRTY-NINE

Police sirens blared throughout the neighborhood, speeding toward the corner of Christopher and Belmont Avenues, where multiple gunshots were fired. The first cop cars arrived on the scene to find two bodies sprawled out on the concrete in front of the schoolyard.

Both victims were black and male. One was shot in the face and chest, lying face down on the ground in a pool of blood, and the second victim, with gunshots to his chest and stomach, was slumped against the chain link fence, looking contorted in pain. Both victims looked DOA. It was a gruesome scene, and only the start of a brutal drug war.

The officers called it in, and within minutes, more police were on the scene, taping off the area. The looky-loos were coming out by the dozens to view the double homicide. Death was nothing new to them. The dead men were well-known drug dealers and gangbangers in the area.

The detectives came to the crime scene to investigate, but once again, all they got from the people living in the area was silence.

The murdered victims were identified as Keeno and Jones, 6-9 Bloods connected to Hassan and Bimmy. Their deaths were retaliation from the upstate incident with Kwan and Cash. Kwan wasn't holding anything back. He wanted both Hassan's and Bimmy's heads impaled on a sharp stick.

Forty-eight hours later, there was another shooting in the lobby of the project building at Blake and Rockaway Avenues. One male was shot in the head, leaving his body twisted near the elevator. There was another body in the stairway, and then inside a fourth-floor apartment three men were sprawled out in the living room, their frames riddled with bullets. They were all 6-9 Bloods. The neighborhood was under siege with a bloody gang/drug war between two drug crews.

A NYPD helicopter hovered above the projects with a bird's-eye view of the complete area, which was shut down. The entire projects was flooded with police activity and cops going in and out of buildings, a stark reminder to the residents that in the blink of an eye, their neighborhood could be transformed.

The media was posted around the area with their cameras and reporters, each news station making it its business to report the Brownsville murders to the world.

Bimmy was observing the chaos from a block away behind the wheel of his idling Beamer. He frowned at the loss of more of their people and one of their spots hit up by a rival crew. He knew Kwan was responsible for seven men being killed in two days. He wanted to hunt him down and end the bloodshed. It was time to strike back with deadly force, with or without Hassan's consent. He felt they'd worked too hard to be attacked by a fledging drug crew. Their reputations were on the line. Hassan needed to understand how serious the situation was. He had warned his boss, "Do not underestimate these men."

Bimmy never thought he would see the day when his friend and mentor would be caught slipping because of a piece of pussy. Hassan had his head wrapped, plunged, and twisted so far up Pearla's ass, it was impossible for him to see clearly.

It was time to make his boss start seeing very clearly. It was time to make some drastic moves and remind everyone, from their rivals to their subordinates, and even the Big Apple, what he and Hassan were about.

Bimmy shifted his Beamer into drive and drove off. First thing first, put a large contract on Cash's and Kwan's heads, and then do the unthinkable, defying his boss, knowing the end will justify the means.

"Baby, are you ready?" Pearla said to Hassan. "The limo is waiting for us downstairs."

"Give me a minute, babe."

Pearla was dressed to kill in diamonds and fur. She walked out onto the soaring terrace overlooking Central Park and the city. It was a beautiful, but cold night with remnants of the previous day's snowfall covering most of the city.

Hassan stood outside smoking his cigar, dressed in a dark Armani suit.

Pearla knew he was under a lot of stress. She had heard the news about the trouble in Brooklyn. He and Bimmy were at war with a rival crew, and things were getting very tense in that part of town. She was however, unaware that he was warring with Cash, since she hadn't been keeping tabs on her ex-boyfriend's life, busy with her own.

Hassan took another pull from his cigar and continued to stare at the city and the park. "She's beautiful, isn't she?" he said.

"Who's beautiful?" Pearla asked, stepping closer and standing next to him, following his gaze.

"This city . . . what it is, and what it has to offer. Like a beautiful woman, you can easily fall in love with her, because she's full of life and glamor. This city can give you everything you dream of—finances, romance, sex, entertainment, make you feel like you belong here. But like a woman, she can break your heart and crush you."

Did I miss something? Pearla thought.

Hassan looked pensive for a moment, and then he said, "Don't mind me, baby. I'm just rambling."

"Well, we're going to be late if we don't leave soon."

Hassan nodded. "I'll get my coat."

The two gathered their belongings and exited the penthouse suite and walked arm in arm to the limousine parked outside the building. Pearla slid inside the plush back, and Hassan was right behind her. The driver proceeded to head toward the lower West Side, where the couple were to attend a high-status charity event hosted at a large art gallery.

Hassan had planned on donating a half million dollars, to impress the prominent, and political players in the city. Hassan had plans of moving forward, extending his money and power into politics maybe.

"You look so beautiful tonight."

"Thank you. And you're very handsome."

Twenty minutes later, their limousine came to a stop in front of the Visual Arts Gallery on 26th Street. In front of the building was an array of limousines and elite vehicles releasing numerous millionaires and even billionaires onto the well-lit sidewalk in front of the gallery.

The couple's door opened, and their driver helped Pearla and Hassan from the limo. The place was flooded with security and the rich, some traveling from as far as London and Africa. Pearla smiled, starry-eyed. This was living. This was who she was born to be.

She and Hassan were arm in arm walking toward the entrance, which was crowded with invited guests. As they walked, from her peripheral vision, Pearla noticed something strange, a man in black that looked like he didn't belong. He wasn't smiling, and he seemed detached from everything happening around him. It was clear that no one else saw this mysterious figure. Something about him sent a creepy chill through Pearla's body.

Meanwhile, Hassan was conversing with another man near them.

Pearla locked eyes with him as he walked toward them. Her heart started to beat faster. He was up to something devious, and she knew it.

And then it happened. He pulled out a gun that looked like a cannon from where she was standing.

Pearla's eyes grew large with panic. It looked like he was aiming for Hassan. He outstretched his arm with the gun, and Pearla quickly screamed, "He's got a gun!"

And as shots were fired, she bravely pushed Hassan away from the danger, and he fell on his side against the concrete.

She immediately felt a bullet tear into her back and then her left leg and collapsed near Hassan. She felt like she was hit by a truck. She couldn't move and was losing consciousness.

The crowd burst into an intense panic with people were screaming and running every which way.

Suddenly, more gunshots were fired from a different gun, and the attacker went down, shot three times by one of the men from the security detail.

Hassan was going berserk. He screamed, "Somebody call nine-one-one! Now!"

Pearla had been shot twice and was bleeding out.

A crowd gathered around them.

Teary-eyed, he clutched Pearla in his arms, hoping to revive her. He wouldn't let her go. "C'mon, baby, don't die on me, please! You gonna live! Don't fuckin' die!" he cried out. "I need a fuckin' doctor!"

NYPD sirens could be heard in the distance, as well as that of an ambulance.

Soon, paramedics were on the scene, and they quickly rushed toward Pearla with a gurney.

Hassan, his eyes full of tears and anger, didn't want to let her go. He felt if he did, then she would die.

FORTY

Pearla opened her eyes to find Hassan by her side. When he noticed she was finally awake, he was overjoyed.

She tried to get up, but Hassan gently grabbed her and restricted her movements. "You need to rest," he said.

"Where am I? What happened?"

"You need to chill, baby. You've been shot twice."

For a moment, Pearla was delusional, not remembering what had happened the night before.

Hassan took her hand into his and said, "You saved my life, baby. I didn't even see that nigga coming. Doctors said you're lucky; the bullet that hit you in the back went straight through and missed all of your arteries. You gonna be okay, just some stitching and rest is all you need."

Pearla couldn't believe she had been shot. It all happened so fast. It was the second attempt on her life. It didn't matter who she was with, Cash or Hassan, her life always seemed threatened.

Hassan said, "The nigga that shot you is dead, but I'm going to find out who was behind this shit and make them pay. You have my word on that, Pearla."

They continued to talk, and Hassan tried to make her feel as comfortable as possible.

There was a knock at the door. It was Bimmy and April coming by to visit Pearla. They walked into the hospital room carrying flowers, a card, and a huge teddy bear for Pearla.

"Girl, look at you. Oh we 'bout to fuck some people up. Got my bitch in the hospital lookin' all crippled and shit," April said loudly. "This ain't right." She went to hug Pearla and gave her the large teddy bear, saying, "It's a little somethin' to have your back when we ain't around."

Pearla laughed. She was delighted to see her and Bimmy. "I'll keep him close," Pearla said about the teddy bear.

"You better, but I'll be closer," April replied.

"I'm fine, April."

"I'm glad that muthafucka was a lousy shooter. If he wasn't dead, I would go and kill him myself," April said.

"You know who it was?" Bimmy asked.

"Nah, not yet, but let's you and me talk elsewhere," Hassan said to him, looking very serious.

Bimmy nodded. Before he left the room with Hassan, he went over to Pearla, kissed her on the cheek and said, "Get better, baby girl. You're in good hands now."

Pearla smiled.

Bimmy turned and followed Hassan out of the room, giving Pearla and April some time to talk.

April was ready to react, go to war and kill. "You family, girl, and whoever tried to take you away from us, believe me, Hassan and Bimmy gonna make them muthafuckas pay."

Pearla was tired of looking over her shoulders, fearing for her life. There was someone out there still trying to kill her. Though Hassan believed she'd saved his life, Pearla strongly felt that they were aiming for her.

Hassan and Bimmy climbed into the truck parked outside the hospital. It was the only place where they felt comfortable to talk.

Right away, Hassan said, "No holds barred on these muthafuckas! I want a fifty-thousand-dollar contract out on Cash and Kwan. I want them dead by week's end."

Bimmy smiled. He felt it was about time Hassan took action. "Consider it done," he replied.

"They wanna play, then I'll show these clowns how the game is played. Anyone connected to them, you take care of them too."

Bimmy nodded.

The test that Hassan wanted to put Pearla through with Cash went out the door once she was shot. He felt Cash and Kwan were gunning for him and missed, but he didn't plan on missing.

"I want their dicks and balls in a glass fuckin' jar," Hassan told him.

"I can make that happen," Bimmy replied with a twisted smile.

"We gonna end this shit."

"It's what I've been waiting for."

Cash loaded up with as many guns as possible—9mms, Glocks, .45s, and assault rifles. If anything came his way, he was ready for it. He wasn't taking any more chances. The incident upstate had him spooked. It was a professional hit. The two hitmen pretending to be cops were serious business.

Like the Mafia does, he and Kwan went to the mattresses. They didn't stay in one place for too long. And when they moved around, they were heavily armed and extra cautious. Cash left the apartment he shared with Sophie, and he and Kwan both agreed that she was safer staying with a cousin in New Jersey until things calmed down. She didn't want to go, but they weren't taking no for an answer. Bodies were dropping all over. The other day Keybo was murdered gangland style, shot to death while seated in the passenger seat of a Honda Civic.

The murders Kwan implemented himself or had someone do made the front-page news and stirred up a hornets' nest. Cash was in the middle of it all, trying to get rich while a lot of muthafuckas were trying to have him die trying.

Cash lingered inside the Bronx basement of a three-story tenement. Below, he and Kwan had a small arsenal and some soldiers. Though they were at war, they refused to stop doing business, and continued selling drugs. The shipment they'd picked up from Albany had been cut, processed, and was street-ready. He sent out his workers to hustle the corners of Brooklyn while staying low and out of sight in the Bronx.

It wasn't supposed to be like this, Cash thought to himself. He took a deep breath and stepped outside for some cold, fresh air. Being cooped up in a basement in the ghetto with a bunch of smelly men wasn't for him. But he had to comply and transform if he wanted to stay alive.

He stood outside the tenement smoking a cigarette, gun in his waist. He looked around. He kept a keen eye on every passing car and every pedestrian that came his way.

Kwan, with two Glocks on his person, stepped out of the building to join Cash in smoking a cigarette and getting some fresh air. He had just ended his cell phone call with someone. He looked at Cash and said, "I just got some crazy news."

"About what?"

"Our beef wit' Hassan almost came to an end last night," Kwan said.

"What?"

"Some muthafucka almost lit his ass up, but they missed him and caught his bitch instead."

Cash felt his heart in his mouth, it was pounding so fast. "You mean, Pearla?"

"That's the bitch he fuckin' wit', right?"

"She dead?" he asked nervously.

"I don't know. I think she's in the hospital. Fuck it! Fuck him and whoever he's associated wit'. Let them all fuckin' die and rot in hell."

Cash didn't feel the same way. Though they weren't together and he had his issues with her, he didn't want to see her harmed or, worse, killed.

"You know what hospital she's in?" he asked Kwan.

Kwan frowned. "What the fuck you care for? I know you ain't thinkin' about goin' to see that bitch. Nigga, she ya fuckin' ex, right?"

"I was just askin'."

"Don't ask, nigga. We at war wit' that nigga and his bitch. If she dies, it's no sweat off my back, and it should be the same way wit' you, muthafucka. Let that bitch be ya ex, and don't forget, you wit' my sister, nigga."

Cash didn't respond. He looked elsewhere, away from Kwan, and no matter what he was saying, he couldn't help thinking about Pearla and hoping she was okay. Shit, it almost felt like he was about to shed some tears for her.

FORTY-ONE

It was discharge day, and Pearla couldn't wait to get home and convalesce. She'd spent five days in the hospital with Hassan and April always by her side. April was helping her with her things, while Hassan and Bimmy were in Brooklyn handling some business. Hassan had called earlier and promised her that he would be there soon to take her home.

Pearla moved around the room with a cane and April's support. She hated hospitals and couldn't wait to relax inside her own place and have her man cater to her. The doctors gave her a clean bill of health, despite being shot twice.

As they were about to leave the hospital room, Hassan called and said he was ten minutes away.

"C'mon, girl," April said. "Let's get you home so we can go shopping and partying again. And I got the good shit for you to smoke."

Pearla got into the wheelchair. "I hate these things."

"It's better to be rolled out than carried out," April told her.

"You right about that."

She and April left the room smiling and joking.

Meanwhile, Chica walked into the hospital frowning and serious like cancer. She was dressed all woman, wearing a black short-sleeve minidress, a short mink coat, high heels, and a blonde wig. She had gotten Pearla's information from the front desk in the lobby and marched toward her room on a mission.

Chica had gotten the news that Pearla was in the hospital after being shot, having survived. Chica was there to finish what the other shooter had failed to do. She looked like a force to be reckoned with, tall and muscular. It was clear to everyone that she was a man. The Desert Eagle underneath her mink was a big gun, but she had big enough hands to hold it and do some serious damage.

Chica strutted toward the elevators. There wasn't a thing anybody could do to change her mind. She was there to kill Pearla.

The corridor was busy with people coming and going, and patients in and out. No one suspected that Chica was armed and dangerous, and that trouble was brewing. Chica was focused and didn't give a fuck.

As she approached the elevators, by coincidence, Pearla and April were coming off, April pushing Pearla in the wheelchair. Both ladies were still smiles and laughter. They unknowingly walked toward the face of danger.

Chica spotted them. Seeing the two of them together, laughing, it fueled such a fire inside of Chica, she pulled out the gun and screamed, "Y'all bitches thought it was over!"

Immediately, she caught Pearla's and April's attention, the large cannon aimed at them.

"Fuck you, Pearla!"

April and Pearla were like two deer caught in bright headlights.

The cannon went off, but it missed the two by mere inches. The lobby turned into chaos as people screamed and scurried away from the danger.

Chica continued firing at them, putting crater-size bullet holes in the walls. The gun sounded like a cannon. *Boom! Boom! Boom! Boom!*

Pearla hit the floor, taking immediate cover, but April had a surprise of her own, pulling out her own pistol and getting into a gunfight with Chica. Several rounds were fired each way.

April wanted to blow that bitch's head off. "I'ma kill you, bitch!" she screamed at the top of her lungs.

Click! Click! Click!

Chica's clip was empty. She took off running in the opposite direction.

April gave chase, but she lost her among the other fleeing and panicking folks. She then turned back around and went to help her friend.

Pearla was in shock, still on the floor, trying not to get trampled by everyone fleeing in different directions around her. It was still difficult for her to move fast.

"Pearla, you okay?" April fearfully asked. "You ain't shot, right?"

"I'm fine! Just get me the fuck outta here."

Pearla wasn't even out of the hospital yet, and once again, someone was shooting at her.

April helped her back into the wheelchair, and they hurried away from the lobby, moving into the cold with April on her cell phone telling Hassan to hurry the fuck there. Once Hassan heard there was another attempt on his woman's life, he went off like a rocket, doing ninety to get to his girl in a hurry.

Pearla was back home and safe. She was recuperating in the bedroom, while Hassan held an emergency meeting with Bimmy and all of his lieutenants in the living room. He stood in the middle of everyone.

One of his lieutenants said, "The hit on Pearla at the hospital, did Cash and Kwan set that up?"

"That was a personal thing between Pearla and some fag," Hassan said. "And I want that faggot dead."

Everyone nodded.

"No up-to-date locations on Kwan and Cash?" Hassan asked the group of men.

His lieutenants shook their heads.

"They haven't been seen around lately," one of his men said. "They're in hiding somewhere."

"Yet their product is still out there, and they're still

making money. I want all that shit to stop flowing. Shut it the fuck down! I want them muthafuckas to starve out there. I want the heat to be so strong they can't fuckin' breathe, and these niggas ain't gonna have a choice but to come up for some air. And when they do, y'all stagnant these niggas! Y'all fuckin' hear me?"

Everyone nodded.

Hassan turned and looked at Bimmy. "Who they gettin' their shit from?" he asked him.

"I'm not sure, but I think it's some nigga from Albany named Tank."

"Well, find out and you let me have a talk with Tank. If it's legit and he cooperates, he can continue to make his money. If he's ignorant and don't, then you already know what to do."

Bimmy nodded. "I'm on it."

"And as for the rest of y'all, y'all primary goal is to hunt these niggas down and make their lives hell, their family's lives hell, and the people they're connected to lives hell. I want it to feel like the devil is breathing fire on their fuckin' backs! Y'all understand?"

"Yes," everyone said collectively.

"Now get the fuck out my place and go do y'all jobs!"

The group scattered and exited the penthouse, apart from Bimmy, who stayed around to continue talking to Hassan.

Bimmy asked, "So how's she doing?"

"She's doing fine, sleeping in the bedroom. And April?"

"You know April—a shootout ain't gonna spook her. She's a soldier."

"I owe her, my nigga."

"We family, Hassan. April was simply lookin' out for family. We take care of each other."

"Thanks for everything, Bimmy."

"We gonna find Cash, and we gon' make him pay for what he did. Don't worry about anything. You and me, we've been doing this for so long, we know the tricks in the trade, and we know how to smoke a nigga out when needed." Bimmy removed his coat from the chair to leave.

After Bimmy left, Hassan went to the bedroom to check on Pearla, who didn't look too pleased with him. She had overheard everything he said to Bimmy and his lieutenants.

"I thought you were sleeping," he said.

"What is going on with you and Cash? He's the one you're warring with?" she asked.

"I am, and he's gonna pay for what he did to you."

"Pay?" Pearla replied, looking befuddled. "You think Cash had something to do with the attempt on my life?"

"I know he did."

"Cash wouldn't dare do such a thing. He wouldn't come after me. He used to love me."

The slap to her face happened suddenly, forcefully whirling Pearla's face around, leaving her in utter shock.

Hassan didn't want to hear it. It pained him deeply to hear Pearla speak up for Cash. He strongly felt she hadn't gotten Cash out of her system.

"You hit me!" Pearla exclaimed, frowning thickly at Hassan.

"Do you still love him?" he growled.

"I don't! But I know Cash wouldn't try to harm me. I know him." Pearla wasn't afraid of Hassan and refused to be intimidated by him. "Whatever problem you got with Cash, it isn't because of me. He's a car thief, not a drug dealer."

"You don't know shit. Your boy, he came up in the game, linked up with a fierce crew from Brooklyn, and is moving some heavy weight on the streets."

"What?"

"That's right, he's in competition with me, and as you know, that presents a problem."

It was still unbelievable news to Pearla. She had to admit, in some kind of way, she was impressed by this.

"He's a dead man!"

It bothered Pearla to hear him say that, but she remained pokerfaced. She told Hassan again that Cash had no reason to want her dead. She then explained to him that someone was out there trying to murder them both, and she believed that the same person was back and trying to finish what they had started.

After her talk with Hassan, she went back into the bedroom and took a deep breath, trying to keep herself strong. She had a few fleeting thoughts about Cash as she looked at the city through the floor-to-ceiling windows. She had no need to worry herself about that man. He'd chosen his way, and she'd chosen hers.

FORTY-TWO

I could have taken care of this on my own, Hassan. You didn't have to come and get your hands dirty," Bimmy said.

"No, I wanna be here and have this fuckin' faggot die by my hands. This is personal for me."

Bimmy shrugged. He replied, "Well, everything's set up. They're just waiting on us."

The two of them were parked outside of Chica's new residence in Queens. She was easy to track down. Hassan only wished that Cash and Kwan were as easy to locate.

Hassan glared at the private home on the suburban block and said to Bimmy, "Let's go have some fun with this Ru Paul-lookin' faggot."

Both men got out of the car and coolly walked toward the back entrance to the home. One of their men was waiting for them to show. He was guarding the back entrance with his pistol. He gave his bosses a head nod as they walked by and into the place.

They trekked down into the basement, where Hassan was greeted by several of his men standing around a naked, tightly-bound Chica. She was sprawled face down across the cold concrete floor with arms and legs stretched and restrained by chains and handcuffs, barely able to move her head left and right. She had been brutally beaten, but it was only the beginning of her suffering.

Hassan walked toward Chica and scowled like he had sucked on a rotten lemon.

Chica cursed, "Fuck you! Fuck you, muthafucka! I hate you all! Kiss my black ass!"

"You have a lot of fuckin' mouth and some big balls for a cross-dressing faggot," Hassan said.

"Fuck you!"

"You know, I'm curious." Hassan scratched his head. "You and your kind, y'all like dick, right? Or it don't matter what y'all put up your ass, as long as y'all are being fucked, right?"

Chica squirmed and wiggled in his restraints, but she was locked down tighter than a nun's vagina. She continued cursing, trying to show a brave face, but deep inside, she knew her fate. These men were serious, and she wasn't going to leave the basement alive.

"You stupid muthafucka!" Hassan shouted. "You tried to take something away from me that was very important."

"Fuck that bitch! She lucky I missed," Chica retorted.

That statement angered Hassan even more. "Fuck my bitch, huh? You said fuck my bitch? The woman I love?"

Hassan motioned toward Bimmy and stuck out his hand. Bimmy smirked and handed Hassan an electric cattle prod. It was long, thick, and black, carrying relatively high-voltage. Hassan gripped the prod in his hand, and it came to life with electricity.

"I heard these things can do a lot of damage if used correctly. If applied to the skin repeatedly, it can cause searing and scarring of the skin at the contact point. You wanna guess which contact point I'm aiming for?"

Hassan crouched near Chica's buttocks and made one of his men spread them wider. Chica couldn't fight or resist; every part of her was vulnerable.

Hassan said, "Let's have some fun." He motioned as if he was about to thrust the prod into Chica's rectum with no mercy but instead he hit up her upper thighs.

Chica's piercing scream was so loud, more from fear than anything else, which ultimately turned into relief that the prod didn't enter her rectum.

Hassan continued to mentally fuck with Chica by toying with the prod near her most vulnerable orifice.

Bimmy looked content, but he was turned off. The last thing he wanted to spend a lot of time on was murdering faggots; he felt that was a job their soldiers could have handled. The main course was Kwan and Cash.

A half-hour later, Chica was dead. Hassan snapped a picture of her broken, tortured body and planned on showing it to Pearla.

FORTY-THREE

Perez sat sulking at the end of his prison cot in disbelief. How the fuck did they fail killing Cash again? It was impossible. He felt like he was in a cartoon, like Wile E. Coyote trying to kill the Road Runner—none of the traps he implemented seemed to work out. Cash was a slick nigga with nine fuckin' lives.

And he'd heard about Pearla's incident.

He stood up and walked toward the end of his cell. He felt like banging his head against the bars. It was making him sick to his stomach that Cash and Pearla were still living their comfortable lives after they'd destroyed his.

The next day, Perez jumped on the jail phone and dialed Spike collect. He wanted to know what had happened. The people Spike hired to do jobs never missed. So what had gone wrong?

"What the fuck happened? I thought you hired fuckin' professionals to do the job, Spike. How the fuck did they miss?" Perez shouted.

"Perez, you forgot where you at? This isn't a matter for you to discuss over the phone," Spike replied coolly.

"Fuck that! Tell me something!"

"I'll see you in a few days, and we'll talk then."

"I don't have a few fuckin' days. I paid these niggas for a job, and I expect results."

"You'll get your money's worth, but until then, goodbye." Spike hung up.

Perez was left on the other end cursing up a storm and banging the phone receiver against the base, wanting to smash it to pieces.

A correction officer told him he needed to calm down.

Perez replied, "Go fuck yourself!"

The officer grimaced and quickly implemented disciplinary action against Perez, who seemed not to care anymore.

Perez fought with the guards, punching, and kicking.

He was quickly subdued and restrained and then carried toward solitary confinement, screaming, "I will have my fuckin' justice!"

FORTY-FOUR

Pearla sat at the foot of the king-size bed watching the evening news, and it was the same shit like always—people dying violently in the raging drug war from Brooklyn and extending to the city and New Jersey.

Tonight's headline was disturbing. A ten-year-old boy had been killed by a stray bullet from two gangs shooting at each other in Brownsville. The media continually showed the distraught family on television. The mother, overcome with grief, passed out in front of the news cameras.

Pearla turned off the TV. She too was disgusted by the story, but she couldn't help but to wonder if it was Hassan's peoples or Cash's goons had something to do with that ten-year-old boy being killed. Her heart went out to the boy's family.

She had come up in the streets and was no stranger to violence herself, but things were out of control in that part of town. Pearla had always considered herself a businesswoman. She'd had her fair share of incidents over the years, but at the end of the day, she had one motive—get money and keep it moving.

She stood up and walked to the window. She was in the twilight zone—her current boyfriend was fighting with her ex-boyfriend, and though the bloodshed between them wasn't because of her, it was still awkward. She lit a cigarette and took in the needed nicotine.

It was another late night, and she was sleeping in a cold bed. She was alone in the penthouse. Lately, most of Hassan's time and attention had been focused on the streets and the war with his rivals. He was gone all day, almost every day. Pearla was living in the lap of luxury, but she didn't have her man to share it with.

Pearla wanted to get into real estate. The economy was rising again, and people were buying homes all over the map. This time, it would be a legit business that she planned on starting from scratch. All she needed was some seed money from Hassan and her own house.

She had been looking in areas like Williamsburg, now heavily populated with whites, and she wanted in. Her last place of residence, Jamaica Estates, was a good area, but not great. There were too many black people, and it was easy for the goons to blend in. Pearla wanted Williamsburg, and she wanted something large—like over a million dollars large.

Her only hobby besides researching real estate was spying on Roark and collecting her taxes. It wasn't much—a thousand dollars here, five hundred there, maybe three or five grand from a good score. Pearla definitely didn't need the money; it was just fun making Roark sweat.

Quite by chance, Pearla had discovered a little secret

about Roark. She had seen Roark and a young girl at a local Starbucks in the city, and they were grinning from ear to ear. Pearla had no idea who Roark's friend was, until she hired a private investigator and learned that Sophie was Cash's new girlfriend. What were the odds? Pearla felt fate was telling her something. She had pictures of Sophie and Roark meeting together, and wondered where they knew each other from, and what they were talking about. Were they talking about her? Was Roark once again stabbing her in the back?

Pearla had hired one of the best private investigators in town, and he found out Roark and Sophie used to be secret lovers. Pearla had no idea that Roark was bisexual. And what were the chances that one of Roark's ex-lovers would be seeing Cash? What was Roark telling Sophie about her? Something was going on, and Pearla was determined to find out what it was.

The following evening, Hassan came in from a busy day. Pearla had a candlelight dinner waiting for him. Her man seemed stressed, and lately, they hadn't been seeing eye to eye. She and Hassan spoke, and she told him about her dream to live in a Brooklyn brownstone, and invest in a few of her own. She was trying to convince Hassan that there was great money in real estate. The market was up. Pearla had learned from her mistake with her last house, a con she would never fall for again.

At first, Hassan seemed skeptical of the idea. Things were hot everywhere, and he didn't want to risk his woman traveling into Brooklyn to fulfill some dream. He had enemies out to get him who would probably use her to get to him.

But Pearla could be very persuasive when she really wanted something. It took some time, heavy talking, and a massage at the end.

Hassan looked at her and said, "Yes, I'll support you in this if you give me something in return."

"And what is that?" she asked.

"I want a baby. I want a family," he said seriously.

Hassan wanted something from her that Cash didn't give her yet—kids. He wanted a son. Pearla thought it over for a minute, and then she looked at Hassan and said, "Okay."

Hassan smiled.

The two kissed passionately, and that same night, they made strong, heated love. Hassan was determined to get his woman pregnant.

The next day, Pearla didn't waste any time. She found a legit realtor and started the process of purchasing a Brooklyn brownstone. The top five neighborhoods attracting buyers were Park Slope, Williamsburg, Brooklyn Heights, Cobble Hill, and Fort Greene. And the average price for a single-family Brooklyn townhouse ranged from 2.2-4 million.

The following week when Roark came around to drop off Pearla's cut, they met in a brownstone in Bushwick that Pearla had been looking at. Roark put $800 in Pearla's hand and then asked, "Why meet here?"

Pearla looked at Roark, knowing the bitch's dirty little secret and said, "I'm thinking about buying it."

Roark looked around the pretty decent-size brownstone, which was under renovation. "So you're moving to Bushwick?" she asked.

"I'm thinking about it."

As Roark was about to leave, Pearla suddenly stopped her and asked, "Roark, do you have anything else that you need to tell me?"

Roark looked Pearla straight in the face and replied, "I don't."

"You sure?"

"I have nothing to hide from you, Pearla. I heard about Chica, and I know you're not the bitch to fuck with."

Pearla didn't respond to the Chica remark. No telling if the bitch was wearing a wire or not. She locked eyes with Roark, who quickly averted her eyes from her. It was obvious she was nervous and had something to hide.

Roark took the subway to the Path train in Lower Manhattan and the Path train took her into Jersey City, New Jersey. From the station she took a cab to the west side of town to a five-story tenement on Bentley Avenue. She paid the fare and climbed out of the cab and went into the building. On the third floor, she met with Sophie.

The two greeted each other with hugs and kisses and then went into the bedroom to talk in private from her cousin.

Roark couldn't wait to tell Sophie the news about Pearla.

While Cash and Kwan were busy with Hassan, Sophie had her own mission, which was with Pearla, whom she was envious of. Roark told her everything, leaving nothing out, from how much percentage she paid her, to Pearla trying to buy a brownstone in Bushwick.

"So that bitch wanna buy a fuckin' house now," Sophie uttered with contempt.

"She was always a businesswoman," Roark said, sounding like she was impressed by Pearla.

"I'm a fuckin' businesswoman, bitch!"

Sophie felt the need to outdo Pearla. Whatever Pearla was interested in, she wanted to do it better. Roark had been her little spy over that way, and she had been very useful. Sophie figured Pearla wouldn't suspect a thing.

"I think she suspects something," Roark said.

"Suspects what?"

"She was asking me some questions. I didn't know where they were leading to."

"That bitch don't suspect shit; she don't even know that we know each other."

Roark was still nervous. She was already on Pearla's bad side, and she didn't want things to become any worse between them.

The starting price for the three-story, single-family brownstone in Bushwick was 1.5 million. Pearla stood among a few other interested buyers wearing a pantsuit and heels. She hadn't come alone, since Hassan had her shadowed by one of his men.

Pearla walked through the home, inspecting it, taking in every little detail. The open house brought in many people: married couples; single men and women; and even a brother and sister. It was one of the properties on her list that she wanted to have. She stood in the living room and was ready to make an offer, when she caught the surprise of her life.

Sophie walked into the house with another woman by her side and locked eyes with Pearla.

Pearla figured Roark had been feeding the bitch some information about her. Pearla wasn't completely taken aback by her being there, but it was awkward, knowing she was fucking Cash, and that Hassan was at their throats.

Sophie looked like a hoochie in her short skirt, stilettos, colorful mink coat, and diamond earrings. It looked like she was trying to outdress Pearla. She had money, and so did Pearla. Both ladies were beautiful, but Pearla was a lot classier.

Pearla knew who Sophie was, but Sophie continued to play this foolish game, like they were strangers at the same open house in Bushwick.

Pearla looked at her sideways. She thought Cash had better taste than that.

Sophie was completely eyeballing Pearla with an attitude. All she could think about was Cash being with her, and how he still had her picture in his phone. She wasn't Gloria, a cougar that Cash was taking advantage of. She was someone Cash loved and held dear to his heart. She had style and was a very beautiful woman, and she was a hustler who made things happen on her own.

The two of them at the same open house, in the same room was like a lion and tiger together in a cage—in a standoff, who would win?

The next open house in Bushwick that Pearla attended, Sophie showed up and was trying to outbid her on the revamped brownstone. Pearla smirked and went on with her business. She knew what Sophie was up to. It didn't matter because she was smarter and more business-minded. In Pearla's eyes, Sophie was nothing but a hood-rat bitch entertaining her leftovers.

The bidding started, and Sophie feverishly kept going higher, like money wasn't an issue and she had it like that.

The price of the brownstone started off at 1.6 million, and it went up to two. When it got to 2.2 million, Pearla smiled Sophie's way, stopped bidding, and walked away, but she had to say something to Sophie before her exit.

In passing, she said, "Slugs that come out at night end up getting salt on them sooner or later." With that, Pearla made her exit.

Sophie stood there looking dumbfounded. *What the fuck did she mean by that?* She frowned. *Did the bitch call me a slug?* She watched Pearla climb into the backseat of a Rolls-Royce and drive away. She had to admit, the bitch was living in style.

Pearla was playing Sophie for a fool, because the real house that she was interested in was located in Williamsburg, a much better neighborhood, and the asking price for it was a lot lower than the price in Bushwick. Sophie could have Bushwick. She belonged in lower class anyway.

Meanwhile, Hassan was able to meet with the owner of the Williamsburg house and pay him all in cash, 1.7 million dollars. He was willing to do anything for Pearla. They were about to start a family. He gave Pearla a half million dollars to decorate and planned on keeping her busy in homes and real estate, while he dealt with the streets.

When Sophie got the news from Roark that Pearla wasn't really interested in Bushwick, after she thought she'd outbid and outsmarted Pearla, she was furious. She felt played. That comment from Pearla had stuck with her, and she knew the bitch was mocking her, and nobody mocks Sophie.

With Cash's ex-girlfriend still around, Sophie would always feel threatened. And with her brother and Cash warring with Hassan, she wanted in on the fun too. She felt she could help her brother out if she had Pearla killed.

The following day, she called up Kwan and told him the news. "I want that bitch dead."

"Who?" Kwan asked.

"Pearla."

Kwan smiled. "I got you, sis, but one problem, how we gonna find her?"

"I already got that taken care of. I have a bitch that knows her moves."

"Who this bitch?"

"You remember Roark, right?"

"That simple bitch you used to fuck wit' back in the days?" he asked.

"She's the one. Pearla got that bitch on a string, making her pay a percentage of everything she makes on the streets. We can use her."

"A'ight, let's do this shit. And your boy, he down, right?" Kwan asked.

"He's my man now. Of course, he's gonna be down."

"I hope so, because the other day when he found out that bitch was shot and in the hospital, he seemed kind of sympathetic to the bitch, like he was ready to rush out there and go see her."

Sophie frowned. "He don't love her anymore. He loves me," she said, trying to reassure herself.

"A'ight, I'll make it happen. Call Roark and let me have a talk wit' her."

"I will."

FORTY-FIVE

Kwan and Sophie had their talk with Roark together, putting much pressure on her to give up Pearla's home location. Roark admitted she didn't know much about Pearla's whereabouts, and that when they met, it was either in public or at a club. Kwan refused to believe that Roark didn't know a damn thing about Pearla. He thought she either was hiding something or protecting her. Kwan was crazy enough to torture Roark if she didn't start becoming useful to him in some kind of way.

Roark finally gave them some useful information. Pearla would be at a certain location the following day in Williamsburg. When Roark had dropped the cash off owed to Pearla, she had overheard Pearla give an address to someone over the phone and then heard her say, "Don't keep me waiting."

The next day, Kwan and one of his goons staked out the Williamsburg location, an area where white folks enjoyed the benefits of gentrification. They didn't have to wait long before spotting Pearla, who arrived in a silver Rolls-Royce. She went into the house with one of Hassan's henchmen.

Kwan waited a half hour and then followed the Rolls-Royce after it left. They made sure to be subtle, not wanting to fuck anything up. They followed the vehicle around the city closely all day, finding out about Hassan's penthouse in the city and their place in Chelsea, which was still under renovation. The final destination was back to the swanky two-bedroom condo on Metropolitan Avenue in Williamsburg.

Pearla didn't stick to the routine Hassan had taught her, knowing how to sniff out if you were being followed or not. She was conducting business in all locations, forgetting her man had enemies everywhere.

From a short distance, Kwan and his man observed Pearla climb out of the Rolls-Royce and walk into the newly renovated building on the street. She was escorted inside by an armed thug.

Kwan nodded, satisfied he had the advantage.

Cash gave the code knock on Kwan's door, and Kwan answered shirtless with a gun tucked into his waistband and a blunt between his lips. Kwan had called him over to talk.

Cash walked inside. The room was filled with guns and soldiers, all smoking weed, preparing for something serious. Every man in the room looked devious and ready for battle.

Cash felt out of the loop. Since that ten-year-old boy was killed by a stray bullet, the streets had been quiet. Cops had inserted themselves on every Brooklyn street corner, making the neighborhoods hot with law enforcement. The carnage between Hassan and Kwan had raged so out of control that the mayor was on TV talking about gun control, curfews in crime-ridden areas, and even bringing in the National Guard to cool things down. The last thing both sides wanted was the feds sniffing around the area and investigating them. So Kwan was ready to take the initiative and turn the tides on their war with Hassan and Bimmy.

Tank from Albany had been murdered. They'd found his body rotting in the trunk of his car, shot twice in the head, his wrists and legs bound. Now Kwan and Cash were desperate to find a new connect.

"What's goin' on?" Cash asked.

"We got some new information," Kwan said.

"On who?"

Kwan didn't answer him right away. Cash's past with Pearla bothered Kwan. "C'mon, nigga, let's talk in the other room," he said.

Cash followed Kwan inside the second room.

Kwan closed the door. He got straight to the point. "We about to run up on Hassan's bitch and do some damage."

"You mean Pearla?"

"Yeah, nigga. What you think? We finally got that bitch. Tomorrow night, we gon' run up in the crib, tie that bitch up, and if Hassan is there too—bingo, muthafucka! Knock two birds out wit' one fuckin' stone, you feel me? We gon' make it look like a home invasion, take cash and jewelry, fuck their shit up, and body these niggas. I ain't fuckin' playin' wit' these niggas. They killed my connect, I kill them."

Cash stood there, looking blank. "Where she at?" he asked very coolly.

Kwan told him about all three locations he had followed her to. "Stupid bitch didn't even know she was being followed."

"That's crazy," Cash replied nonchalantly.

"We need you on this, my nigga. You down, right?" Kwan asked brusquely, staring at Cash like he was trying to peek into his soul.

Cash's heart was racing. Kwan was telling him everything, but why? Kwan could have done the hit without him knowing. Cash could tell Kwan was testing him, trying to see where his heart was truly at. If he showed any resistance and tried to defend his ex-girlfriend, he was sure Kwan wasn't going to allow him to leave the apartment alive.

Cash returned the same hard gaze Kwan was giving him. "Yo, fuck that bitch! I'm definitely down, my nigga! I'm about my damn money, nothing else. But I don't like the way you lookin' at me, like you tryin' to question my loyalty."

"I'm just lookin' at you, my nigga. Sometimes you never know."

"Well, I'm here, nigga, wit' you and Sophie. I've been riding wit' you this far, what the fuck I'm gonna go back to? You ain't gotta fuckin' question or doubt me, a'ight?" Cash stepped closer to Kwan, not breaking eye contact with the man.

"A'ight, my nigga," Kwan replied dryly.

Cash then left the apartment. He climbed into his BMW and drove away, feeling certain ambiguity with Kwan's response and feeling ambivalent toward the following day's event Kwan had planned. He lit a cigarette and glanced through the rearview mirror. He was almost certain Kwan was following him.

He continued to drive, heading toward the Holland Tunnel and then New Jersey. Kwan was still behind him. They were now in Jersey City.

Cash drove to Sophie, where she was still staying with her cousin temporarily, despite buying a house in Bushwick. When he parked on the block and went into the building, that's when Kwan finally got off his tail and turned back around.

Cash exhaled. He went to the third floor and met with his woman. As he and Sophie talked in the bedroom, Kwan called. She answered.

He heard Sophie say, "Nah, he right here."

Cash shook his head, knowing Kwan didn't trust him. It was obvious Kwan had asked about him, to confirm his whereabouts. But Sophie was his alibi. After she hung up, he and Sophie made passionate love, and after some good dick and smoking a phat blunt, she was fast asleep.

In the wee hours of the morning, Cash slipped away from her side and left the apartment. He got into his ride and sped toward one of the three locations Kwan had told him about. His gut feeling told him to try Williamsburg first, and he did. He couldn't let Pearla be slaughtered because of the man she was dating. The war was with Hassan and Bimmy, not her.

It was cold and still dark when Cash parked on the block and stared at the building Pearla was supposedly residing in. He was nervous. He wasn't stupid. If Hassan or Bimmy saw him creeping around, he was a dead man. He was willing to risk his life to warn Pearla. He owed her that. She needed to know they were coming for her the following day.

Cash took a deep breath and got out of his car, armed with a 9mm and a backup .380 holstered to his ankle. It was quiet and still, and the cold weather was nipping at his skin. He crossed the street and approached the building with stealth. It was simple to enter. The hard part was wondering if she was alone or not. If he knocked, and Hassan or one of his henchmen answered, then it would be World War III right there and then.

An armed thug was posted right outside Pearla's door. He was in enemy territory, and there was no telling how

Pearla felt about him. He'd left her high and dry, so he knew she had to be really upset with him. Who's to say she wouldn't kill him herself?

Cash made a slight noise and the thug perked up. He was on alert as he cautiously approached the exit. Cash jumped out at him from the dark and knocked him upside the head with the butt of his gun. The man winced and stumbled from the blow, but he wasn't knocked out.

Cash didn't want to knock him out. He just needed to disarm him, which he did, and then he said to him with his gun to the back of his head, "You move, nigga, and I'll blow your fuckin' brains out!"

The man frowned.

"You gonna help me. Two questions—is she home, and is she alone?"

The man refused to answer.

Cash cocked back the pistol placed to the side of his head as he gripped the man in a fierce chokehold. "I'm not gonna ask you twice."

"She's alone."

"Okay, come wit' me." Cash forced the guard toward the apartment door and made him knock. Cash stood out of view, his 9mm aimed closely at the thug's head, just in case. One wrong move, and Cash wasn't going to hesitate to kill him.

The man knocked a few times to awaken Pearla from her sleep.

Moments later, Cash heard her voice.

"What is it, Reno?"

"It's an emergency. We need to get you out of here," Reno said.

"I haven't heard anything from Hassan," Pearla said through the door.

"He called, told me he was trying to reach you. This location has been tainted. We need to get you packed and ready to go," Reno said convincingly.

"Okay."

Cash could hear her turning the locks to allow the guard inside. He was ready to react. The moment her door opened wide enough and he saw an opportunity, he forced the thug into the apartment with brute force, pushing Pearla back and off her feet.

Pearla fell to the floor, and Cash struck the thug with the butt of his gun repeatedly until he was unconscious.

Pearla was wide-eyed and in shock, as she gazed at Cash. She didn't know what to think. It'd been a long time since they last seen each other. It wasn't a comfortable feeling for her.

Pearla jumped up from the floor and tried to flee from Cash. She ran toward the bedroom, where she kept her pistol. Cash chased behind her, caught up with her, and tossed her on the bed roughly.

He pointed his gun at her and shouted, "Chill! I'm not here to hurt you, Pearla!"

"Then why are you here?" she shouted back.

"He was right. You're not safe here. They're coming for you."

"What are you talking about? Who's coming for me?"

"Kwan and his men."

"How the fuck do they know where I'm at? How did they find me? How did you find me?"

"Because you were sloppy. Most likely, they followed you from somewhere. But they know about all three locations, this one, the penthouse in the city, and your Chelsea address."

Pearla was dumbfounded. "What!"

"Where's lover boy?" Cash asked.

"He won't be back for a while. He and Bimmy left to take care of something in New Jersey."

"Well, we need to get you out of here."

"And go where, Cash? And how I'm supposed to tell Hassan? What am I supposed to say to him?"

"Fuck him! I'm only worried about you."

"Well, my life has changed, Cash, and I'm with him now. And you think I'm supposed to believe you, after what you did to me, leaving me when I needed you the most? You abandoned me, Cash. What kind of man are you?"

He responded quickly, "The one that's trying to save your life and make it up to you."

Seeing Cash again was heartrending for Pearla. She couldn't help but shed a few tears.

"Look, we don't have much time. Kwan and his goons plan to come here or the penthouse tomorrow night. They want to hurt you to get to Hassan. I'm not gonna allow that to happen," Cash said.

"Oh, now you care about me."

"Look, I'm sorry, okay? I'm sorry that I abandoned you. I got lost and scared, and I just didn't know how to handle it. I fucked up. But you definitely came out okay."

"And you're a drug dealer now."

"I had to step my game up."

Pearla had to admit to herself, she still found Cash attractive. She caught herself looking at him from head to toe as he stood in her bedroom. But she couldn't make that mistake again. She had to fight her feelings.

Snapping back to reality, Pearla said to Cash, "Leave here and go where, Cash?"

"Go stay at a hotel."

"You think it's that easy? What about Hassan, and my life with him?"

Cash didn't want to hear about Hassan. "He's gonna get you killed!"

"And leaving with you tonight, that's gonna make things better for me? It's not happening." Pearla sat on her bed and folded her arms across her chest.

"So what am I supposed to do, Pearla? Your life is in danger. Kwan's a fuckin' sadistic killer, and he won't stop hunting down you and your man until y'all are dead or he is. I know him."

"Let him come then."

"Baby, you can't be that stupid."

"Maybe I am. I've changed, Cash, and unlike you, I don't run away from my problems."

Cash sighed. Exhausted from her stubbornness, he said, "Okay, then we need to come up wit' a plan."

"Like what?"

"I don't know yet."

Pearla came up with a suggestion. "Why don't you duck Kwan and let him still come as planned, and I'll have Hassan and Bimmy waiting on them? Kwan won't even know it's coming."

"It won't work. He's not stupid. If I come up wit' an excuse and try to back out of it, he'll know he's being set up."

"Then why don't you kill him yourself?"

"What?" Cash was taken aback. "I can't."

"Why not? You've killed before."

"This is different, Pearla."

"What's so fuckin' different about it?"

Cash had his reasons, but he couldn't explain it to her. He needed Kwan right now for business and muscle. He wasn't ready to take things that far.

"You always been so fuckin' stubborn, Pearla!"

"And you always been an asshole," she countered.

They locked eyes, and then their aggression toward each other rapidly turned into passion. They collapsed into each other's arms in a strong, passionate kiss.

"Fuck! I missed you," Cash said.

"I missed you too."

She tore his clothes off, he peeled away her robe, and their mouths hungrily devoured each other's lips.

As they fell against the bed, Cash quickly positioned himself between her inviting thighs. His lips latched onto her breast as he penetrated her slowly.

Pearla closed her eyes, knowing she was doing the unthinkable as Cash fondled her body and was about to insert himself into her. She gripped him tight, feeling his huge erection open her up like a good book.

Cash groaned with the sudden jolt of pleasure, feeling like he was inside of Pearla for the very first time. With every deep thrust, he felt her tremble around his dick. Pearla's arms gently wrapped softly around his shoulders as their faces neared each other, and they kissed passionately again, her legs sliding up and over the back of his own.

Pearla cooed underneath him, her pussy pulsing nonstop around him. "You gonna make come!" she announced.

Cash continued thrusting and grinding, until she cried out loudly, pulling him tightly against her naked frame. Her moans echoed off the bedroom walls, hopefully not leaving a trace of her infidelity.

Cash continued to fuck her, pushing her to another orgasm.

After their post-coital moment, they looked at each other and, with their eyes speaking, said, *What now?*

FORTY-SIX

Cash hurriedly got dressed and realized that Reno wasn't unconscious. He was dead. Shit was getting too complicated.

"How this nigga gonna die?" Cash asked, as if it was the dead man's fault.

"Well he didn't kill himself," Pearla replied, sarcastically.

These two couldn't stop themselves from bickering.

"Not now, Pearla. Cure ya slick mouth for a moment. Any minute now niggas could be at your front door. We gotta get his nigga into my trunk or else you gonna have problems."

Pearla had to bite her tongue from lashing out. Instead, she jumped into action and grabbed her shopping cart. It took every ounce of their strength to load the dead body into the cart and get him into Cash's trunk, but they did. Both were winded and sweaty.

Cash finally left Pearla's place. He had been gone for too long, and it was about to be dawn soon. He hurried back to New Jersey to be with Sophie but not before dumping the body, quickly, and haphazardly on a random residential block not too far from Pearla.

Luckily, when Cash arrived, Sophie and her cousin were still sleeping. He had snuck the key and placed it back where he found it. He climbed back into bed with her and pretended like he'd never left.

A few hours later, Kwan showed up. He walked into the living room, where Cash was nestling with Sophie. Kwan looked at Cash and said, "Yo, let's go for a ride. I need to head to the Bronx, and we need to talk."

Cash had no idea what they needed to talk about. "Nah. Now is not a good time."

"Why not?"

"I got some shit to do."

"Like what, nigga? What the fuck you gotta do today?"

Cash looked at Sophie, looking for her to back him up, but it appeared she was siding with her brother.

Cash went reluctantly, and Sophie didn't say a word.

Outside, Cash got into Kwan's Audi, and they drove off to the Bronx. For what, Cash had no idea.

For a few minutes, they rode in silence. Cash was staring out the window, wondering what was going on. He thought he'd made a mistake leaving his pistol at the apartment.

They drove around Jersey City, going toward the GW Bridge. It was early afternoon, and a nice warm day, though it was still the heart of winter.

Finally, Kwan turned to Cash and asked, "Yo, what's good wit' you, my nigga?"

"What you talkin' about, Kwan?" Cash replied civilly.

"I mean, you've been moving kinda shady lately."

"I've been moving like the same ol' me. You just paranoid and shit. Yo, you need help, nigga. This war wit' Hassan got you trippin'."

"It got me trippin', huh?"

"Yeah, it got you buggin'."

"So let me ask you a question then."

"What?"

"You still down wit' tonight?" Kwan asked.

"Of course, I'm still down. Why wouldn't I be?"

"Yeah, I've been asking myself that too."

Kwan steered his Audi toward the New Jersey Turnpike. He removed a half-smoked blunt from the cup holder and lit it. He took a strong pull and looked as cool as a cucumber. He took another hit and then passed it Cash's way, asking, "You smokin', nigga?"

"Nah, I'm good right now."

"You sure, nigga?"

"Yeah, I'm sure, nigga," Cash replied dryly.

"A'ight, my nigga. So we talkin', right, and we real wit' each other. Right, my nigga?"

"Yeah, we real, nigga."

"So let me ask you another question."

"What?"

"Yo, where the fuck were you last night?"

"What? What you mean, where was I? I was wit' ya sister, went there right after I left you, and we fucked our brains out, nigga."

"Nah, nigga, you fuckin' lyin'!"

"What the fuck you talkin' about, Kwan? You know I was at your sister's, because you followed me there, nigga. You think I didn't know?"

"Yeah, and you left in the middle of the night too, nigga," Kwan countered. "Where the fuck did you go?"

Cash knew he was busted. It was obvious Sophie had told her brother that he'd left while she was still asleep. Cash had noticed that Kwan had driven them to a secluded area in New Jersey, where there was a row of dilapidated, abandoned buildings.

Kwan stopped driving and pulled to the side. He glared at Cash and said, "Talk, nigga. Explain yourself, muthafucka!"

Cash had no reasonable explanation. The way Kwan looked at him, it was clear he had already made up his mind. Cash knew the deal. It got very tense inside the car.

Cash matched Kwan's hard stare, and before Kwan could react, Cash quickly elbowed him in the face, pushed open the door, and took off running. He wasn't going out like this.

Momentarily dazed, Kwan jumped out his car and gave chase. He pulled out his gun and fired multiple shots. *Bam! Bam! Bam! Bam! Bam!*

Cash ducked and zigzagged away from bullets flying his way as he ran for his life.

Kwan continued to chase him down several city blocks, where there were people everywhere, even children. He continued shooting at Cash, as Cash did the flash from block to block, ducking between cars, bullets whizzing by.

Cash made a hard right at the next corner, while shots rang out.

Kwan stopped the chase for a moment and daringly aimed at him a half block away and fired. *Bam! Bam! Bam!*

Three shots tore into Cash: one in his right leg; the second shot in his right arm; and the third in his side, causing him to tumble to the concrete.

He screamed out in pain. *Not like this*, he thought. *Please, not like this.*

Kwan reached Cash, who was sprawled out on the sidewalk. He scowled down at him. He aimed at Cash's head and fired.

Click! Click! Click! Kwan's gun was empty.

"You lucky muthafucka!" Kwan yelled. "Yo, this shit ain't over, nigga!" He turned and fled, leaving Cash in bad shape on the sidewalk.

FORTY-SEVEN

A puzzled Hassan looked at Pearla and asked, "What the fuck you mean, we're in danger here? How? And what happened to Reno? He was supposed to be guarding the door. Where the fuck did he go?"

Hassan was losing his cool. There were too many questions, and he wasn't getting any reasonable answers. It was hard for Pearla to explain to him how she came to know about the threat on their lives. She couldn't tell him that her ex, the nigga he was at war with, came to save her life, that she refused to leave, and that they had sex on their bed.

"Tell me something, Pearla. What happened here while I was gone? Who warned you that we need to leave here and the penthouse in the city? I need to know."

Pearla could see the anger in his eyes. She had to be smart. She couldn't afford to piss him off and let him know the truth. "I fucked up."

"How?"

"While I was out doing business, Kwan's men had been following me. They came here. I noticed some strange men lurking outside last night. I got scared and told Reno about it. He went to go check it out, and he never came back," Pearla lied. "I think they kidnapped him, probably took him to torture him for more information. That's why I kept calling your cell phone. I'm scared, Hassan."

Hassan stood silent, putting it all together. He then screamed out, "Fuck!"

One thing bothered Hassan.

"Why take Reno and leave you behind, alone and vulnerable?"

"I called nine-one-one and locked the door then took out my pistol. It's not safe here for us, Hassan, or the penthouse, or Chelsea. We need to leave."

Hassan agreed. He made Pearla pack up everything. He was moving her to a secure location in Long Island. He then got on the phone and called Bimmy and a few other men to come by. Enough games. He was going to murder Kwan once and for all. Cash too.

Cash had little to no visitors while being treated for his gunshot wounds in Jersey City Medical Center—except for Jersey City PD. They came to question him about his wounds. Every day was a nervous day for him, not knowing whether Kwan would come visit him while he was incapacitated in the hospital and finish the job. He knew he was lucky to be alive.

He cut off Sophie completely. He didn't trust her. She, without a doubt, had told her brother that he had left out that night.

Cash felt like he had no one. What he'd worked so hard to build with Kwan and Sophie was gone overnight. Their drug connect was dead, Pearla was with Hassan, and the two people who'd had his back wanted him dead.

After his release from the hospital, Cash was convalescing at a hotel in Queens. He wasn't fully healed and walked with a minor limp. He had a lot to worry about.

While he was resting, his cell phone rang. He answered cautiously, not recognizing the number, and was shocked to hear Pearla's voice on the other end.

"Hey," Pearla said softly.

"Hey." Cash was damn near speechless. Hearing her voice again created some vigor and faith inside of him. It was the most comforting thing he'd heard in weeks. He perked up in the bed and took a deep breath. He didn't want her to hang up.

"I heard what happened to you. I'm so sorry, Cash."

"You don't need to be sorry. Shit happens, right?"

"You could've died."

"But I'm still here, tough as nails, baby. I'm not going anywhere. I'm around another day to get on your nerves."

Pearla chuckled. Through a grim time, he still had a sense of humor. It's what she missed most about him, his affable personality and his charm. She and Hassan didn't joke around like she and Cash did.

For a moment, they shared small talk, and then she asked, "What happened?"

"Kwan shot me."

"No, I mean, what happened between us, Cash? Why did you leave me? Why did it go the way it went? I needed you, and you just left. I loved you so much, and you dissed me," she said sadly.

Cash sighed heavily into the phone. "I was still immature and stupid. I blamed you for everything that was happening, and then the thing wit' the house kinda pushed me over the edge. I just needed to escape. I thought there was a better life out there for me. But I shoulda stepped up to the plate and handled it wit' you. I'm so sorry, Pearla," he said sincerely.

"Well, you were right about the house. We shouldn't have dumped all of our money into it, and it turned out that the realtor was running a scam. She was a straight bitch; you read her correctly."

"It was crazy, right? We've been through so much—both been shot and in the hospital, and we're still here."

She laughed. "Yes, we are. We definitely now how to survive and handle ourselves."

They continued to laugh and talk nostalgically.

Cash regretted everything he did to her. Pearla always had his back, through the good times and bad.

While they talked, a beep came through Pearla's phone. "Cash, I'm gonna have to call you back. Someone's trying to get through on the other line."

"Okay, I love—"

Pearla immediately clicked over to the other line. Bimmy was calling her. The first thing he said to her was, "Hassan got locked up."

Pearla was in shock. "What?"

"I'm on my way to you now. Don't worry. Everything's okay." Bimmy hung up, leaving Pearla stunned by the news.

And how is everything okay with him locked up? she thought.

Pearla sat in her living room in tears. Things were quiet and still. She ignored phone calls and wanted to be by herself. It had been a long day for her. She had been in court at Hassan's arraignment and felt completely lost and angry.

Hassan had gotten knocked in the truck with two of his soldiers. He was looking for Kwan personally. He had gotten legit information on his whereabouts and wanted to kill the man himself. But NYPD pulled over the truck, did a thorough search of the vehicle, and stumbled across three guns, one of which was connected to two homicides in the past year.

When the judge denied everyone bail, Pearla screamed out and had to be removed from the courtroom. No one was receiving bail until one of the three men owned up to the guns. Hassan's lawyer was planning to appeal the decision.

Pearla continued to grieve outside of the courtroom. She didn't know what to do. There were people out there trying to kill her and take away everything she had. She was in a new, bigger house deep in Long Island, and once again, with Hassan incarcerated, she found herself sleeping in a cold bed.

For weeks, Pearla barely slept. It felt like history was repeating itself. Hassan was in jail, and she was all alone wondering if this was her karma. How many people had she hurt to get to the top when she was with Cash? *Too many to remember*, she thought. And how many people fell victim to one of her schemes before she had gotten with Hassan? The crimes she had committed weren't victimless, and for what? There were so many hustles out there that she could have exceled in without hurting others. Instead of going after corporations she went after the elderly. Shame on her.

And what about her friends? When Hassan showed her the picture of Chica, her body burned and shot once in the head, her heart lurched. She felt something. Something she should have felt a long time ago when she killed Jamie. Pearla finally began to feel remorseful. Who was she? What had she become? She and Hassan began to discuss having children. She now felt that if she continued on this path that she would be no better a mother to her child than Poochie was to her.

Pearla convinced herself that if she didn't change her selfish ways that Hassan would rot in jail and she would be left to once again fend for herself. You get what you give. So the next day Pearla went on a giving spree. Each elderly person she had scammed would receive triple what they had paid out to Pearla.

Next, she anonymously sent a FedEx box to Roark containing all cash. It was double what Pearla had extorted from her.

Chica and Jamie couldn't get their lives back, but Pearla made a fifty thousand dollar donation in Chica's name to a transgender charity that helped teens who struggled with identity. A fifty thousand dollar donation was made to Jamie's high school in her name to renovate the computer lab. The principal said they would add a plaque in lab with Jamie's name, which Pearla was sure Jamie would have liked.

Pearla was done with bad karma. She hoped that all her good deeds would buy her and Hassan a drama-free future. It wasn't practical thinking, but she didn't do things sensibly. She promised herself that she would try to really change. But she also knew that Rome wasn't built in a day.

Rebuilding all she had destroyed would take time.

EPILOGUE

Pearla was just stepping out of the shower when she heard the doorbell ring. It was almost midnight, and she was expecting company. She quickly toweled off and hurried downstairs to answer the door.

She opened the front door, and Cash smiled at her, holding flowers and champagne. Tired of living inside an empty house while Hassan was in Rikers Island, she had invited him over. She wanted to catch up with him, to talk and enjoy his company.

They hugged and kissed at the entrance, and he walked inside with a minor limp, still in slight pain from his injuries. They went into the living room and comforted each other.

Pearla nestled against Cash and cried on his shoulders, and he didn't want to let her go.

"I'm here for you, baby," he said. "I got your back."

It's what Pearla needed to hear.

Soon after, they went upstairs to the bedroom to have sex. The lights clicked off, they climbed into bed, and Pearla gave herself to Cash completely.

Meanwhile, parked outside in the shadows of the mini-mansion was Bimmy. Smoking his cigarette, he frowned at Pearla's infidelity. She was sleeping with the enemy. He had grim news to report back to his boss.

Bimmy started the ignition and slowly drove away.

Two Down, One To Go.

Time to Make a House a Home

As Pearla prances around the house that Hassan's hustle built, she doesn't know that someone is watching her. Carelessly sneaking around with Cash – her past, and being financially supported by Hassan – her present; she's playing a dangerous love game.

Hassan sits behind the iron bars of New York's Rikers Island correctional facility contemplating how to deal with all that he has on his plate. His right-hand man Bimmy, and trusted advisor, wants him to do the unthinkable.

Narrowly escaping yet another attempt on her life, Pearla knows that it's time to grow up and chose the right man to grow old with, whoever that may be in hopes of living happily ever after in The House That Hustle Built.

Available Everywhere.

FOLLOW NISA SANTIAGO

FACEBOOK.COM/NISASANTIAGO

INSTAGRAM.COM/NISA_SANTIAGO

TWITTER.COM/NISA_SANTIAGO

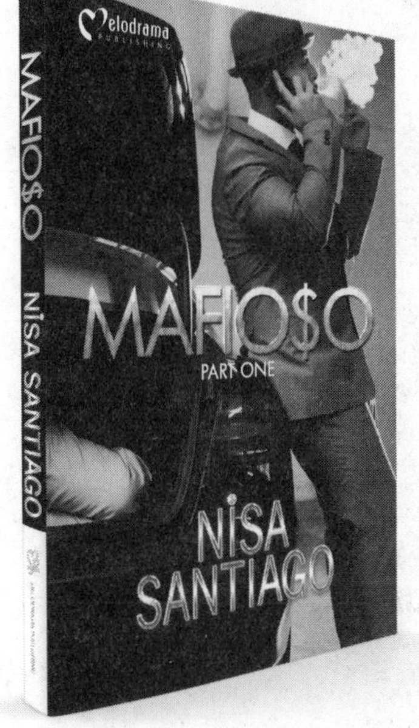

Ambitions as a Mobster

Scott West and his wife Layla have an infatuation with the Mafioso way of life. Armed with what they've learned, they assemble their own family based on the careers of the most successful mobsters and are now in charge of a powerful crime family. Their six children—Meyer, Bugsy, Lucky, Bonnie, Clyde, and Gotti—are all being groomed to manage the family business.

Al Capone's legacy taught Scott to run his drug empire upon fear, helping him prosper as a daunting opponent. When challenged by Danger, the daring Baltimore crime boss, Scott has to play the game for real as they clash in a mob-style power struggle. When the smoke clears, only one will have a seat at head of the table.

The enthralling new series by Nisa Santiago

Things are about to get Dirty...